CAPTIVE

OF THE

HORDE KING

ALSO BY ZOEY DRAVEN

Warriors of Luxiria

The Alien's Prize

The Alien's Mate

The Alien's Lover

The Alien's Touch

The Alien's Dream

The Alien's Obsession

The Alien's Seduction

The Alien's Claim

Warrior of Rozun

Wicked Captor

Wicked Mate

The Krave of Everton

Kraving Khiva

Prince of Firestones

CAPTIVE OF THE HORDE KING

HORDE KINGS OF DAKKAR BOOK 1

ZOEY DRAVEN

PROLOGUE

I t all began with a burning field.

Black plumes of thick smoke rose high above our village, cries of horror lifting with it. Higher and higher, black against the backdrop of the grey sky. A dreaded beacon. *A mistake.* Because no one in their right mind would ever willingly signal the Dakkari, to bring their wrath on us all.

Bile filled my throat and I dropped my basket and ran to the fields, as others did. Because somehow I knew. I *knew* who was responsible.

When I reached the fields, a group had formed. Water was rushed out in steel buckets to suffocate the blaze that had spread wildly. It was hot. So hot, but it didn't stop me from running towards it, from forming into the line as water passed from villager to villager.

I watched my younger brother at the end of the line, watched him desperately throw the much-needed resource onto the flames. A waste, but a necessary one. In between bucket passes, I saw the way his face was drawn tight. And I knew.

Fury and fear filled me.

It squeezed my chest, making it hard to breathe. My hands trembled as I passed more buckets down the line.

When the fire had finally been extinguished, silence filled the air, thick and heavy, like smoke that still lingered. There were at least twenty villagers in the line, with at least twenty more watching in horror from the edge of the dead, now burned, field. The intelligent ones were probably already preparing to hide because they knew what would happen next.

They'd all heard the stories, the rumors. It was only a matter of time, only a matter of which Dakkari horde was closest to us.

I broke the silence with that fury and I rounded on my younger brother, stalking towards him.

"You fool!" I hissed, useless tears filling my eyes before I blinked them away. I was five years older than Kivan, but he still towered over me. I pushed at his broad shoulders. His cheeks were blackened with ash from his latest 'experiment.' "What have you *done?*"

"I—I," he stuttered, his gaze darting from me to the villagers watching, to the blackened field, a field which hadn't produced crops in at least five moon cycles. "I was just trying to…to…"

He was always *just trying to.*

My gaze flashed to the sky, seeing the smoke. It could probably be seen from the Dakkari capital. I looked at the field, at the darkened, destroyed earth, my throat tightening.

"They'll kill you for this," I whispered to him, to myself, filled with fear so potent it made saliva pool in my mouth, made nausea churn in my belly. I had heard they'd killed humans for less.

Because they would come.

The Dakkari would come…

They would demand retribution.

1

I'd seen the Dakkari twice before in my lifetime.

The first time, I'd been a child, no older than six or seven. Our mother had still been alive then.

A horde had passed directly next to our village, but didn't set foot inside. The memory of them, though I'd been young, was forever imprinted on my mind. From afar, the Dakkari horde had seemed like a black cloud passing over the land. As they'd grown closer, I'd discovered that they were similar to men, to *us*, though so very *dissimilar* at the same time.

I remembered the black-scaled beasts they rode, gold paint glittering in the sunlight across their flanks, beasts that sometimes traveled on two legs, or sometimes utilized all four. Beasts that looked like monsters to my young self, that gave me nightmares until I woke screaming.

My mother had dragged me away from my spying place before I could take a closer look at the Dakkari males riding those beasts. We'd hidden in a corner, wrapped in fur blankets —my nervous mother, a crying Kivan, and I—until the horde passed without incident.

However, my curiosity about the Dakkari's appearance

would be assuaged years later when they came to our village for another purpose.

I'd been fourteen at the time. Part of the horde had broken off and walked through, leaving their black-scaled beasts at the single entrance to our walled village while the rest waited on the peak of a nearby hill. They'd come upon us so suddenly that for most, there had been no time to hide.

It was then I'd gotten my first real look at the Dakkari.

Up close, they were massive beings. When one passed me, I'd only come up to the center of his bared waist. They wore hides and furs to cover their bottom halves, some in pants that encased their legs, others in small pieces of cloth that revealed the expansive muscles of their thick thighs. My mother had told me the Dakkari hordes were nomadic warriors serving their king...and they looked like warriors. Primitive warriors so strong and big that no one dared to breathe in their presence as they walked through our village.

Unlike the other alien species that were spread out on the surface of Dakkar, the Dakkari—the native species, the species whose will we *all* had to obey—had a similar skin color to humans. Like darkened honey, tanned from the sun from their nomadic lifestyle. Golden tattoos across their flesh flashed as they walked, their long, black, coarse hair swaying around their waists as they inspected the village. Behind them, long, flexible tails flicked as they walked, slightly curled so they wouldn't drag on the ground.

Their eyes were like black pools, their circular irises a golden yellow that contracted and widened with light. They had no whites in their eyes like us. It was eerie, spine-tingling to look into them. But a strange part of me had been fascinated. A strange part of me had thought them beautiful.

That day, a day that had started out like any other, had taken a shocking turn when one of the Dakkari males saw Mithelda—

a young, timid blonde eight years older than me, who'd always been kind—and promptly taken her.

He'd captured her, torn her away from her aging parents and young sister, and the Dakkari had left as quickly as they'd come.

No one spoke of it. No one in our village saw Mithelda again, though news from another human settlement, four days' travel away, had seen her with a horde as they'd passed, riding one of the black-scaled beasts, in the lap of a Dakkari male. The human settlement had reported she'd looked beaten, abused. Yet, no one dared to interfere.

From that day on, if the lookouts saw evidence of a horde approaching, all women in the village donned cloaks and hoods to conceal our faces. Just in case.

Which was why, on that evening after the burning field, after a lookout had come running into the village with news of a horde approaching *fast*, I put on my thick cloak, tied back my brown hair, and pulled up the hood.

Kivan watched me, his fingers fumbling nervously.

"Luna," he said, his voice trembling. "I—I just want you to know that I—"

"Shhh, Kivan," I said, going to him. He was seated at our modest table, rocking the broken chair back and forth on its three legs. Crouching in front of him so that we were eye to eye, I squeezed his shaking hands and said, "I will always protect you. Mother made me promise, remember? You have nothing to fear."

"I was only trying to bring life back to our crops," he explained, as he had a thousand times since that afternoon. "I heard that on Laperan, they burn crops to—"

"We are not on Laperan," I replied gently, squeezing his hands, meeting his eyes. "We are on *their* planet. We must respect their ways. And today, we did not."

Tears filled his eyes, which shocked me. I'd never seen him cry since Mother died. Not once.

"I didn't mean for it to burn so much," he rasped. "You're right, Luna, I *am* a fool."

"Stop," I whispered, guilt eating at my chest, wanting to comfort him. It may very well be the last time I saw him, no matter what happened that night. "You were only trying to help us. It was an accident. I will speak with them. I will make them understand. Yes?"

Kivan shook his head, unable to meet my eyes, as his tears slowly dried up. But I stayed crouched at his feet, listening to the silence of our home, the silence of the village outside our doors.

"I love you, brother," I said, lifting his face. "It will be all right."

"They will give us up," he said. He meant the villagers, our friends and neighbors, in an effort to spare themselves from the Dakkari's wrath.

Truthfully, I couldn't even blame them for it.

"I will make them understand," I repeated, my tone hardening. Because I had to.

It wasn't much longer before we heard the horde approaching on their black-scaled beasts. It was like rumbling thunder, which sometimes boomed across the planet during violent storms.

Closer and closer they came, until the thunder stopped all at once and I heard the sounds of heavy bodies dismounting outside the walls of the village, of deep, gruff voices that easily penetrated our flimsy door.

I looked at Kivan and then slowly stood from my crouched position.

"Stay in here," I told him.

"Luna—"

I walked out of our home before he could say another word

and closed the rickety door behind me. The village street was empty and eerily quiet. Some villagers had even left earlier that evening, to hide out in the mountains until the horde passed on. But most remained, though their homes were dark and silent.

Through the one small, dirty window of our home, I could see Kivan watching me from the table, his eyes wide. Taking a deep breath, I turned and walked to the center of the single dirt road that connected the entire village together. It was there I waited with a pounding heart.

The creaking of the village gates met my ears as they were forced open, like a shrill cry cutting through the darkness. Then I heard the unmistakable sound of Polin's voice, perhaps the only person in the village brave enough to meet the Dakkari willingly. He was our leader, the head of our small village council. Polin saw it as his duty to meet with the Dakkari, but I had no doubts that he would direct them to our door, to wash his hands of Kivan once and for all.

But I would not give up my brother. Ever.

There were only two possible outcomes I would accept. One being that I would exchange my life for Kivan's. It was simple enough. I promised our mother that I would protect him and I *always* kept my promises.

The second option...well, I couldn't stop thinking about Mithelda. And that the Dakkari male had taken her for an obvious purpose.

It was rumored that the Dakkari sometimes took prizes. *War prizes.* Females—not necessarily humans—from other villages or settlements spread across Dakkar that had wronged them.

Perhaps they would take me instead of taking my brother. It was a trade I was willing to offer.

The moon was full and bright enough that I didn't need a lantern to see the Dakkari approaching.

I'd forgotten just *how* big they were. Readjusting my hood, I blew out a long breath through pursed lips, pressing my suddenly trembling hands flat against my cloak.

As I peered at the small group of Dakkari approaching, I saw that there were seven in total. All were bare-chested, exposing cords and planes of tanned muscle, of gold ink embedded into their skin in intricate, yet bold lines. No one knew what those markings meant. I saw their tails flicking behind them, obviously agitated, restless.

My eyes caught and held on the Dakkari leading the pack, my lips parting unseen within the shadowy confines of the hood. His own gaze was fixed on my cloaked figure, though his alien features were expressionless, those black eyes reflecting nothing in the moonlight.

But he moved swiftly, those long legs eating up the distance between us. Polin was nowhere in sight.

Seven Dakkari suddenly surrounded me in a circle, drawing their blades from the sheaths that crisscrossed their backs with a smooth *swish*. All except for *him* and the male next to him.

And I knew right then that he was one of the horde kings, one of the six that led the hordes across Dakkar, keeping order, patrolling their lands, and punishing those that threatened the Dakkari way.

He stood, stance widened, bulging arms at his sides, his long fingers—six on each hand—tipped with deadly claws. His thick, black hair was half-braided down his back, keeping it out of his face, exposing sharp, shadowed cheekbones, a flat nose with slitted nostrils, and wide-set eyes with yellow irises. His hair was decorated with a few gold beads and wrapped metal. On his large wrists—which were the size of my upper arms—were gold cuffs.

I could hear my swallow echo within the small circle, bouncing off their massive bodies as they towered over me.

The Dakkari male next to the horde king addressed me in the universal tongue, the only tongue I could speak, with, "Were you the one who burned our land, who disrespected and defiled our goddess, Kakkari?"

The messenger's voice was nothing more than a growl, a deep growl that made the hairs on my arms stand on end.

The Dakkari revered their land above all else. To destroy their land, especially with *fire*, was to disrespect them all, including their deities.

I thought of Kivan, sitting just a few feet away at the table in our home. He would be able to hear through the door and I prayed to all the gods and goddesses in the universe that he stayed inside.

"It was an accident," I said softly, resisting the urge to look down at their feet. But I kept my eyes level on the smooth column of the horde king's throat, though I knew they would not be able to see my face unless I tilted it towards the moon.

"Is that a confession, *vekkiri?*" the messenger growled again, next to the horde king.

My breath whistled out from my nostrils. "Please listen to what I have to say. Our village is hungry. Our crops have withered. We were only trying—"

The messenger slashed his arm through the air to silence me.

"We?" he repeated. "You did not act alone in this crime? Name your partner and I will ensure that both of your blood spills over the scorched land, to replenish Kakkari in full. You take from her? Then you must give in return."

My stomach lurched. For some strange reason, I looked up from the horde king's throat, though he had not spoken yet, directly into his eyes...because I knew that it was *him* I spoke to. Not the messenger. It was *him* I needed to appeal to. His eyes were still on me, as if his gaze could penetrate the shielding shadows of my cloak, freezing me in place.

The door of our home burst open and I cried out in alarm as Kivan flung himself into the circle of armed Dakkari,

9

moving to stand before me, blocking my view with his broad shoulders.

"Kivan!" I hissed, moving to step in front of him again.

"It was me," Kivan exclaimed. "I started the fire, not my sister. She is only trying to protect me."

The Dakkari messenger finally unsheathed his blade then and I saw Kivan's shoulders tense tight when the sharpened edge glinted in the light. The gold was so reflective that I saw my hooded figure in it, saw Kivan's drawn, frightened face.

To draw attention away from him, I shoved him behind me, putting myself within arm's reach of the horde king, and said, "Our village will starve if we cannot replenish the crops. *You* do not let us hunt game. We are surviving on Uranian Federation *rations*. So, I'm sorry that we burned your land, but know that it was only in a desperate attempt to feed ourselves before the cold season comes and the ground freezes over."

"It is not our concern how the *vekkiri* feed themselves," the messenger growled out.

Before I could reply, a rumbling, deep voice thundered within the group, making all of the Dakkari straighten, even the messenger.

Because that rich, dark voice belonged to the horde king.

"Take off your hood, *kalles*," the horde king ordered in the universal tongue, still looking straight at me. "Let me see the face of the female who dares to challenge the Dakkari."

2

The horde king wanted me to take off my hood?

I didn't hesitate, though Kivan began to protest. Anything to save him, to take the attention away from him, I would do readily.

The horde king's nostrils flared and the singular yellow ring of his irises contracted with a visible pulse when I pushed back the thick hood, letting it settle around my shoulders.

My chin lifted, meeting his gaze, though he towered over me.

"Brave *kalles*," the horde king murmured and I could actually *see* the way his pupils studied me, how they shifted over my face. "Foolish *kalles* too."

I stiffened at the slight insult. I assumed *kalles* meant 'woman' or 'female' in the Dakkari language. Either way, it set my teeth on edge.

My spine went taut like a bow string, all too aware that Kivan still remained within the circle of gold swords, in front of a horde king that wanted his blood in exchange for burning their land.

"Call me what you wish," I said, the cool night air brushing my face like a soft touch. "But my brother's life is not yours to take. I will not let you."

The Dakkari surrounding us shifted, the movement hardly perceptible, ever so slight.

As for the horde king...he didn't even twitch.

"*Let* me, *kalles*?" he repeated, his voice sharp. "I will do whatever I wish."

Perhaps that had been the wrong thing to say.

"Please," I said, my hands trembling from adrenaline and nerves. The yellow band around his pupils contracted again, his head cocking slightly to the side. "Take my life in exchange."

"Luna—" Kivan tried to cut in, but I pushed him back when he made to grab for my arms.

"I am responsible for my brother," I rushed out, "and therefore I am responsible for his actions. *Please*. He is young. He will never do this again. I promise." Even though we were only five years apart, sometimes I felt ten or twenty years older than Kivan. "Take me instead."

"*Luna*, no!" Kivan growled, frustrated, swinging on the horde king. "Don't listen to her."

But the horde king never took his eyes from me. I felt trapped by them, like I could never look away.

The messenger beside the horde king addressed him in a low tone with, "*Vorakkar, kivi vekkiri dothanu un kevf?*"

The horde king didn't respond immediately to whatever the messenger asked. As the moments stretched on, my blood grew hotter and raced faster until I heard it rushing in my ears. Still, we watched one another as I wondered what he would decide.

Because I knew his words to be true...he could do whatever he wished. The Dakkari had the authority and power and strength over any being that found a home on their planet, however unforgiving that home might be. It was the deal the Uranian Federation had made with the Dakkari for access to their closed planet.

"*Vorakkar*," the messenger repeated after a long moment.

I stiffened when the horde king stepped forward. In one fluid motion, he unsheathed a small dagger from the thick band around his waist. His movements were surprisingly graceful, smooth, and yet still impatient as he gripped my cloak.

I didn't have time to feel fear—for surely he meant to end my life, as I'd requested—before that dagger dragged down with one quick motion.

Instead of pain, I felt cool air shift across my skin. He'd cut the front of my cloak and he pulled the sides away for a better glimpse...of my *body*. Humiliation, or perhaps relief, made my cheeks hot as I realized what he was doing, even with my nonexistent experience with males.

Kivan, however, didn't seem to know since he demanded, his voice surprisingly outraged in front of the Dakkari, "What are you doing to her?"

The horde king didn't answer him. It was as if Kivan didn't even exist in his world. Though I was wearing old, worn pants and a dirt-smudged tunic underneath the cloak, the way he looked at me...I felt naked under his gaze, bared for him, as if he could see every inch of my flesh.

Outrage slowly began to burn in my belly, but I kept it leashed within. He was inspecting me like I was something to be bought at the marketplace, a new tunic or a shiny bauble.

"*Kassikari*," the horde king said suddenly. His tone was low, the words like a rough caress across my flesh. My eyes flashed up to his, surprised by *something* I heard in his voice, though I couldn't identify what. I found he wasn't looking down at my body any longer, but at *me*.

The tension in the circle suddenly doubled, the Dakkari males straightening even further, their golden swords dipping.

The messenger said, "*Vorakkar? Erun kalles vekkiri?*"

"*Lysi*," the horde king replied. The gold beads in his hair clinked together when he tilted his head. Addressing me in the universal tongue, he asked, "You wish to offer your life in exchange for your brother's offense?"

I was proud my voice didn't tremble as I said, "I do."

"You are willing to die for him?" he asked next.

The memory of my mother's last moments, begging me to protect Kivan even as she choked on her own blood—so red it looked black on the ice—made my voice hoarse as I said, "I am."

"Luna, *no*—"

"If I decide not to end your life or your brother's," the horde king murmured lowly, his gaze dropping down to my body again, his voice deepening even more, "will you serve me, *kalles*?"

There was no mistaking the meaning behind his words or the way his eyes roamed over the modest curves of my body. Goosebumps broke out over my flesh as I whispered, "Serve you?"

"*Lysi*," he rasped.

He wanted me as his whore, wanted me to warm his bed, wanted to use my body for his pleasure...in exchange for my brother's life.

There was no choice. I'd already made up my mind before they'd entered the village gates. This had always been the second possibility.

Dread swarmed in my belly. I felt like I was floating outside my body as I whispered, numb, "I will."

Movement behind me made the horde king's gaze snap away. Before I realized what had happened, Kivan had yanked one of the gold swords from one of the Dakkari's grip and pushed me aside, his sudden strength surprising. But the sword was too heavy for him, sagging in both hands even as he tried to swing it at the horde king, who easily dodged the clumsy maneuver.

Horror filled me. I cried out, "Kivan, stop!"

Fool, fool, fool! Surely they would kill him *now*.

"*Nik, pyroth!*" the horde king ordered his Dakkari when they raised their weapons. They halted immediately, though they didn't lower them, just stopped their advance. The horde king's hand flashed out, gripping the sword by the *edge* and he flung it out of my brother's grasp with ease. He seemed to grow in size, his expression darkening, my brother's actions yet again an insult to the Dakkari.

I swung on the horde king, stepping between them, holding my hands out in supplication. "P-please. I will go with you now. Please just do not...do not hurt him."

His nostrils flared wide, but at least his attention was on me, not on my brother.

"Please," I begged, and I had never begged before in my life. I had no pride when it came to my brother, the only family I had left. "*Please.* Just take me. I promise I will serve you. I will do whatever you want, just do not hurt him."

Long moments of thick tension lapsed. Even the Dakkari males seemed to wait for their horde king's decision with bated breath.

He finally growled, "We ride out *now.*"

Relief made me sag, but my reprieve was short.

In one swift movement, all the Dakkari sheathed their gold blades as the horde king turned back towards the entrance. My lips parted when I saw the scars across his back, as if he'd been whipped. Brutally.

"Come now," he barked over his shoulder and halted, waiting for me.

Kivan stood, still encircled by the Dakkari, frozen from shock, fear, disbelief. I went to him, embracing him, which I never did.

Softly, I whispered, "I *will* see you again. I promise."

His arms were still at his sides. He didn't want to accept this, but I wished he would return my embrace.

"Come," the horde king commanded again. My heart

15

squeezed in my chest, tears burning my eyes, but I refused to let them fall.

"Go inside," I said finally, pulling back. "Be safe, Kivan."

I looked at him one last time, saw that his pupils were dilated, his face pale. He was in shock. I turned away before I started crying. I had to be strong now. For him. And for myself.

Halting just behind the horde king, I saw him look at me before ordering, "*Vir drak!*"

His Dakkari fell away from Kivan, the messenger falling into place beside him. We walked down the village road, their footsteps vibrating the ground beneath me. In a state of shock, I followed, clutching my ripped cloak around me as if it would protect me like a shield from what was happening. I caught sight of a few faces peeking out from windows of homes we passed, usually small children, before their mothers ripped them away. Otherwise, the village was drenched in night and darkness.

The entrance of the village, the only place I'd ever known, was in sight. I saw Polin standing there, watching with narrowed eyes. That was when I heard Kivan shout, "Luna! Luna, *no!*"

I looked over my shoulder, saw my brother running towards the Dakkari. Looking back to Polin, I pleaded, "Take him! Take him away!"

Polin didn't move.

Desperation rose in my throat and I cried out, "You *owe* me, Polin. You owe it to me! Now take him back inside!"

Something came over Polin's face. The horde never stopped moving, despite my outburst, despite the horde king looking back at me with an unreadable expression in those yellow-rimmed eyes.

Finally, Polin slid past the Dakkari, careful not to step in their path, and moved to intercept Kivan. Despite Polin's age, he was still stronger and larger than my brother and managed to hold him back. I heard my brother's struggles, however, the way he called after me, his voice clogged with tears and fury and sadness. It would always haunt me, I knew.

The entrance gates creaked open when the messenger pushed them aside roughly. And waiting at the entrance were the black-scaled beasts of my nightmares.

The Dakkari slid around me, each going to their respective monster, except for the horde king. He appeared at my side, grasping me around my waist and leading me over to the only creature that remained without a rider.

I knew it was *his*. It was by far the largest, most battle-worn beast of them all. It was standing on all four of its legs, which were tipped in sharp, talon-like black claws. Its scales were painted in thin gold strips, looping up and around in the Dakkari way, similar to the tattoos adorning the horde king's flesh. Also like its master, the beast had a plethora of scars—across its sides, the front of its legs, around its tall, thick neck.

And its eyes...they were *red*. Blood red. Like blood on ice. Like my mother's blood.

Panic began to rise in my belly and I stumbled away from the beast, though the horde king's chest prevented me from going anywhere. He stood behind me, a wall of unmovable strength.

He didn't give me a choice. He gripped me around my waist, hauled me up high like I weighed nothing, and settled me on the back of the monster, my legs dangling over both sides of its massive, cold body.

It felt like a rock underneath me and when it shifted on its feet, I felt its tendons and muscles flex too. When I started to slide off, I placed my hands at the base of its neck, though the cool touch of its scales made me want to recoil in horror.

The horde king swung up behind me a moment later, not allowing me time to adjust. He scooted forward until I was wedged between his strong thighs, until his groin was pressed against my lower back. The heat of him, and how much stronger he was than me, registered.

Strong, tanned hands appeared in front of me, grasping onto the thin, gold metal chains that were secured around the beast's snout, looping up around its neck. The horde king fisted them in one hand and used the other to press against my belly, anchoring me to him.

I refused to cry out when he made a sound in the back of his throat which set the beast into motion. Swallowing my panic, I held on as best I could as it jolted into a high-speed run. I felt the horde king's thighs tense around me, bracing, obviously comfortable being on the back of it.

But I was not. I didn't think I ever would be.

That hand pressed tighter into my belly. It was so large that I felt it span across my ribs. I knew it wouldn't be the last time those hands were on me.

My face burned, my throat tightened. I stared at the empty darkness of Dakkar in front of me, framed by the beast's long, pointed ears, at the empty, wild lands beyond my village that not many dared to venture into.

What had I done? What would my life be like from this moment forward?

I'd sold myself to a horde king of Dakkar to save my brother's life. I'd sold myself to a horde king to serve him...as his human whore.

That knowledge sunk in.

It sunk in deep and festered.

3

It seemed like hours until I spied lights in the distance.

An encampment, I realized, as we drew closer and closer.

The moon was already sinking into the star-speckled night sky. It had to be the early hours of morning and though I was exhausted from the day's events, I hadn't been able to relax or sleep. The jostling, rough movements of the black-scaled beast had ensured my discomfort and it had been hours since I could feel my legs or my backside. Surely I would be bruised in the morning.

The camp was mostly quiet once we reached the perimeter, but I spied many Dakkari males still awake, huddled around tall, gilded cauldrons of fire. The Dakkari didn't believe in burning the earth. Seeing that enclosed fire made my belly churn. I never wanted to see fire again.

The encampment was surprisingly large. It surprised me that there *was* a camp, a base for the roaming Dakkari. No one had ever heard about one. The camp alone was larger than my entire village and we had a population of eighty-six.

Eighty-five now, I thought silently to myself.

Large, domed tents of tanned animal hide dotted the flat land, the camp positioned at the edge of a darkened forest of black trees. I had only seen trees once before and I stared up at them, amazed at their height.

Loud trills echoed in the night sky, making me jump. The horde king's hand tightened on my belly briefly before he made a responding trill, loud and deep, from the back of his throat. I felt it vibrate through his body, against my back. The rest of the horde that traveled with him followed suit.

A signal, I realized.

More Dakkari emerged from their tents, some completely nude, which embarrassed me. But what surprised me the most was that females and children were among them, traveling with the horde.

As the horde king guided his beast into the camp, winding around the tents towards the forest's edge, Dakkari surrounded us, lining up along the makeshift road. My head swiveled from side to side, looking at unfamiliar faces. I felt their eyes on me, felt their curiosity, or perhaps their animosity.

But the males cheered with that loud trill as we passed and I jumped when I felt foreign hands on my legs. The Dakkari people—males, females, and children alike—reached out their hands to pass them over the horde king's creature, over the horde king's legs, and by extension, my own.

Finally, once we passed most of the tents, he stopped his beast with a firm tug of the golden chains near a wide enclosure. My lips parted, my chest squeezing, when I realized it was an enclosure for the beasts, with numerous troughs of raw, pink meat and clear water filled to the brim. I stared at that raw meat, thought of my hungry village with our dead crops and withering Uranian Federation rations, and turned my head away. Their beasts were eating better than we were.

There were hundreds of them, all enclosed within the single pen, but they had ample space to roam. The enclosure was larger than the entire encampment. I saw hundreds of red eyes in the darkness, their hides glimmering in gold paint.

The horde king dismounted with a surprising grace, handing the gold reins to a Dakkari male who came to greet him. Reaching up for me, my new keeper grasped my waist and easily swung me down, setting me on my feet beside him. I swallowed a hiss when the pain registered, everything stiff and sore from my waist down.

The horde king turned from me and gently took his beast's snout in his wide palm. He leaned close, looking into its red eyes, and murmured something in Dakkari, his voice soft. The beast made a chirring sound in its long neck and was led away by the other Dakkari male. Once inside the pen, it immediately went to eat from one of the nearest troughs.

Without a single word—he hadn't said a single word to me since we'd left my village—the horde king led me to the largest domed tent in the entire encampment. Stationed outside were two Dakkari males, who inclined their heads in greeting to their leader, ignoring my presence completely.

The horde king jerked his chin at the thick flaps of the tent, his eyes on me. Then he turned to the guards and spoke in Dakkari, probably something along the lines of 'make sure she doesn't escape.'

Like I could.

There wasn't a doubt in my mind that if I escaped, the horde king would return to my village and kill my brother as retaliation, and perhaps more villagers in the process. I had accepted my fate, had agreed to it, had *promised* that I would serve him. I intended to, but I felt my soul slowly begin to wither at the prospect of it.

With that in mind, I stepped through the tent flaps, under the watchful gaze of the horde king. He was testing me, I realized. He wanted to see what I would do.

Screw him, I thought. There was a fire still within me, an anger. As long as I held onto that, my soul would stand a fighting chance.

Warmth enveloped my cloaked body when I stepped inside the tent. I hadn't quite known what to expect, but my widened eyes took in luxurious surroundings, some luxuries I had never seen before.

Like plush carpets that lined the floor, soft beneath my booted feet—the soles of which were failing. Like wax candles that drenched the tent in golden light, and little vases of hot oils that filled the space with a light, delicious fragrance. Like an actual *bed* set up on a low pallet draped in soft furs and cushions, not a simple pile of blankets on the floor like back home. Like a row of chests on the floor that glimmered with gold and the horde king's treasures.

For a long moment, I simply stood on the threshold of the tent, taking in my new surroundings. My new prison. Because I couldn't forget that this tent was still my cage, one I'd willingly chosen.

I didn't dare to touch anything, though my fingers longed to stroke the soft furs on the bed. So I simply stood, waiting, glancing at the front entrance of the tent every so often. But the horde king didn't appear, which relieved me.

Just when my eyes started to droop, when I swayed on my feet with my exhaustion, the flaps pushed open suddenly and a large bathing tub was brought in by two Dakkari males, not the guards stationed at the entrance. They didn't meet my eyes. They simply deposited the tub in the empty space to the right, the space that wasn't carpeted, left, and returned with huge basins of hot water. It took them multiple trips in and out of the tent to completely fill up the tub and once it was filled, they exited.

Then two Dakkari females appeared. I straightened at the sight of them, watching them warily. They were smaller than the males, with plaited black hair that ended at their waists.

Both females were dressed in flowing gray shift dresses that brushed the tops of their six-toed feet. Behind them, small slits were cut out to allow for their tails, which were tipped in dark tufts of hair.

"What are you doing?" I asked in alarm when they approached me and began to tug at my clothing, one kneeling to take off my boots, the other pushing the tatters of my cloak off my shoulders.

"The *Vorakkar* sent us," one of the females said in the universal tongue, the one trying to unlace my boots. "He requests that you bathe after your long journey."

"Orders, you mean," I muttered, cheeks reddening. "I don't need one."

It had been four days since I last bathed. Water was precious in our village and wasn't needlessly wasted. I eyed the hot water in the bathing tub with longing, but I wondered if I could keep the horde king at bay for a few days if I refused to wash. Just a few days, to come to terms with my new life, my new purpose.

"You need one," the female said, her lips pursed as if it was obvious. "The *Vorakkar* will not be disobeyed, even by you."

What did *that* mean?

I was just about to protest again, but then bit my tongue. It was inevitable, just like my eventual relations with the horde king, whose name I still did not know.

Be brave, I told myself, *and endure.*

A thought occurred to me suddenly.

I would fulfill my promise and maybe when the horde king eventually tired of me, he would allow me to return to my village, to Kivan. Perhaps if I pleased him enough, he would take mercy on me and consider my debt paid.

I knew the likelihood of that was slim. Mithelda once again crossed my mind. She had never returned to our village, though there wasn't a doubt in my mind that she'd been taken for the same purpose as the horde king had taken me for.

Shoulders sagging, I let them undress me without a fight. Truthfully, I was too tired to fight them, too sore.

Guilt filled me when I slid into the bathing tub…because it was wonderful and because Kivan, or anyone in my village, would never experience anything like it. A moan of surprise left my throat, which embarrassed me, because I'd never felt water that hot, never felt the way it could relax aching muscles and envelop me like a warm, comforting blanket.

Pain seared me as well, however. My inner thighs were chafed and raw from riding for hours on end and it stung like hell when the water soothed over the wounds.

I tensed when the two females knelt next to the bathing tub with cloths in their hands. They lathered them with soap, but I said quickly, "I can do that," when they closed in.

As expected, they ignored me. With thorough strokes that left my cheeks flaming, they washed me from head to toe with efficiency, even scrubbing underneath my fingernails and toenails. They washed my dark hair twice with soap and I saw how quickly the water turned brown from dirt and dust.

One of the females suddenly yelled something towards the tent flaps, making me jump.

"Up," she told me and wrapped me in a large fur blanket. "The water needs to be changed."

"I'm clean," I protested.

"*Nik*, the water needs to be changed. Look at the color."

And so, I stood as the tub was carried out by three Dakkari males this time, returned once they'd tossed out the dirty water, and I watched with a tight throat as more hot basins of water were brought in.

Such a waste.

Once the bathing tub was full again, the female ordered me back inside and I went through another scrubbing. The water remained clear, however, and I let out a little sigh of relief.

"Do you ache from the *pyroki?*" the female suddenly asked.

I met her eyes. They were so dark I could see the reflections of the candles in them. The other female still hadn't spoken a word to me yet.

"The *py...pyroki?*" I asked, the word feeling strange on my tongue.

"You are raw here," she noted, reaching beneath the water with her cloth to touch my inner thighs.

Realization dawned on me. "The *pyroki* are those creatures?"

Her eyes narrowed when I said *creatures,* but she said, "*Lysi. Pyroki.*"

Lysi must mean *yes*, I decided.

"I've never ridden one before," I told her softly, "or anything like it."

"Your body will adjust in time," she told me simply. "Dip your head again."

"Why are you being so nice to me?" I couldn't help but ask when I resurfaced, catching her gaze. Did all of the horde king's whores—of which I was certain he had more than one—receive this kind of attention?

She blinked at the question, her eyelids painted gold. "The *Vorakkar* has tasked us with your care," was all she would say.

Not a moment later, the tent flap pushed back, the horde king in question appearing.

The two females scrambled to their feet, inclining their heads, but not speaking. I froze, naked in the bathing tub. All the air seemed to leave the room as my heartbeat tripled its rhythm in my throat.

"*Rothi kiv,*" he said in his dark voice, his eyes finding me in the bathing tub and holding.

Immediately, the two females left after draping their washing cloths over the edge of the tub.

And suddenly, I was alone and naked with the horde king.

4

"*Kalles*, you look frightened," the horde king said. His voice sounded almost...mocking.

I stiffened in the bathing tub, indignation rising, but I tamped it down. I still had the presence of mind to recognize that he held the power over me and it would be best not to anger him.

He turned from me, which gave me a momentary sliver of relief, but it was to rummage through one of the closed chests I'd spotted earlier. Sinking lower into the bath water, making sure it covered my jutting nipples, I watched carefully as he crouched, his back muscles shifting in the golden light as he searched for something.

I let my eyes linger on him longer than I should have. Just because he was my new master, it didn't change the fact that he was visually intriguing. The gold beads and wraps in his hair flashed, the golden, swirling tattoos adorning his dark skin glimmered, those scars, long and deep, bringing questions to my mind, though I didn't dare voice them. He was strong and large and powerful and dangerous, a cautionary tale I'd heard since childhood made flesh.

When he stood, I saw he had a silk shift night dress in his large hands. It was practically transparent and it confirmed my suspicions that he had more than one female 'serving' him. Why else would he have that in his private possessions?

When he approached, I leaned forward, hugging my knees to my chest in an attempt to shield my nudity, looking up at him warily. I cursed the fact that the water was clear now, instead of the dark brown it'd been earlier.

"Stand," he ordered.

I froze. "What?"

"You are clean now. Stand, *kalles*."

There was a challenge not only in his voice but in his eyes. He was testing me again. Why?

He'd called me brave back in my village. He'd also called me foolish. Perhaps I *was* both because that challenge steeled my spine and set my teeth on edge.

Slowly, I unwrapped my arms from around my knees and stood as I swallowed past the nervous lump in my throat. Would he take me this night? Was that why he wished for me to bathe? Was I to start 'serving' him immediately, though we'd ridden through the night, though I was chafed raw between my thighs?

The horde king's gaze tracked over my naked body, lingering on my breasts, the curve of my hips, and the dark tuft of hair between my legs. He made a rough sound in the back of his throat and it made me jump.

"Step out," he ordered, though his voice was considerably deeper than it'd been a moment before.

I licked my dry lips and did as he commanded, though I couldn't suppress my wince as a twinge of sharp pain shot through my backside.

The horde king stilled. "What is it?"

Pride made me say, "Nothing."

His eyes narrowed and he grabbed my wrist, hauling me

towards him. The sudden movement made me grit my teeth, but he turned me, inspecting me.

He growled out something in Dakkari when he saw my flesh, the redness of my backside, no doubt, and then he turned me, peering between my legs, at my inner thighs.

My cheeks flamed with humiliation. I'd never been naked with a male before, not since my mother used to bathe my brother and me together when we'd been children. I wasn't used to baring my body so freely, especially in front of rapt, attentive, yellow-rimmed eyes.

I gasped and jumped when he brushed his fingertips across my reddened, sore flesh.

"Don't," I protested, trying to twist away from him. But he held me still, though I squirmed.

Finally, he released my wrists. His face was tight when he turned me back around to face him and he scooped up a spare fur blanket, using it to roughly dry off my body, though his touch gentled when he reached my hips...and below.

It surprised me, but I was too nervous to let out a single breath, so I stood, frozen.

"Put this on," he commanded, dropping the transparent night dress in my hands.

My eyes bulged. "But...but it's..."

Not that it mattered. I was already naked in front of him. I had no dignity left, it seemed.

"Sleep bare then," he said, with a shrug of his massive shoulders. "I would prefer it, *kalles.*"

That had me scrambling to pull it on over my head. I would take whatever I could get. Besides, it was clean and it was possibly the most luxurious item I'd ever felt against my skin. The material was so light it felt like air, so it wouldn't rub against my raw skin.

Again, guilt swamped me. I shouldn't appreciate these luxuries.

The horde king studied me, though I avoided his gaze. Finally, he shifted to untie the laces of his pants, which looked to be made of the same material as the tent—tanned animal hide.

My alarmed eyes flashed up to his. "What are you doing?"

"I need to bathe after the journey," he told me, stepping out of his pants until he was nude, except for the gold cuffs around his thick wrists. "You will wash me."

My face burned with so much heat that I wondered if my eyeballs were red too. Actively, I avoided looking at his groin, keeping my eyes level with his neck.

But it was unavoidable. When he stepped into the bathing tub, I caught a glimpse and my mouth went as dry as the earth around our village.

He was massive. Long and thick, with a heavy, dusky, full sack swaying just below. There was a large bump just above the root of his shaft that protruded slightly, something human males didn't have. And just like the rest of his body…he had two, intricate stripes of gold tattooed around his sex. One near the base of his cock and one just underneath the rounded head.

What made dread pool in my belly most was that he was erect. So hard that his cock bobbed against his taut abdomen when he stepped into the tub. I also caught a glimpse of his perfectly sculpted backside, of the strong tail that jutted out above his buttocks.

He groaned, the sound strangely erotic, when he leaned back, fully enveloped in the warm water. His eyes closed briefly, his arms coming to rest on the lip of the tub, the size of which was obviously meant for a Dakkari male, since he fit perfectly.

Despite the situation, despite what happened that night, and my pain and exhaustion from riding the *pyroki*…my heartbeat stuttered at the sensual sight of him.

I swallowed with difficulty, looking away, shame burning deep in my chest for finding him attractive. He'd almost killed my brother, had taken me as his whore. I needed to remember that.

His voice made me jump. "Bathe me, *kalles*. You promised you would serve me, did you not?"

Slowly, I knelt beside the tub, ignoring my aching soreness. I took up one of the washing cloths the Dakkari females had used on me, dipping it in the water quickly to wet it.

Then, taking a deep breath, I smoothed it over his skin, trying to copy the efficient motions the females had used on me. Otherwise, bathing him felt too…intimate.

So, with rough, quick circles, I washed his shoulders, his arms, cleaning away the dirt that had accumulated during our ride to the camp. His eyes remained closed, thankfully, and he remained still. It gave me the courage to wash below the water, to wipe across his chest, his abdomen. He lifted slightly so I could wash his back.

But washing below his waist seemed unavoidable once I'd finished.

He grunted lightly when I made one light pass over his cock. I bit my lip, looking away, and then blew out a silent breath of relief when I moved down to his long, muscular legs.

"Relax, *kalles*," he murmured. When I chanced a look at him, I saw his eyes were on me, heavy-lidded. "I will not fuck you this night."

My body went tense at his words, though I also felt relieved that I'd escaped my 'duties' for that night. He said it so crudely, so matter of fact.

I'd always heard that the Dakkari were like barbarians, primitive beings that did nothing more than fuck and ride their beasts and wage war on unsuspecting settlements.

Something told me that I'd been fed untruths. At least partial ones. There was more to the Dakkari than the tall tales I'd heard since childhood, as evidenced by this very encampment, by the females and children that traveled with the horde, by the gentle luxuries that the horde king seemed to enjoy. Nothing in that tent told me he was a primitive barbarian.

But still...

I did not know what prompted me to say it, but I told him, "Can you blame me? I'd expected to be rutted on the floor the moment you came inside. That was what I'd agreed to, was it not?"

I cursed myself once the words left my tongue.

He made a sound in the back of his throat. "Do not give me tempting ideas, *kalles*."

That surprised me. He said it with no venom behind his words.

I moved on to washing his hair. It was surprisingly soft, though it looked coarse, and I threaded my soap-covered fingers through it, washing away the dirt. Once it was clean, the horde king did one final rinse and then stood from the tub, water sluicing off his body.

He looked down at me, his magnificent flesh on display, his cock still hard in front of me. And I kneeled before him in my transparent shift.

His jaw ticked and he growled, looking away. He stepped out of the tub, calling out in Dakkari towards the entrance, and I gasped when the same three males appeared, taking out the bathing tub so quickly I didn't even have time to shield my almost-nude body from them. Not that they looked. They kept their eyes averted.

The horde king had no hesitations about his own nudity and simply dried off with the same fur I had used before draping it over the back of a steel rack at the side of the tent.

When we were alone again, I stood, wrapping my arms around me to hide my modest breasts. My hair was wet, however, drenching the fabric as it dripped, and parts of the shift molded to my body.

I tensed when he approached me and despite the heat in the tent, I shivered, my nipples pebbling against my arm.

He unthreaded my arms, placing them at my sides, looking down the front of my body the same way he had at my village. Like he could see all of me. And I supposed he could.

Tension, at least on my part, thickened the air between us.

"I had intended to rut you on the floor this night like a beast," he murmured suddenly. "I thought of nothing else as we rode."

I inhaled a sharp breath.

"I will wait until you heal," he finally said.

That...surprised me.

The way he was gazing at me...no male had ever looked at me like that before. And when he reached out a hand to touch me, in desperation, in a clumsy attempt to maintain some sort of distance between us, I hurriedly asked, "Do the Dakkari often take humans as their whores? I would think your own females would suffice for that purpose."

The horde king stilled and my blood rushed in my ears, wondering if I'd gone too far.

Silence spread thin between us.

"You believe you will be my whore, *kalles*?" he finally asked.

Confusion made my brows furrow and I licked my lips as I said, "Isn't that what you meant?"

The horde king grinned, though it was small and dark. Still, it made my breath hitch.

"*Nik*, you will not be my whore," he rasped, his voice deepening. I gasped, my body going tight, when he brushed his fingertips over my pebbled nipple before thumbing it back and forth in a way that made my hands shake, the sensation foreign and new. "*Nik*, you will be my *kassikari*. You will be my *Morakkari*."

My head went foggy as he continued his caress over my other nipple but when I tried to squirm away, his tail wrapped around my waist, holding me fast and firm, surprising me with its strength.

"What…what is that?" I asked, trying to focus.

"I will claim you in the old way, in the old Dakkari tradition," he told me, which only confused me even more. "You will not be my whore, *kalles*. You will be my queen."

5

When I woke up the next morning, the horde king was gone.

Emerging from a restless sleep, I felt even more exhausted than I had the night before. And when I shifted my legs, turning over in the wide bed, I hissed. The pain was even more severe as well.

I sat up gingerly, looking around the empty, dark, domed tent. I already knew he was gone. I had woken briefly when he'd roused from bed in the early hours of morning, but it didn't prevent me from scanning the quiet space warily.

When I was convinced I was truly alone, I blew out a small breath, pushing my wild, still-damp hair away from my eyes, my mind replaying the events of last night.

I picked at the fur blanket covering my thinly dressed body.

He'd told me I would be his queen.

His queen.

Not his whore.

Though truthfully, perhaps to the Dakkari, they were one and the same. He still expected access to my body, as evidenced by his admission last night. But he'd also said something about claiming me in the old Dakkari tradition, whatever that meant.

And he hadn't allowed me to question him afterwards.

After he'd told me I'd be his '*kassikari*,' he'd brought me to his bed, covered our bodies with the furs, and told me to sleep. I'd been tense, wanting answers, but he remained mute on the subject, had simply lain next to me, his long, bare side touching mine. Then he slept, his breathing evening out in a slow rhythm. Awake one moment and dead to the world in the next.

Now, he was gone.

I had no knowledge of what a horde king of the Dakkari did during the day. Was he gone on another 'patrol'? Was he somewhere in camp? Was he raiding another innocent settlement, taking treasures like the ones he had stored in his chests? Was he with one of his other whores?

Questions and more questions piled up in my mind until I thought I would scream. The events of yesterday were finally catching up with me and in the light of day, on the first day of my new life...I felt despair. I felt hopelessness. I longed to see my brother, to walk the quiet road of my village to the head seamstress's home where I worked, to see the familiar hills just beyond the village gates.

Yet, I was here. Alone, in the domed tent of a horde king, among a people I knew almost nothing about.

Pushing off the furs, I looked down between my thighs and saw they were even redder than the night before, the sensitive skin chaffed and rubbed raw. When I touched the flesh, it stung and I prayed to all the gods and goddesses in the universe that I wouldn't have to ride one of those beasts again.

It was a blessing in disguise, perhaps, I admitted to myself. After all, the horde king said he wouldn't demand my body until I healed.

I didn't know how to take his unexpected reprieve.

Begrudgingly, I was thankful for it, though I knew it was only a matter of time before he expected my repayment in full.

I jumped when the tent flap pushed open, my head snapping up.

A female appeared, the one from last night, the one who'd spoken to me. She was followed by the other, the one who had not spoken to me. Both were still dressed in their gray shift dresses, their hair neatly plaited down their backs. One of them balanced a white bone tray, inlaid with gold, filled with small, steaming bowls of fresh meat and broth.

My mouth watered, my stomach growling. I hadn't eaten since yesterday morning, before Kivan had set our crop field on fire.

Had that only been yesterday? It seemed like weeks ago.

"Come and eat, *Missiki*," the Dakkari female said, setting the tray down on a low table near the horde king's chests. There were no chairs, only cushions on the floor. "Gather your strength."

Desperate hunger filled me when I eyed the food. Five separate small bowls filled the tray. One bowl held braised meat, another dried meat. One held a creamy, steaming broth that filled the tent with a delicious aroma. Another held some kind of root vegetable and the last was filled with a fluffy grain, a deep purple in color.

It was more food than I'd eaten at once in years. I hadn't had meat since the Uranian Federation had included it in their rations, but that had ceased two years prior. *Fresh* meat...I'd never had it. It was a luxury we were not allowed on Dakkar. We were not allowed to hunt *their* game.

My own mother had died in an attempt to give us fresh meat. We'd been starving and she'd been desperate. The memory of her lying in the icy snow, mauled but still clinging to life, made nausea churn in my gut.

"I'm not hungry," I said, blocking out that memory, looking away from the food.

The two females exchanged a look. "The *Vorakkar* will be displeased if you do not eat. You must eat, *Missiki*."

"I don't care," I said. I knew I was being petulant, but the thought of eating meat, of eating such a lavish meal when my own brother, my own village, was hungry made me sick.

I'd obviously stumped them because the female changed tactics. "You can eat later. Let us get you dressed."

For what purpose? I wanted to ask. I might as well stay naked in the horde king's bed. That was where he wanted me, wasn't it?

Stop, I told myself. I was sulking, feeling sorry for myself. They were only trying to do what they'd been tasked with. Would they be punished if I didn't obey?

Nodding, I swallowed the sharp, sore pain that made it difficult to move as I swung my legs over the side of the bed.

"Oh, *Missiki*," the female said, her features contorting when she saw the redness between my thighs. In Dakkari, she said something to the other female, who immediately left the tent. "Do you wish to bathe? Will it help?"

My brows furrowed. "I just bathed last night." It seemed like a lavish waste of water to bathe again so soon. But of course, the Dakkari probably had endless resources at their disposal. It was their planet, after all.

The female frowned but didn't say anything. Instead, she went to the bundle the other female had been carrying when they'd walked in and unwrapped it.

"This will not irritate your flesh," she said, holding up a short skirt, followed by a top that looked entirely too short.

My cheeks heated, thinking how revealing the clothing was. "Er, I would prefer the clothes I came in."

The female scrunched up her nose, blinking. "You want those

rags over this?" She shook the top and the gold beads that adorned the front jingled musically. It looked heavy but well-made. I couldn't imagine how long it took to sew those beads on.

"Yes," I said, bristling. I'd made those 'rags' myself, a long time ago.

"They are being cleaned, *Missiki*," she said simply. "You must wear this until they are returned."

I was about to protest but the other female, the silent one, returned with a small jar of a white, milky substance.

"What is that?" I asked warily.

"Salve for your *pyroki* burns. It will help the flesh heal, take the sting away."

"No," I said quickly.

"*Nik?*" the female asked, obviously dumbfounded that I would reject it. "Why?"

"I…" I trailed off, but then decided I would tell her the truth. There was no way around it and perhaps a female, even a Dakkari one, could sympathize. "He said he wouldn't touch me until I healed."

Both females looked even more confused.

"I want to avoid it as long as possible. I'm not ready to have sex with him, though I know that is my purpose now. I agreed to it," I whispered, though I said the last part more to myself.

A cautious understanding finally entered the female's eyes. She looked embarrassed, actually, and returned her attention to the clothing in her hands, inspecting the beads as if her life depended on it.

"Come, *Missiki*," she finally said, raising her eyes. "We will dress you."

She didn't speak of the salve again as they went about their duties.

Though the shift dress the horde king had given me last night barely concealed my nudity, I would have preferred it over what they helped me dress in.

The skirt was made out of animal hide, similar to what the horde king had worn the night before. Tan in color, it was cleanly made, the stitching impressive. However, it came to my mid-thigh, exposing the majority of my legs. And I feared that if I bent over, my sex would be on display, exposed.

The gold beaded top was also too short, stopping just above my navel, molding to my breasts. Thankfully, the material was thick and the plethora of beads that decorated the front helped hide the outline of them. However, it left my shoulders and arms bare. The worst part, however, was that the neckline was attached to a thick golden band, which secured around my neck like a collar.

After helping me into sandals with very impractical, intricate, thin straps, the Dakkari females seemed pleased with their work. When I looked down at myself, my cheeks flushed with mortification because I felt every inch like a kept whore. Collared and exposed. All that was left was to be painted and coifed.

Which was apparently to be next, when I saw the females pulling out little pots of black and red pigments, a white bone brush, and gilded hair pins from their bundle.

"No," I said, shaking my head, taking a step away. The beads on my top jingled and the collar around my neck felt too tight. "That's quite enough."

The Dakkari female frowned, looking down at the cosmetics in her hands. Her own eyelids were painted gold, her already dark eyes rimmed in a solid black powder. I didn't want any of that on my face.

"Please," I said, "just hand me the brush. I'll brush out my hair, but that's all I want."

"I will do it," the female said finally, gingerly setting her pots of cosmetics back into her bundle, though she didn't seem happy about it. "It is my honor to serve you, *Missiki*."

"My name is Luna," I snapped, that overwhelming feeling

returning full force, my voice sounding sharp to my own ears. I felt confined, on display. Nothing was in my control. I had been dropped into a world where nothing made sense and I just wanted someone to call me by my actual *name*. Not *Missiki*—whatever the hell that meant—not *kalles* or *vekkiri* or *kassikari* or *Morakkari.*

Luna.

The name my mother had given me. An old name of our race. An ancient name.

Both of the Dakkari females blinked and exchanged a look with one another, freezing in place, their tails flicking behind them wildly. I blew out a breath, lifting a shaking hand to my wavy hair, which I usually kept pinned back since it curled around my cheeks.

"We cannot call you by your given name, *Missiki*," the female said, her tone surprisingly gentle. "It is forbidden. Just as we do not call the *Vorakkar* by his given name."

A name I still did not know, though I shared a bed with him. Though I'd bathed him and he'd caressed my breasts and told me I would be his queen.

Silence stretched out and the females seemed uncomfortable as they waited for me to speak.

"I'm sorry," I finally whispered. "I didn't mean to snap."

Again, they seemed uncomfortable, even with my apology. "You are our *Missiki*. You should not apologize to us. We are here to serve you. It gives us purpose and is a great honor bestowed on us by the *Vorakkar*," the female repeated.

This was going nowhere. For whatever reason, these females thought they should obey me. They *wanted* to.

I sighed, looking at the brush the silent female had grabbed. "Very well," I said softly. "No cosmetics, but will you brush my hair out and pin it back?"

"*Lysi, Missiki*," the female breathed, seemingly relieved.

"Will you tell me your names at least?" I asked next, sitting on a nearby cushion. "Or is that forbidden too?"

"We are only *piki*. You may know our names," the female said, though hesitantly, as if I wasn't supposed to ask, as if it was strange. The customs of this culture would be difficult to learn, I realized. And what were *piki*? "My given name is Mirari."

Mirari said something in Dakkari to the other female, who finally spoke, her eyes meeting mine for a brief moment before they darted away, and she said softly, "Lavi."

It was then I realized that the silent female simply didn't know the universal tongue, which was why she hadn't spoken.

Nodding, I gave them a small, strained smile in return and felt Lavi move behind me to brush out my hair.

"What are *piki*?" I asked Mirari.

She was fiddling with the gold pins as she replied, "We are like...helpers. We are unmated females that travel with the horde. We help the wives of horde warriors with these things."

"You *like* traveling with the horde?" I asked, hoping that my question wasn't offensive. It seemed like a hard lifestyle to me, constantly on the move, no permanent roots.

Mirari said, "*Lysi*. It is our hope to become horde brides one day and this is how we attract warriors. It is how it has always been done in the hordes. One day, we will have *piki* of our own."

I nodded, but I didn't truly understand.

Mirari continued, a thread of excitement in her voice, or at least what I believed to be excitement, with, "Now that the *Vorakkar* has given us this honor, surely we will be brides soon. All of the horde will know us."

Was this about the 'queen' thing?

Wisely, I kept my mouth shut, though questions raced in my mind. Truthfully, I wasn't certain I wanted to know the answers. A part of me was still hoping the horde king would tire of me when he realized just how inexperienced I was when it came to sex and would allow me to return to my village. And, well, if what I feared he'd meant came true, then I knew he would *never* let me return.

The domed tent was silent as they finished brushing my hair. A few moments after that, Lavi had my hair braided and then pinned up in an intricate way, so it was off my face and neck.

"Will you eat now, *Missiki?*" Mirari asked once Lavi was done, casting a glance over at the food still on the tray, though it had gone cold. "You must be hungry now."

I was famished. But the thought of eating made acid burn in my belly.

"No," I said, shaking my head.

Mirari looked at the food and then back at me. "The *Vorakkar* will be displeased if you do not eat. He told us specifically that you needed sustenance."

Closing my eyes, I asked, "Have you ever been hungry, Mirari? Truly hungry?"

The Dakkari female seemed surprised that I'd used her given name but she answered, "In the mornings after I wake, *lysi.*"

I shook my head, but she had answered my question regardless. The hordes had never known the hunger that plagued the settlements and villages spread across Dakkar. Of course they wouldn't know. They fed fresh meat to their beasts, which told me they had meat to spare. They were nomadic. They followed their game across Dakkar, while still denying that opportunity to the settlements under penalty of death.

Though the foreign races had begun to settle on Dakkar over thirty years ago, we still struggled to produce crops and find fresh water. We still had an elementary knowledge of the land. All we knew was to never destroy it or else the Dakkari would come.

Mirari said something in Dakkari to Lavi after several moments of silence. Lavi stood and left the tent once again.

"What was I meant to do today?" I asked, exhaustion weighing on my shoulders again. I felt the collar around my neck whenever I swallowed.

Mirari studied me and then replied, "The *Vorakkar* was to take you out among the horde, to present you."

Present me.

I wondered what Kivan was doing at that moment. I'd never been away from him this long before. I had promised him that I would see him again, but I wondered...was that a promise I could keep?

How would he survive? Without my credits coming in from my seamstress work, would he be able to save enough to buy rations? We had a few ration packs saved, but that would only be enough for a couple weeks, if that.

Grief made my throat burn. I had always taken care of him, protected him. Now he was alone, likely an outcast in the village for his reckless actions yesterday.

The tent flap slapped open and I sucked in a startled breath when the horde king ducked inside, tense anger written on his face. Behind him, I saw Lavi, though she stayed outside.

"*Rothi kiv, piki*," he growled, his voice dark and ominous.

Mirari inclined her head and hurriedly scuttled out. I watched her leave, a sense of betrayal making my lips press together.

They'd ratted me out to the horde king. And he was *pissed*.

6

"You refuse to eat, *kalles*?"

His voice was measured and controlled, but quiet in a way that sent alarm bells through my head.

I didn't answer him.

And he didn't like that.

The horde king stalked towards me in three angry strides. Though I was still kneeling on the cushion, I tipped my head back to look at him. I was still frightened of him, unsure what to make of him, whether he truly was the primitive brute I'd heard stories of or not, but I would never let that fear show.

Unlike yesterday, he was wearing nothing more than a draped cloth that attached to a wide, gold belt. His thick boots creaked when he crouched in front of me and I caught a glimpse of his cock, swaying underneath the loose cloth. He was still bare-chested, his wide cuffs flashing on his wrists.

"You," he said quietly, "*will* eat now."

"Why?" I hissed, just as quietly, back.

"You are malnourished," he snarled. "I will not have you wasting away."

"I will eat what my village eats, what my brother eats. Uranian Federation rations and nothing more."

The horde king burst out with a Dakkari curse and his large hand flashed out, wrapping around the side of my neck, just over my collar. His strength was undeniable and I let out a small, surprised breath when he tilted my head back to look at him.

"You are a part of the horde now. You will eat what the horde eats!" he growled, those yellow eyes flashing. My temper was rising. Whenever I felt backed into a corner, I came out fighting.

"I will *never* be part of the horde."

"You are!" he roared. "You will be my *kassikari*, I will fill your belly with my heirs, you will be my queen, and *you will eat when I tell you to!*"

Sucking in a breath, anger pulsing through me, I hissed out, "Or else *what?*"

Something dark came into his narrowed eyes. His hand flexed on my throat and he rasped, "If you refuse to eat, I will consider it a slight. I will return to your little village and do what I should have done last night. I will let Kakkari feast on your brother's spilled blood as retribution."

I froze. He was threatening me, using my brother's life as leverage.

However, he would lose me if he took that course and for some reason...he wanted me. A horde king of the Dakkari wanted *me* and I could use that to my advantage.

Narrowing my eyes, I called his bluff.

"Do it then," I said softly, pressing my neck into his hand further, rising to my knees so that we were eye to eye, ignoring the pain from riding the *pyroki*. The beads on my top swayed as I moved. The horde king stilled, his eyes flashing to my lips as I spoke. "But if you do, I swear on your goddess that I will *never* eat again. I will die here and be reunited with my brother and mother in the afterlife. *Nothing* would make me happier."

The horde king's nostrils flared.

Then, without warning, he grabbed me around the waist and hauled me up, striding over to the tray of food on the low table.

I gasped, struggling against him, my skirt riding up in the process. My thighs rubbed together as I squirmed, but I didn't care about the rough pain. Not right then. Desperate sounds, small and frustrated and animal-like, emerged from my throat as I fought against his hold.

But he was unmovable. Like a mountain.

"Enough!" he bellowed, dropping us both down to the table. He maneuvered himself behind me, pinning my legs down with his own, bracketing my arms at my sides until I couldn't move, but I still continued to struggle, finding energy and a fire inside me that I *needed* to keep fueled. No matter what.

When I realized what his intention was, my eyes widened. "You wouldn't dare," I hissed.

"If you will not eat," he rasped, "then I will make you, *kalles*."

I watched with frustration as he plucked a piece of dried meat from one of the dishes. Immediately, he pressed it to my lips, but I kept them tight together, keeping my teeth clenched, and turned my face to the side. He followed and I whipped my face to the other side.

And it continued. I don't know how long I continued to fight against him, but soon, I grew tired. I was expending too much energy, my weakened muscles straining against him as I fought his hold.

"Stubborn *kalles*," he growled. "I will break you like a wild *pyroki* if I must."

You can try, I goaded in my mind, but kept my teeth firmly clenched.

He was growing more and more frustrated too and I would

hold out for as long as I could. In my mind, it wasn't even about the food anymore. It was about so much more and I couldn't let him succeed. I wouldn't.

Even when I felt something harden beneath my lap, even when he used his tail to keep my head still, even when I started panting from the exertion, I still fought.

Finally, the horde king let his hand fall away, though he kept me pinned. Relief went through me, thinking I'd won that battle. And if I could win one battle, I could win another.

"It seems you are feeling much better this day, *kalles*," he finally rasped, something entirely different in his voice. Sucking in a sharp breath through my nostrils, I felt dread pool in my belly when he maneuvered our position, dragging my legs apart wider with his own, wrapping his strong, flexible tail around my arms, holding them in place. I felt cool air rush over my sex and when I glanced down, I saw my skirt was barely concealing me. "Let us forget about the food then."

I made an alarmed, muffled sound when his other hand came to cup my exposed sex. Biting my lip, I resumed my struggles when one of his fingers stroked over my slit, teasing the flesh.

I was all too aware that he still held the dried meat in his other hand, hovering just on the edge of my vision. The battle wasn't over, he was just employing very different methods than before. That frustrated me, made me desperate to get away.

"*Lysi*," he hissed, "you are making me ache, *kalles*."

Stop, I screamed in my mind, *please stop!*

But he continued to slowly, almost languidly stroke me between my thighs. He found my clit, pressing and rolling it with the rough pad of his finger.

And goddess help me...I felt my treacherous body responding to his surprisingly gentle, expert, exploring touch.

No, no, no!

Whimpering, I resumed my struggles tenfold, trying to

scratch at his legs like a caged animal, muffled noises emerging from my throat.

But he never stopped. And I never gave in.

Soon, panic sank into my gut, my breathing going ragged, trying to fight against the heady pleasure that was building between my thighs.

In my ear, he rasped, "You are growing hot for me, *kalles*." A dark chortle came next and I felt my cheeks heat with humiliation, with shame. "*Vok*, you need this. I need this too, *kassikari*."

It was building and building, the heat growing hotter and hotter. I feared what would happen next.

Finally, desperate, I pleaded, "*Stop*."

"What, *kalles*? I did not hear you."

"*Please*, st—"

He shoved the piece of dried meat between my open lips.

Disbelief shot through me but before he could clamp my mouth shut, I spit it out, though the delicious flavor burst on my tongue, making my stomach cramp with even more hunger. But I was used to it.

The horde king growled in dark frustration and, to my surprise, released me entirely, pushing me forward so he could stand.

The pins in my hair had fallen out, all of Lavi's hard work destroyed, and I pushed back a tendril of escaped hair when I looked up at him, stunned. His expression was thunderous, though his cock tented the cloth covering him. Behind him, his tail flicked dangerously, back and forth. He was so large, he seemed to take up all the space in the palatial tent.

"Go hungry then, *kalles*. It is your choice," he rasped. "Rest today. Because when I return tonight, I will have what you promised me. It is obvious you have recovered your strength and I will not wait another night to claim your cunt."

Glaring up at him, I felt my heart racing in my throat.

The horde king turned and stalked out of the tent, letting in a brief, blinding chunk of sunlight before it closed. Then it was dark once more. Outside, I heard him bark something in Dakkari before his footsteps retreated.

Alone, I stared at the cold food on the low table in disbelief, at the dried meat I'd spit out, which had landed on the plush rug. Slowly, I picked it up and placed it back in the bowl.

My body was still humming from his touch. My body felt like a stranger's.

I may have won that battle between us, but I felt like I'd won nothing at all.

7

L ater that night, Mirari and Lavi prepared me for the inevitable.

They bathed me again, though I'd protested that I was clean. Naturally, Mirari insisted, saying that all the horde bathed daily, which seemed like a great waste to me.

After my bath, they dressed me in the night dress the horde king had given me, which had already been cleaned, though my old clothes still had not been returned to me.

The *piki* brushed my hair until it fell in softened waves down my back, and lit the wax candles and fragrant oil pots to burn for the remainder of the night. The tent was cast in a golden light, the gentle flames flickering and swaying.

When they finally left, Mirari took the tray of food she'd brought that morning with her, casting a frown over it, obviously inspecting it to see if it'd been touched. Ever since they returned that afternoon, she'd been pressing me to eat, telling me how pleased the *Vorakkar* would be if I did.

Wisely, I'd held my tongue and eventually, she'd stopped pressing, though every time my stomach growled and she cast me a speculative, hopeful look, it made me blush.

I was alone then, clean, practically naked, sitting on the edge of the bed facing the tent's entrance. I'd decided that afternoon that I needed to be brave, that this was the cost I'd willingly paid. The horde king wanted me in his bed and I would be. My brother was alive because of his mercy and while he couldn't make me eat...he could make me do this.

It didn't matter that my stomach was in knots—and not just because of my hunger. It didn't matter that I worried he would tear me in two or that he would be rough. It didn't matter that I was a virgin, inexperienced with males and sex.

I'd made a deal with the Dakkari devil and I would hold up my end.

Heavy footsteps approached the tent and I sucked in a breath. I heard him, his unmistakable, deep voice speaking in Dakkari to the guards stationed at the entrance. After a moment, I heard their footsteps retreat, dismissed from their duties for the night, and my spine straightened, my heart tripling its beats in my breast.

There was silence for a moment, as I waited for him to enter. But he took his time, as if composing himself, before he suddenly ducked inside.

Across the tent, his eyes found mine, his yellow irises contracting and then widening. He straightened to his full height, swallowing the space with his broad shoulders and massive bulk.

Gone was his anger from earlier in the day, I noticed. It had been replaced by desire, by lust, the same expression on his face that he'd had when he'd cut open my cloak in my village.

I'd been right. For some strange reason, the horde king wanted me. I didn't know why.

My nipples pebbled tighter underneath the transparent shift, but thankfully my long hair covered them. Warily, I watched him as one might a predatory beast, studying him for a weakness. His hair was plaited down his back, his skin looked even more honeyed from his day in the sun, with a slight shimmer of sweat gleaming on his bare chest, though the sun had long set. Not for the first time, I wondered what his duties were during the day, when he wasn't patrolling the lands of Dakkar.

His hands went to the gold belt at his hips, which he unclasped. With it went the piece of cloth that shielded his sex. He dropped it to the floor of the tent with a small *thud* and then he was naked, his cock already hard, his dusky, dark sack hanging low beneath it.

I sucked in a small breath when he approached, my hands twitching against my legs. I'd had Mirari smear some of the healing salve on my thighs after all, since it was obvious I wouldn't be able to rebuff the horde king's attentions. It had helped take the stinging pain away, which I was begrudgingly thankful for. It would make this easier.

Though there was a fresh, steaming bathing tub in the corner waiting for him, it was clear that he didn't intend to use it. At least not yet.

"Leika," he rasped, his voice brushing over my skin when he pushed me back onto the bed, the furs beneath me tickling my arms. *"Rinavi leika, rei kassikari, rei Morakkari."*

With one decisive tug, the horde king pulled my shift over my head until I was as naked as he was, dropping it onto the floor beside the bed. Out of habit, my arms crossed immediately over my breasts, but he pulled them away a moment later, bringing my arms over my head, securing my wrists in one large palm.

He adjusted me so I lay in the middle of the bed, bare and exposed to him. Then he crawled over me, his head ducking low, those eyes searing me as his pointed, dark tongue flicked out, licking a single line from my navel to between the valley of my breasts, to my collarbone. I couldn't contain my gasp.

"Rinavi leika," he rasped again, though I didn't know what

those words meant. That head ducked a second time and then he was suckling one of my breasts, that hot tongue flicking over my peaked nipple.

My breathing went shallow as my treacherous body began to respond to him once more.

Foreign sensations battled within me. Pressure began to build as my nipple tingled between his lips and I ground my teeth together against the pleasure when he switched breasts, laving his tongue over it.

No, no, no.

I'd told myself I would allow this. But I didn't want to enjoy it. *That* seemed like a betrayal, *that* seemed like a true violation. It was not something I ever wanted to give him, that satisfaction.

The scent of his musk reached my nostrils, rising from his skin after his long day. He smelled like the earth, heady and warm. I smelled his sweat. Instead of repulsing me, it made my head swim.

When I squeezed my eyes shut, trying to block everything out, I felt him move down my body, releasing my wrists above my head in the process. Something hard and hot brushed my stomach and I knew it was his cock.

My eyes flew open when he pulled my thighs wide. When I looked down, I saw he was lying between my spread legs, his head just inches from my exposed sex.

But he hesitated.

His eyes tracked over the dark bruises that had begun to bloom across my lower buttocks. He saw how red my inner thighs still were, how chafed the skin was. Though the salve helped, it would be another few days until the pain was gone completely, until the flesh healed over.

The horde king made a sound in the back of his throat, but he didn't hesitate any longer. I bit my lip to keep from gasping when he licked the slit of my sex slowly.

His deep groan of pleasure, his rasped words in Dakkari, made my body tense tight. I gripped the furs beneath me, staring up at the canopy of the domed tent, where the supports met in the very center. I focused on that spot.

But he wouldn't even give me that.

"Look at me, *kalles*," he growled between my thighs, parting my lower lips with his fingers. I felt cool air dance over my clit.

I had to do what he said so I met his gaze, though I kept my expression carefully shuttered. His yellow-rimmed eyes darted back and forth between mine and then he ducked his head.

This time, I couldn't stop the choked moan that slid from my throat as he lapped at my exposed sex, flicking my clit back and forth with that stiff, pointed tongue.

It felt good. And I hated that. I hated it and liked it so much that to my mortification, I felt tears well in my eyes. They pooled before rolling across my temples, dropping onto the furs beneath my head. Tears of frustration, of physical need, of grief, of fear of my new life, of confusion.

To make matters worse, right at that moment, my stomach growled.

Loudly.

The horde king froze between my thighs.

I couldn't stem my tears in time. When he looked up at me, he saw them.

He cursed low in Dakkari, a whispered, anguished curse, before dropping his warm forehead above my pelvic bone. I felt his breath against my skin when he blew it out roughly, his shoulders moving with it.

A moment later, he rolled off me before sitting on the edge of the low bed, his scarred back to me, those golden tattoos glittering. Silence stretched between us but I didn't dare move.

Finally, the horde king rose.

"*Veekor, kalles*," he growled before heading to his bathing tub, which was most likely lukewarm by now. "Sleep."

"What?" I whispered, shocked.

"Go to sleep," he repeated, stepping into the tub, assuming the position he had the previous night, his eyes closing, his arms resting on the edge, his head tilting back towards the canopy.

I stared in disbelief at his sharp profile. My legs were still splayed wide, my chest was heaving, my cheeks were wet from my tears. Confusion warred within me.

Slowly, I sat up and reached for my shift dress on the floor. Pulling it over my head, I snuck another glance at the horde king, but found his eyes were still closed.

My hands shook when I smoothed the dress into place, my nerves still jittery, my body still warm from his touch. I felt like a stranger in my own skin, my emotions all over the place.

He stopped, I thought in disbelief.

He could have taken my body just now but he stopped.

Why?

Hesitantly, I looked over at him in the bathing tub. Water trickled as he began to wash, lathering up the soap in the coarse cloth before scrubbing over his skin, a duty I'd had the previous night.

Could it...could it be that he'd felt unease? Guilt? He'd seen my tears, heard my growling belly and he'd stopped, though he'd been so aroused he groaned when he first tasted my sex.

I was still sitting in the bed, wondering about his actions, hugging my knees to my chest, when he finished and stepped out of the bathing tub. My eyes caught his as he dried off, but he didn't say a single word. I continued to watch him as he went around the tent, putting out the little flames from the wax candles with a sizzling twist of his fingertips, still naked, *still* erect.

The horde king came to bed. Just like the previous night, he pulled the furs around him, around me, warding off the slight chill in the night air that threaded its way through the tent flaps.

Unlike last night, he tugged me towards him in the darkness when I lay down beside him.

His skin was shockingly warm after his bath and smelled clean, not that musky, heady scent from before. The ends of his damp hair slid over my shoulder as he tucked me into his side, pushing my face into the column of his neck, resting his chin on my temple. I felt his cock settle and press into my belly.

I blinked at the intimate embrace, torn between wanting to pull away and wanting to accept it. I'd never been held this way before, by anyone.

Neither of us slept yet, though long moments passed.

And maybe the darkness made me brave, maybe it was because I couldn't see his face, could only feel his warmth, but I whispered, "Will you tell me your name, horde king?"

My future was uncertain. At the very least, I knew that my immediate future would be tied to his. It was only fitting I knew his name, so I could call him by something other than 'horde king' or '*Vorakkar.*'

"You do not know much about the Dakkari, do you, *kalles?*" was his answer. I felt his vocal cords vibrate against my forehead.

"No," I replied truthfully, wondering why they tiptoed around something as simple as names. "I do not."

"Except one, no Dakkari among my horde knows my given name," he told me. "None ever will."

"I'm not Dakkari," I pointed out.

He made a sound in the back of his throat. For a moment, I thought he sounded amused. "*Nik, kalles,* you are not."

I waited for a long time, but eventually decided that I would have to call him *Vorakkar.* Just like everyone else. A strange part of me found disappointment in that.

Which was why I was surprised when he finally said, "I will offer you my given name on two conditions."

Curiosity and wariness made me ask, "What are they?"

"You never speak it where it can be overheard by my horde," he said.

"And the other?" I asked.

"You will eat once you wake."

I inhaled a small, surprised breath through my nostrils.

Logically, I knew I couldn't go even another couple days without eating *something*. But I still felt an incredible guilt weighing on my shoulders when I thought of eating fresh meat and having a full belly. What did that even taste like, feel like?

Softly, I said, "I will have the broth." The horde king made a noise of protest and I said, "We have broth in our rations. I will eat that and nothing more."

"Stubborn *kalles*," he murmured. But he let out a deep sigh. "You will eat the entire portion I give you?"

"Yes," I whispered. "I promise."

The horde king pressed his hand to the back of my head and I felt his lips brush my ear, felt his tail curl around my calf.

"Arokan," he rasped softly, sending goosebumps over my arms. "My given name is Arokan of Rath Kitala. Now, sleep, *kalles*."

Arokan.

I did as he asked with his name ringing in my mind.

8

When I woke, Arokan was gone again. Only this time, I hadn't heard him leave the bed.

In the light of day, some of which filtered through the very top of the domed tent, casting little pools of light on the furs, I was even more confused than I'd been the previous day.

The furs tickled my bare legs since my shift dress had ridden up during the night. I could distinctly remember the heat of his tongue running up my body, the feel of it between my thighs.

The absence of it when he stopped.

I exhaled a sharp breath through my nostrils.

Whatever thoughts I had about the horde king, however, I didn't need to dwell on, so I pushed them from my mind as I pushed up from the bed I'd shared with him.

As if waiting for any sign of movement within the tent, my two *piki* entered without hesitation. Mirari was carrying another tray of food and Lavi had her bundle of supplies they would no doubt use on me again that morning.

Was this what my life would be like until the horde king tired of me? To sleep beside him and stay sequestered in a tent during the day, to be bathed and clothed and coifed for no reason at all?

"The *Vorakkar* sends you this," Mirari said with a slight incline of her head in greeting. She set the tray down onto the same low table as yesterday. Except this time, I saw that instead of numerous bowls of food…there was a single bowl filled with steaming broth. "He says you are to eat it all and if you do not… then we must tell him."

It was a *giant* bowl of broth.

I pressed my lips together, remembering our agreement. He'd said he would give me his name in exchange for eating the *entire portion* he would give me. Only, he hadn't mentioned that the portion would be four or five times larger than what it normally was in our ration packs.

"Right," I said softly, pressing a hand to my empty stomach. Then I sighed as I walked to the low table and sat on a cushion.

Mirari watched me out of the corner of her eye as I picked up the bowl in both hands and brought it to my lips.

Flavor burst on my palate, delicious and savory. It was possibly the best thing I'd ever tasted and I only felt a slight twinge of guilt as I swallowed the mouthful I'd taken in. I could feel how the broth traveled to my waiting belly, how it warmed a path inside me.

Closing my eyes, I drank more and I hated that it tasted so good, nothing like the bland, watery soup we were given in our rations. It was rich and fatty and delicious.

It took me only a few moments to finish the entire bowl. By the time I was done, I felt…full. A strange, foreign, even uncomfortable sensation. I felt like my stomach would burst.

But the hunger was gone. That was something.

After my meal, I let the *piki* do what they did yesterday without a fuss. From their bundle, they dragged a fresh outfit— two different outfits in two days, when I'd had two in total for the past couple years—just as revealing as the last.

It was a gold-collared top, just like yesterday, that showed my navel and left my arms and most of my back bare. The skirt was asymmetrical, long on one side while short on the other, so short that it barely covered my backside. The same pair of sandals were strapped to my feet and Lavi did what she did yesterday with my hair.

Thankfully, Mirari didn't touch the cosmetics, nor did she try to convince me to use some.

I stayed silent through the whole process. Even when Mirari put some salve on my inner thighs.

However, she hesitated as she asked, "Would you like some for inside?"

Inside? I thought, my brow furrowing in confusion.

It took me a moment to realize what she meant and when I did, my cheeks flamed.

She assumed Arokan mated me last night, seeing as how she'd prepared me for it.

She thought I was sore, or perhaps that he'd been too rough or too large.

I cleared my throat and shook my head. "He didn't...we didn't do that."

Mirari blinked. "He will wait until the black moon?"

Black moon?

"I don't know," I answered, because it was the easiest answer to give. Arokan had told me little about my purpose here. And what he *had* told me...scared me.

Yesterday, he'd told me again that I would be his queen, that he would fill my belly with his seed and get me heavy with his heirs.

He must have thought that humans and Dakkari could procreate. Was that my purpose? To be his breeder? Why didn't he sire heirs with a Dakkari female? Surely that would be easier.

Mirari didn't say anything in reply but she murmured something in Dakkari to Lavi, who stood and left the tent.

"Do the Dakkari often take humans from their settlements?" I asked softly.

Mirari jerked her head to look at me.

"You speak the universal tongue," I commented. "So do others. For what purpose other than to speak to us?"

"To communicate," Mirari said, as if it were obvious. "Most who have lived in *Dothik* can speak it. It is not just humans who live on Dakkar now. Even beyond our planet, the language is useful."

"*Dothik?*" I asked.

"Our capital. Where the *Dothikkar* lives, our king."

My lips parted. "I thought the horde kings ruled over your lands."

"They do," Mirari replied. "The *Dothikkar* stays in the capital. He handles...other matters, political matters. Our king was born into his rank. The *Vorakkars* earn it. They are our protectors and providers, celebrated kings in their own right."

I thought of Arokan and wondered what he'd done to 'earn it.'

I knew nothing about him. I knew next to nothing about the Dakkari, which Arokan had commented on last night.

But how could I? We knew of the Dakkari through rumor and whisperings only, none of them good.

"Why do the Dakkari not like to give their names?"

Mirari blinked and her gold-painted eyelids flashed.

"We believe," Mirari started slowly, "that names have power over us. Dakkari give their true names to those who are important to them, who they trust not to abuse that power. Sometimes, however, names are given for just the opposite reason, to show that they do *not* respect the one they give it to, as an insult, to show that they are so low in their eyes as to not warrant concern."

My lips parted. How would I *ever* understand this contradictory culture?

"And the *Vorakkar*?" I asked softly.

"Horde kings keep their given names especially close," Mirari said. "No one needs to know it because the *Vorakkars* wield the ultimate power over their hordes. To know the *Vorakkar's* true name would be an insult to him."

But he gave me his name, I thought. For nothing more than my promise to eat a bowl of broth.

I didn't think I understood. At least not entirely.

"Did I...did I offend you when I asked yours and Lavi's?" I asked, wanting to know.

Mirari tilted her head to the side. "*Nik*. You are our *Missiki*, our Mistress, and soon to be our *Morakkari*. We serve you and it is a great honor to do so."

"Even though I'm human and not Dakkari?" I couldn't help but question.

She hesitated. "We respect the *Vorakkar's* decisions. It is our duty as members of his horde."

Her answer left me a little uneasy.

"But are there those that resent me being here?" I asked.

Again, she hesitated. It told me what I needed to know.

A moment later, Lavi appeared, pushing past the thick tent flaps. She held one open, however, allowing light to pool inside.

"Come, *Missiki*," Mirari said, guiding me over to the entrance. "The *Vorakkar* is ready for you."

Ready for me?

Sunlight blinded me when I stepped out of the tent. It was unusually warm for the season that day and I felt that heat across my bared flesh, like fingers against my skin.

Two guards were positioned at the front entrance of the tent, on either side, but they didn't look at me. They kept their gazes averted.

Arokan stood a short distance away from the tent, speaking

with the Dakkari male that had also come to my village, the messenger. Their tones were low and Arokan's gaze met mine the moment I stepped outside.

The messenger's eyes cut to me as well and I watched his lips press together. Perhaps *he* was one of the Dakkari that resented me being there.

Arokan said something and the messenger left him, stalking towards the pen of the *pyroki* that lay a short distance away. The horde king approached me and I couldn't help the shiver that raced up my spine at the sight of him...couldn't help remembering his heat and his tongue between my thighs.

He was dressed as he was yesterday, in nothing more than a heavy cloth that covered his genitals, held up by a golden belt, and thick boots. His exposed shoulders and chest were bronzed from the strong Dakkari sun, those intricate, swirling designs of gold ink glittering as he moved towards me.

He looked every bit the barbarian Dakkari warrior I'd heard of from rumors. Only now, I knew his scent. I knew his warmth and the feel of his body against me as he slept.

Arokan of Rath Kitala.

Feeling flustered, I looked from him, past him to the horde settlement spread out across the land.

In the sunlight, it was even larger than I'd originally thought.

Dozens and dozens and dozens of domed hide tents were spread across the settlement, slightly smaller than Arokan's. I saw smoke rising between them with mild alarm, but I saw that the fires were contained, raised off the ground in golden barrels so they didn't scorch the earth.

Some Dakkari were working the *pyroki* pens, hauling in meat and fresh water for the black-scaled beasts of my nightmares. There were over a hundred of them enclosed in the pen, just a short distance away.

"You ate the broth?" Arokan asked me when he was within arm's reach.

My eyes flashed up to his and my spine straightened ever so slightly. "I said I would, didn't I?"

"Every last drop?" he asked softly, those yellow-rimmed eyes on me.

"Yes," I said. "Although if you made the portion any bigger, I wouldn't have been able to."

"Come then," Arokan said, seeming satisfied with my answers. "My horde will see you now."

He turned and began walking, those scars across his back pulling. I looked behind me, saw that Lavi and Mirari remained in the tent, and hesitantly began to follow Arokan.

When I caught up to him, I asked, "What do you mean?"

He didn't answer me. Yesterday, Mirari had said something about Arokan 'presenting me.' Was that what this was?

Letting out a small sigh, I simply walked with him because I didn't know what else to do. Slightly behind him, actually, because his legs and strides were much longer than mine.

At least I'm outside, I thought, deciding to enjoy it. The air was fresh, the sun warm. Every so often, I caught a stray whiff of *pyroki*, whenever the wind changed. Sometimes, I even caught Arokan's scent.

Within the settlement, it seemed like a flurry of activity. I spied many Dakkari milling between the spaces of each tent, hauling baskets of wood, or food, or cloth. I heard the distant, strange laughter of Dakkari young, saw some dart between the tents as we walked, peering at us curiously. I heard metal clanging together, like a blacksmith shop, like swords were being forged. I saw what looked like a training ground, with young Dakkari males sparring with spears and blades.

The further we walked into the settlement, the more notice we drew. Every Dakkari we passed stopped and stared at me, though I noticed that whenever I returned their gaze, they darted their eyes away. It didn't matter if it was males, females, or children...no one would look at me directly.

Many had already seen me. I remembered that first night, when Arokan's horde had greeted him, touching his *pyroki*, his legs and mine, as we rode through the camp.

But perhaps in the light of day, it was different.

It was intimidating.

I was the only human in a camp full of Dakkari. And I stuck out like one.

It didn't help that I was practically naked. The clothes covered my breasts and my collarbones and my lower half, but not much more.

I did notice, however, that many Dakkari females also wore revealing clothing, despite their age. Some females were even topless, baring their large breasts to the sun. Most of the males only wore a cloth over their sex, just like Arokan.

It was something else I would need to get used to, a difference, of which I was sure there were many, between Dakkari and human culture.

We made multiple passes throughout the entire settlement, so many that by the end of it, my thighs were rubbed a little raw again.

Arokan had said his horde would see me and he'd been right. I didn't think a single Dakkari hadn't by the time we were finished.

Throughout it all, Arokan didn't look at me once. Whenever I tried to ask him a question—about something we passed, about how many Dakkari lived in his horde, about the training grounds, about the bustling cooking area I spied—he remained silent. He ignored me—*completely* ignored me—like I hadn't spoken at all, like I didn't even exist.

It was dismissive and humiliating, especially considering that his horde was witness to it.

So by the time we returned to the tent, after we both

stepped inside and Arokan dismissed Mirari and Lavi, once we were alone, I was irritated and unsure and my face was burning in embarrassment.

His eyes finally turned to me and he watched me for a brief, silent moment. It felt strange to finally have his gaze on me.

"What was that?" I asked quietly.

"I presented you to my horde," he said, as if it was obvious.

"Not that," I said. "You expected me to follow you like I was an animal and you ignored me like one."

Arokan's eyes narrowed. "Do not question my actions, *kalles*. I expect you to obey me, especially among my horde."

I bristled. "Am I just a—a pet to you? You feed me and touch me and clothe me and brush my hair and I'm expected to do whatever you want?"

"You agreed to it," he rasped, taking a step towards me. "Even if I did consider you my 'pet' as you call it, you agreed to it, *kalles*."

"Do you even know my name?" I asked, surprisingly stung by his words and I didn't even know why. "Do you even care?"

"Luna," he answered swiftly. My lips parted, my body stilling as I heard it curl off his tongue. "That was what your brother called you, was it not?"

Stunned, I looked down to my feet, slightly dirty from the walk around the camp. Hearing my name on his lips felt... wrong. Different. Strange.

"Whether I care," he hissed next, "does not matter. You are not Luna anymore. Not here. You will be my *Morakkari*. You will be the *Morakkari* of my horde and you will show your respect of me when we are among them. Whatever I demand of you, you will do without question because I am still their *Vorakkar*. It does not matter what you want. It matters what they *see*, what they *think*. I will not have you threaten that. Do you understand me?"

Disbelief made my head swim. He wanted to take my identity away, my past. He wanted my only purpose to be *him*, his people.

"Go to hell, Arokan," I whispered, deliberately using his name.

His hand flashed out and he gripped my arm, just above my bicep, dragging me towards him until he loomed over me. His eyes were furious, his slim nostrils flaring.

But I wasn't afraid. I glared up at him and rasped, "I agreed to be your whore, not your queen, and certainly not your obedient little slave."

"You said you would serve me," he corrected, "and you will. However I want. I *own* you, *kalles*. And when the black moon comes, I will show you just how much. In three nights, you will truly be *mine*."

9

Arokan didn't return to the tent.

After the first night and next day when he'd 'presented' me to his horde, I didn't care that he hadn't returned. I welcomed the space as I got my head sorted, as I came to terms with the fact that I'd let my temper get the best of me.

Though Arokan had been a cold bastard, he'd been right. I'd agreed to it all.

I remembered that just in time too, considering that I'd just begun to think that Arokan of Rath Kitala might not be so bad after all, that he wasn't the cruel monster that the horde king rumors had made him out to be.

It didn't matter that he'd given me his true name, that he'd stopped his advances because I was uncomfortable, that he'd wanted me to eat and not to go hungry.

I was still his pawn, his plaything. For a reason I hadn't yet discovered, he'd chosen me to be his obedient little wife. He wanted me tamed, he wanted me quiet.

I could be neither.

I refused to be.

As I was granted the space I needed, it became more and

more apparent to me that I couldn't get out of my promise. Arokan wanted me as his queen, his wife...and I would be.

Whatever my role would be, whatever my duties would be still remained to be seen. However, I was still in control of my actions. I wasn't going to be diminished by a horde king of Dakkar—I wasn't going to be erased so that he could command the respect of his horde.

I would be his wife but I wouldn't be his victim. I wouldn't let him break me. That had never been part of the deal.

So on the second day of Arokan's absence, I asked Mirari and Lavi to bring me hide, cloth, a needle, and cordage.

After my request, Mirari cast a long look at Lavi, like the other female understood what I'd said.

"I want to make my own clothes," I said, looking at her, dressed in my sheer shift dress. "Since my other clothes seem to have been lost in the wash."

Mirari didn't even have the decency to look embarrassed. "They had holes in them. I had no choice but to burn those rags."

I took a deep, calming breath and gave her a small, hopefully charming smile. Then again, I'd never been good at charming anyone, so it most likely fell flat. "Please. I don't blame you for throwing them away, but I'd like to make other clothes that I'm more...myself in. I don't feel comfortable in Dakkari outfits."

"Why not?" Mirari asked, like it was a personal insult.

"If I bend over, all of the horde would see my backside," I said bluntly. "I don't like feeling exposed."

"The *Vorakkar* said you were not to have weapons," Mirari said quietly.

My brow furrowed. If I wanted a weapon, I could have stolen one from Arokan's belt during his baths, or when he slept at night. I'd had the opportunity before. It wouldn't have been difficult.

"A needle is hardly a weapon," I countered, "and I can't stitch if I don't have one."

Mirari still didn't look convinced. Lavi simply looked confused about the exchange and kept looking to Mirari for guidance.

"Please," I said again. I licked my lips, clearing my throat as I said, "If I'm going to stay here, if I'm going to be part of this horde... I need to do it my way. And I know it seems silly, but something as simple as making my own clothes, as feeling comfortable walking through the camp, will make a difference to me."

Mirari watched me, as if trying to discern if I was telling the truth or not. Finally, she nodded. "*Lysi*, I will get them for you."

She said something in Dakkari to Lavi, who seemed to protest, but then she left the tent, returning a short while later with the supplies I'd asked for, along with a few...embellishments. Like gold beads, clasps, and strips.

We set them out on the low table and I got to work under their dutiful watch.

After I'd taken my measurements, I started cutting the hide I would use to make pants. Mirari, despite her protestations, had brought me a small razor for the purpose, though her gaze was sharp on me as I made use of it and she took it away the moment I was done with it.

"I worked as a seamstress," I said quietly, my eyes rapt on the cloth, "back in my village. As an assistant to one, actually."

"Then why were your clothes in such disrepair?" Mirari asked boldly.

I almost laughed. "Because I made clothes for others, not myself. Cordage was hard to come by. I didn't want to waste it."

"We have heard little of human settlements," Mirari said softly, surprising me. "We know there are many spread across Dakkar, but we hear tales of their disrespect to Kakkari, of their uprisings and violence."

70

I sobered. "My village was peaceful. We were poor, but we were peaceful."

Mirari made a sound in the back of her throat. "We all saw the black smoke the day the *Vorakkar* brought you here."

"That was an accident."

"How is setting fire to Kakkari an accident?" Mirari asked. Her tone wasn't angry. It sounded like she simply wanted to understand. I was learning that despite her insistence that she was there to serve me, that she was there as my *piki*, she spoke her mind. She wasn't afraid to. I liked that about her.

"My brother set the fire," I told her.

"Your brother? Yet the *Vorakkar* brought you in his stead?"

"I made a deal with him," I said. That night seemed like so long ago. But it had only been a handful of days. "He spared my brother in return."

"Why did your brother start the fire?" Mirari asked, watching me. "Burning our land, our Kakkari…it is the ultimate insult."

"I know," I whispered. "He knew too. But our village is on the verge of starving."

Mirari blinked at the knowledge.

"He heard that burning the land for crops makes the soil healthier, makes the possibility for life greater. He was only trying to help our village, in his own foolish way."

Mirari went quiet for a brief moment, watching me begin to stitch the hide after I threaded the needle.

Finally she said, "You said 'our' village. Not 'their' village."

My needle stilled. "What?"

"Loyalty to the horde is a concept that is driven into all Dakkari from a young age," Mirari said softly.

"What are you saying?"

"That you hold onto your life, your past life, when you should not."

"It was my home," I argued. "It was where I grew up, with my mother, with my brother."

"You cannot be our true *Morakkari* if you choose them over the horde," Mirari said. "You were not born Dakkari, but you are Dakkari now. You have a responsibility to us now, to our *Vorakkar*."

"You're asking me to change my allegiance to him?"

"*Nik*, to us all," Mirari said softly. "To the *horde*."

My lips parted as I argued, "It does not have to be 'them' versus 'us.'" Mirari's brow furrowed. "You have heard stories of humans? We have heard stories of Dakkari too, of terrible things. We cannot hunt, we cannot plant, we cannot forage. We cannot leave the area of our settlement though the land is dead. And if we do, we die. We *all* share this planet now. There does not have to be a division."

"It is our *Dothikkar* who has ultimate power over these matters," she finally said, after a long silence. "There will always be division because of it."

My shoulders slumped and I returned my eyes to the clothes, similar in style to the pants I'd made for Kivan a couple seasons ago.

"The *Vorakkar* is still a male, however," Mirari said next, quietly.

Something in her tone made me look at her. "What do you mean?"

"Do you know of Drukkar?" Mirari asked.

I frowned. "No."

"Drukkar is Kakkari's counterpart. Her other half. Drukkar is our god and Kakkari is our goddess."

I'd never heard of a male deity, only Kakkari.

"Kakkari is the earth—solid, nurturing. She gives us life. Drukkar is everything that supports *her*, a foundation for her to stand on. Rains, seasons, storms, heat. He can be violent and merciless at times, but she always opens for him, accepts him.

Because of that, he loves her, he cares for her, and he punishes all who harm her."

"I don't understand," I said softly, watching her carefully.

"A Dakkari male is the same as Drukkar. He worships his female when she opens for him. He can be swayed."

Realization hit me like a punch.

"You think...you think Aro—the *Vorakkar*," I corrected quickly, "can be persuaded to help my village?"

"I am saying," Mirari said carefully, "that if anyone can sway a male's actions, it is his female."

"How?" I asked softly. "I'm not...I'm not experienced in things like this. How do I 'open' for him?"

Poor Lavi had no idea what was being said, though she was obviously trying to follow the thread of conversation, watching our mouths, her brows furrowed in confusion.

Mirari's lips curled and she asked Lavi something, who blinked, huffing out a small breath. Lavi replied in Dakkari and Mirari translated, "Lavi says satisfy his needs. Opening for your male is both literal and figurative."

My cheeks flushed. "That's a given."

Mirari's expression sobered a little as she said, "Support him. Males need comforting, no matter what they say. Every being needs comfort, needs warmth and affection. The *Vorakkar*...I do not envy his position. He works hard, he has sacrificed much, and he makes difficult decisions that most cannot fathom making. All horde kings do, to keep their horde safe and free."

I swallowed, nodding slowly, my heart thrumming in my chest.

"Perhaps the *Vorakkar* needs your warmth most of all," Mirari whispered quietly. "He has chosen you for a reason, when he has forsaken many."

All I'd done was fight with him instead, I thought.

"There were other Dakkari females who wanted him?" I asked, pressing my lips together briefly.

Mirari nodded. "*Lysi*. Of course, especially in *Dothik*. Many vie for the attentions of a horde king, though in my opinion, it is distasteful."

My eyes strayed over to the chests of treasures along the far wall of the tent. The shift I wore had come from them and I'd always assumed that he had his choice of females, probably had others who 'served' him, if he had a stock of clothes and trinkets for them.

"He has chosen you to be his queen," Mirari said, "and you hold power because of that. Power over him."

"Couldn't you get into trouble for telling me that?" I teased softly.

Mirari's laugh sounded beautiful. "Females always have power over their males. That is a truth."

I thought of a couple back at my village. A middle-aged man and woman—Jerri and Lysette. Jerri was mean to his core. Everyone knew he beat Lysette behind closed doors, taking out his frustrations on her. But she never left. She always took it.

She had no power over him.

I sobered. Were the Dakkari any different? Was Arokan different? Would he beat me, hurt me if I refused to obey him?

Did it matter?

I wouldn't be cowed, wouldn't be threatened. If he beat me because of it, I would fight back. I never wanted to be like Lysette, never wanted to be powerless and frightened of the male I joined my life with.

I nodded to myself. Blowing out a breath, I resumed my work on my pants.

"I'll try," I said softly. I would do anything to help my brother, my village, though I could do without helping Jerri.

Could I truly sway Arokan's thoughts and decisions?

I would find out.

"Where is he?" I asked next, after I resumed the stitching. "I haven't seen him since he took me out among the horde."

Mirari asked, "He did not tell you?"

Part of me had assumed he was with another one of his females, which was why he hadn't shared his bed with me for the past two nights.

"No," I said softly. "He didn't."

"A scout brought news of the Ghertun. A group was seen camping towards the west, close to *Dothik*. The *Vorakkar* rode out with a part of the horde to eliminate them."

What?

"Ghertun?" I asked, frowning, sitting up straighter.

Mirari cut me a look. "You do not know the Ghertun?"

"No," I said. "Are they some sort of beast?"

"A race," Mirari corrected. "A vile race who settled here centuries ago after a corrupt king allowed them in. They stay to the east, in the Dead Lands, but have been testing our borders of late."

My mind raced. "How do we not know about these beings?"

"Because the hordes have kept you safe," was what Mirari replied with.

My breath hitched. "How so?"

"I guarantee that if a Ghertun pack descended on your village, there would be nothing left. They rape females and burn settlements and kill young. It is their way. Then they consume the land, defile Kakkari, until there is nothing left. They move on to the next place. You would know their faces, know their war cries. The horde kings and our horde warriors keep us safe. They track down and kill any Ghertun outside of the Dead Lands to eliminate threats before they begin. However, sometimes they are too late."

Heart racing, I blew out a breath. "And this is *normal*? How long has this been going on?"

"Since they settled here," Mirari answered. "There used to be two hordes that patrolled our lands, that hunted game to send back to *Dothik*. Only two. Now there are many hordes. It is necessary."

The needle fell from my grip and I ran my cold fingers over my lips, trying to absorb the information.

Arokan had been right. I knew *nothing* of the Dakkari, knew next to nothing about this planet, though it had been my only home.

Had they truly been keeping us safe all these years? Perhaps inadvertently? If what Mirari was saying was true, if a Ghertun pack happened upon our village, we wouldn't have been able to defend ourselves. Had the hordes been protecting us all along?

Mirari was studying me. Lavi spoke, asking her a question, probably wondering what was wrong with me.

"When do you think he will return?" I asked after a long moment of silence.

Mirari tilted her head. "I suspect before tomorrow night."

"Why?"

"The black moon comes," she said. "I do not think anything could keep him from you once it does. Even bloodthirsty Ghertun."

10

Mirari had been right.

Arokan returned with his horde warriors the next afternoon to a camp in chaos.

At least that was what it seemed like to me, though Mirari told me that the camp was only preparing for the *tassimara*. The joining celebration, scheduled for later that night under the black moon.

All of them returned—Arokan and the ten horde warriors he'd taken with him. I was outside the tent when they came back, in my new pants and tunic top that I'd stayed up through the night to make with Mirari and Lavi. The two *piki* hadn't complained once about the late hour, but I knew that they wouldn't leave me alone with the blade or the needle either.

So they'd stayed.

And by the time they showed up at the tent the next morning, I was already dressed in my new outfit, with my hair braided down my back. I drank the bowl of broth they'd brought me, refusing the meat once more, and then we'd gone outside.

I felt more like myself than I had since I'd arrived at the Dakkari camp.

It was simply ironic then that later that night, I would never be the same again. I knew what was coming. Arokan had told me himself. After that night, I would be his wife, his queen. He would own my body and my life would be tied to his from that night forward.

Husband.

The word seemed strange to describe him, but that was what he would become.

My mother had often told me to be strong. It was such a general saying, two words that had no meaning to me until I found myself in a situation where they made perfect sense.

I'd had to be strong when I found my mother lying in a pool of her own blood. I'd had to be strong for Kivan, to protect him, working long hours to keep rations coming in. I'd had to be strong when I made a deal with a Dakkari horde king.

Be strong now, I thought as I watched Arokan and his horde warriors ride into camp. Behind me, I heard Lavi make a sound, a sound like *relief*, when the males guided their *pyroki* to the pen a short distance away. I watched Lavi approach one of the male warriors, watched her speak with him, watched her touch his hand.

The warrior was tall and broad and handsome, much like Arokan. And Lavi was obviously smitten.

As if of their own accord, my eyes found Arokan. Our gazes had connected when he rode into camp, but he'd looked away to attend to his *pyroki*, to give orders to the male in charge of the beasts, and to address an older Dakkari male that approached him from a nearby tent.

I watched them speak and studied the horde king, whose flesh was streaked in black blood and dirt. Some of the other warriors looked worse. One had a particularly nasty gash on his thigh and a female came forward to attend him almost immediately, leading him away.

Other than that brief pause, however, the camp continued to prepare for that night, as if their males and their horde king returning all bloodied was a usual occurrence.

When Arokan broke away from the older male and began his approach, my heart stuttered in my chest, remembering how angry he'd been the last time we spoke.

"You should attend to your male, *Missiki*," Mirari said quietly. "Remember. He is just like Drukkar."

I nodded to her, though my eyes never left Arokan. Quietly, she slipped away, weaving towards the front of the camp, where I was sure she could find something to occupy her time. It seemed like there was still much to prepare.

His eyes tracked over my body, taking in my hide pants and cloth tunic, before settling on my face. Arokan didn't say anything about the clothes, however, just held the tent flap open for me as I ducked inside and he followed behind me.

When we were alone, I took a deep breath and turned to him, though my tongue felt tied, knotted in my mouth.

It was possibly the first time I'd ever been at a loss for words as I looked at him. Up close, he looked like a bloody mess. Black splatters of blood adorned his body, covering parts of his golden tattoos. His left side was covered in grime and dirt, as if he'd fallen *hard*. The pants he wore would probably take multiple washings to clean.

As if on cue, the tent flap parted and males brought in the bathing tub, followed by buckets of steaming water.

We were silent as they filled it and I only moved once they left us in peace. Arokan was watching me and I moved towards him slowly, remembering Mirari's advice, remembering the story of Drukkar. Remembering that perhaps the horde king needed warmth most of all, considering the crusted and cold blood that decorated his flesh, remembering that he had the power to help my village, if I gave him reason to.

He would be my husband. Nothing would change that. And if we entered into this partnership, however unequal it might be, on good terms, perhaps we could be of use to one another.

Arguing with him, fighting against him would accomplish nothing. Unless he *really* pissed me off, and then I would give him an earful, the consequences of that be damned.

He watched me with thinly veiled suspicion as I removed the golden belt around his waist, only fumbling with the clasp for a brief moment before letting it fall to the floor.

My cheeks heated a little as I untied the laces of his pants. Before I pushed the waistband down, however, he caught my wrists, his narrowed eyes on me as he rasped, "What are you doing, *kalles*?"

"Helping you," I replied, disturbed by how much I liked his voice. It was rich and dark and deep. Sinful and decadent. "You need to bathe."

His fingers gave my wrist a squeeze, like he didn't trust my intentions, like a warning, before he released them.

Taking that as his answer, I pushed his pants down his long, thick legs, swallowing the lump in my throat when his cock made its appearance.

I turned to walk towards the bath and he followed, his heavy footsteps padding on the plush rugs spread across the floor. I prepared the washcloth and soap as he got in and I heard him hiss in satisfaction at the warmth.

I knelt by the side of the bathing tub and waited for the warm water to soften the blood and dirt coating his skin. Arokan's eyes closed and I felt a twinge of strange compassion for him. What Mirari had said, about the Ghertun, had surprised me. It made my thoughts about the Dakkari shift ever so slightly. It was obvious that Arokan wanted to protect his horde, his people…that he would do whatever it took to keep them safe. How could I judge him for that?

"Why didn't you tell me you were leaving?" I asked softly.

His eyes opened and he regarded me carefully. "Would you have cared?"

"At the time…" I said and then decided to answer honestly, "I don't know. We were both angry before you left."

Arokan made a sound in the back of his throat, an acknowledgment. The water trickled when he lifted his arms, scooping it up to wet his shoulders and upper chest.

"Mirari told me about the Ghertun," I said, my eyes going to his throat, to the little nick there scabbed over with blood. "I had no idea that there were beings like that living on Dakkar."

"I have seen some humans do worse things than the Ghertun," Arokan said. "I have seen Killap and Nrunteng do worse things too. And Dakkari. Beings like that have always lived here."

The Killap and the Nrunteng were other races that had arrived on Dakkar around the same time as humans, though I'd never seen them. Their settlements were farther to the east.

"Still," he continued, "as a race, the Ghertun are the most dangerous. Dakkari, humans, Killap, and Nrunteng? Their dangerous ones are outliers."

"I'm assuming you found the pack you were looking for," I commented, my eyes trailing his flesh. The blood had just started to soften, so I dipped my washcloth into the water, soaking it.

"*Lysi*," was all he said.

Smoothing the cloth over his forearm, I focused on scrubbing the grime away as I said, "Next time, I would like to hear about your leaving from you. Not Mirari."

Arokan stilled, his eyes cutting to me, glinting like ice. "*Neffar?*"

I ignored his word, focusing on cleaning his skin. But

Arokan wasn't to be denied for long because he caught my hand, tearing the washcloth away before tilting my chin up to look at him.

"*Neffar?*"

I assumed, by his tone, *neffar* meant something like *what*.

Taking a deep breath, I said, "I don't like being kept in the dark."

Arokan was studying me, those yellow-rimmed eyes darting back and forth between mine, as if I'd asked him a riddle and he was trying to decipher the answer.

"I will tell you next time," he finally said, dropping my chin, his gaze turning away.

I nodded, snagging the washcloth again. "Thank you."

"Have you eaten?" he asked next.

"Broth," I answered.

He shook his head, muttering something in Dakkari. "You need meat. You cannot survive on broth."

"I have for a long time," I informed him.

A sharp breath through his nostrils told me he was frustrated. Probably tired too. I wondered if he'd slept since he left.

We lapsed into silence again as I washed him. Once his arms were clean, I moved to his chest, where a thick coat of blood remained just above his right pectoral muscle.

However, as I washed the area, Arokan stiffened and I gasped, seeing that the blood surrounding it wasn't Ghertun blood, it was his own. Underneath the crusted blood was a deep slash that probably needed stitching.

"You're hurt," I whispered. "Should I go get—"

"*Nik,*" Arokan rasped. He pointed to a tall dresser near the entrance of the tent. "There are sutures and dressings in there."

I pushed up from the bathing tub and retrieved them—thin golden thread, a hook needle, a clear salve, and clean padding.

I placed them on the bed, knowing that I wouldn't be able to stitch him in the water. It would have to wait until he was clean.

So, I quickly resumed helping him bathe, gently cleaning the wound before scrubbing the rest of him down. Only after his hair was clean did he rise from the tub. The front of my tunic was wet, but I paid it no mind as I watched him dry himself. It didn't escape my notice that his golden tattooed cock was hardened, bobbing against his abdomen.

Strangely enough, my eyes lingered on it before I forced myself to look away. I would know it well soon enough, I thought, knowing that the joining celebration drew near.

Once he was dry, he sat on the edge of the bed, still nude, which I tried my hardest not to notice as I cleaned the wound for a second time...though my face burned.

Arokan noticed and commented, "Humans are strange about bare flesh. Why?"

Swallowing, I kept my eyes on the slash, making sure there was no debris or dirt inside it. "I don't know. We just...cover ourselves around other people." I gave him a pointed look. "It's polite."

Arokan made a sound like a snort. "I am not 'other people,' as you call it. You will know my flesh like it is your own soon enough."

Goddess help me, I thought, my ears burning then. He said it so nonchalantly, like it was a given. In a way, it was.

"Humans are strange about mating too, it seems," Arokan commented next, eyeing my expression. "Why? It is natural."

I cleared my throat, reaching for the hook needle and easily threading the gold strand through, despite my trembling fingers. "I don't know. It's just...it's a private matter. We don't usually discuss it so openly."

"There is no one here now," he murmured. "This is private."

Startled, my eyes met his and for the second time that afternoon, my tongue was tied. To give myself an excuse not to answer, I quickly pierced his skin with the hook needle and made the first stitch. He didn't even flinch, which made me wonder how many times he'd done this.

"You know how to do this well," Arokan commented, looking down at my neat stitches, when I didn't reply.

"I worked as a seamstress in my village," I told him softly. "Flesh and fabric are not so different."

"I see you made your own clothing while I was gone," he said.

"I didn't steal the razor or the needle. I won't have a way to kill you in your sleep if that's what you're worried about, horde king."

He huffed out a small, startled breath and I felt it across my cheek. I hadn't realized how close we were until that moment, but I could feel his heat along my side, could smell his scent.

"*Nik, kalles*, I am not worried about that," he murmured. We lapsed into silence as I finished up the stitching. Only when I cut the thread and spread salve over the closed wound did he say, "You will need to wear the Dakkari ceremonial dress tonight."

My lips pressed together as nerves stuttered my heartbeat. Softly, I said, "I'm sure the *piki* already have it prepared."

Arokan grabbed my wrist gently when I finished placing the padding on his chest. It looked like he wanted to say something, but then his jaw ticked and he looked away, releasing me. He stood and pulled on a pair of fresh pants from his trunks.

Then he said, "I will see you at the *tassimara* tonight."

With that, he ducked through the entrance and left.

"You're welcome, *Vorakkar*," I grumbled to the empty tent, wondering what the hell had just happened.

11

"You can't possibly want me to wear *this*, Mirari," I exclaimed, eyeing the 'ceremonial Dakkari outfit' in horror and dread.

Or rather the *lack* of an outfit.

Stomach knotted in nerves, I pressed three of my fingers to my lips, trying to keep it together. It was bad enough that I was going through with this *tassimara* at all, bad enough that I would freely give my body to a horde king who seemed cold and surly most of the time. Bad enough that I would most likely live out the rest of my life among the Dakkari, never to see my brother again.

And now *this*.

The ceremonial outfit was only a short hide skirt, embroidered with beautiful gold swirling stitching, accompanied by a heavy gold necklace. The necklace had one wide strand that wrapped around my throat and one thick plate that hung at the level of my breasts. My *bared* breasts.

"Where's—where's the top?" I asked, my voice sounding breathless and light.

"No top, *Missiki*," Mirari replied, taking a pot of gold paint from Lavi. She dabbed her fingers into it and then smeared it over one of my pebbled nipples, making me screech in surprise and dart away, rounding the bed. The necklace bobbed against my breasts, cold and heavy.

"What are you doing?" I cried, looking down at my nipple.

Mirari eyed me carefully and then let out a long sigh. "This is the Dakkari way, *Missiki*."

"N-no," I said, holding out my hands when she approached me. "Stop."

"*Missiki*, this is for the *Vorakkar*. You must."

"How does this have *anything* to do with him?" I cried out, my voice climbing higher and higher in my panic. My heart was racing fast and my rushing blood was loud in my ears.

This might just be my breaking point. Out of everything, a short skirt and painted nipples had broken me.

"He will take the gold into his mouth tonight, consume it so it is a part of him," Mirari explained, as if she were talking about how clear the skies were tonight and not about Arokan *licking* my nipples clean. "It is the Dakkari—"

"The Dakkari way, I know. I know," I whispered, staring at the little gold pot like it was a blade in her hands.

Goddess help me. What was with the Dakkari and *gold*?

I knew there was no escaping this. Just like everything else that had happened thus far.

Inhaling a sharp breath, I snatched the pot from her grasp and said, "I'll do it myself."

Mirari let me have the pot and shuffled backwards to stand next to Lavi, who I thought looked a little *amused*.

Hands trembling, I painted my nipples and areolas gold until they glittered in the candlelight of the tent. Once I was done, I tugged the necklace plate, encrusted with red jewels, so that it helped cover my breasts. But it wasn't enough.

"You are ready," Mirari announced and another jolt of fear and nerves shot through me.

I felt like a stranger again, that desperate emotion rising inside me. I'd allowed Mirari and Lavi to have their way with me. They'd brushed and dried and volumized my hair until it fell in soft, big waves down my back. Into the strands, they'd threaded little gold beads and cuffs that I heard jingle whenever I moved my head.

To my face, they'd taken a surprisingly light hand, only outlining my eyes with thin gold strokes, bringing out colors in my irises I hadn't even known I'd possessed. On my cheekbones and lips, they'd dusted a shimmery gold powder.

When I looked at myself in the small mirror they'd brought, I hardly recognized myself. My chest was heaving with shortened breaths as I took in their handiwork. My hair had never been fuller and my face seemed softened by the gold powder. My eyes looked desperate and wild and I couldn't stand to look at myself for long, so I turned the mirror away.

"I'm ready," I whispered, taking in a long breath. Better to get this over with.

Night had fallen hours ago. One of the darkest nights too, considering it was a 'black moon.' Or a new moon, as the humans called it. Mirari and Lavi guided me from the tent and when I stepped outside, shivering a bit in the cool air, my eyes found Arokan's. He was waiting for me.

Breath hitching, I took him in. He'd gotten ready elsewhere, considering that he wore a hanging fur cloth and not the pants he'd had on when he'd left the tent earlier. His hair was loose and long down his back, his tail was decorated in gold cuffs, and his eyes were lined in black, making the yellow ring of his irises that much more intense.

My belly quivered. He was watching me with a silent ferocity that made me feel like prey, and when I straightened, the necklace bobbed at my bare breasts, drawing his gaze there.

Even from a distance, I heard him make a sound, almost like a growl. It made my nerves jump even higher, especially when I noticed he stood next to his *pyroki*, which was freshly painted with gold lines and whose reins he held in his large, six-fingered grip.

My palms went sweaty at the sight of the beast.

A part of me, the cowardly part, wanted to turn and dart back inside the tent, to hide there for the remainder of the night and bolt from the camp at my next opportunity, to try and brave the wild lands to navigate my way back home.

That was suicide, I knew, but I was afraid enough to want to *try*. At least, the unreasonable and emotional part of me wanted to try.

I'd made a promise, I reminded myself.

With that thought, my feet—which were bare and unpro-tected—guided me to Arokan, though I stumbled a bit. The clearing in front of the tent was empty, the whole camp was quiet, though a gentle yellow glow emanated from it, which seemed strange. Silently, Mirari and Lavi slipped away, threading around the quiet tents, disappearing from view.

Until it was just Arokan and I. And his beast.

He didn't speak. He held out his free arm, extending his hand towards me, and with a final breath, I took it. His hand was warm and mine was cold. My whole body trembled though I desperately tried to stop shaking.

Arokan gripped me to him, pulling me close so that I felt the fur cloth covering his genitals brush against my bare belly. The fur tickled, it was so soft.

But I was beyond laughter when I looked up at him.

"Are you frightened, Luna?" he asked me and I stilled when I heard my name fall from his lips, so unexpected that for a moment, I forgot my nerves. Forgot everything.

Then I remembered. Remembered who I was, why I'd come here. Remembered the young girl that had been forced to grow up too soon, remembered the years of hard work, of struggle, to provide for Kivan in an unfair universe.

I was strong.

I *was* Luna. Not *kalles* or *Missiki* or *Morakkari*. At least not yet.

Luna.

Bright stars shone down, glimmering in the absence of the moonlight. Some of the stars I didn't recognize. Some of them only made their appearance when the moon was dark.

"I am," I whispered, which was difficult to say. I *was* frightened. I wouldn't pretend otherwise.

I'd grown up trying to put on a strong face, trying to lie to myself that everything was all right, for Kivan's sake. But right then I realized I didn't need to lie anymore. I didn't need to protect Arokan from the truth and I certainly didn't need to impress him.

It was...freeing.

I could be strong and still be frightened. That night, I just needed to be brave, and I would be.

Arokan inclined his head in acknowledgment, but didn't say anything in reply, which I was surprisingly thankful for. Instead, he made a clicking sound in the back of his throat and his *pyroki* inclined his head, bowing so that it would be easier for me to climb on.

Remembering the unforgiving hardness of riding a *pyroki*, I hesitated. Truthfully, I would rather parade myself naked around the entire camp than get on the back of the intimidating creature again, but Arokan was watching me, studying me.

So I climbed on with the help of the horde king, though I surely flashed him in the process. The short skirt barely concealed my lower half and with my thighs splayed wide over the *pyroki's* back, I felt exposed and on display.

With grace and experienced ease, Arokan swung himself up behind me, those thick thighs bracing on both sides of my body, encasing my own.

Stiffening in the seat, I gasped when Arokan reached around

and pressed his hand to my bare sex, cupping it. Warmth from his hand heated me, registered, and my cheeks flamed when I asked, "What are you doing?"

"No male will see you here," he growled. "This is only for *me*."

"Then maybe you should have given me a longer skirt," I returned, though my voice sounded a little strangled.

Arokan made a grunting sound and curled his fingers, making me straighten, making my nipples tighten even *further*, if possible. "I did not want to."

My eyes narrowed—*maddening* male—but I bit my tongue when he urged the *pyroki* forward.

The jolting, rocking motion of the *pyroki* was both familiar and strange, but every step it took pushed Arokan's hand against me more, making me swallow, making me aware of my shallow breathing.

Perhaps it was best that I focused on that hand, as opposed to everything else that would come that night. Perhaps that was part of the reason why he'd done it. To distract me from my nerves.

So, I stayed, rigid and still, on top of the *pyroki* as Arokan guided it towards the front of the camp.

That glow that I'd noticed earlier became more and more pronounced and when the *pyroki* rounded a tent, riding onto the main alley of the narrow road, I realized what that glow was.

My breath hitched, startled, when I saw all the Dakkari, all the members of Arokan's horde, lining the makeshift road of the camp. Females, males, children, all holding glowing, parchment-thin lanterns with something bundled inside them that I couldn't make out.

All roads of the camp, the same route that Arokan had taken when he'd presented me, were filled with Dakkari.

The warm glow was reflected in their dark eyes as his *pyroki* led us through. It was completely silent and the only sounds were the gentle breeze whistling through the tents and the crunch of the *pyroki*'s hooves on the dirt.

It was beautiful. Surprisingly peaceful and dizzyingly beautiful.

The Dakkari reached out with their free hands as we passed, pressing them over the *pyroki*'s side and over both our legs, just like that first night. Hundreds of hands brushed my flesh but I continued to look around at all the surrounding Dakkari, into their eyes, searching for *something*.

They would only meet my eyes for a brief moment before they looked away, but I realized that they did the same for Arokan. It wasn't discomfort that had them unable to hold my gaze, I realized.

It was…respect.

We rode through every possible road that connected the camp together until we reached the end. It was there that I saw a celebration area had been erected. A raised dais with one golden throne stood off to the right, underneath the starry sky, against the backdrop of the silent landscape of Dakkar. Before the dais were rows and rows of tables filled with food and a cleared area for dancing, I assumed.

Arokan halted the *pyroki* when we reached that area and turned to face his horde. With his hand still pressed to my very core, with all of their eyes still on us, Arokan bellowed out words in his language, which reverberated in my ear. Whatever he said was short. I heard *kassikari* and *Morakkari*, but the other words were alien to me, frustratingly so.

When he was done, the Dakkari cheered in their strange way, like war cries, rolling their tongues, the sound rising into the quiet night, as jarring as it was mesmerizing. Then, all at once, they released their lanterns and they rose into the black sky, lit by little flames that would flicker out long before they touched the earth.

My lips parted, watching the subtle glow within each of them shine through the thin, colorful lanterns. More than a hundred rose, some faster than others, until it seemed like the sky was peppered with a hundred new stars.

I'd never seen anything more beautiful. It was so beautiful that it made me forget what was to come that night.

Soon, the breeze picked up and the lanterns scattered and drifted away, still high in the sky. In the back of my mind, I wondered if one would be carried all the way to my village, if my brother would see it.

Suddenly, drums started up and excited cries came from the Dakkari, who all started towards the celebration area.

Arokan's hand suddenly left from between my thighs as he dismounted his *pyroki*. I swung my leg over and he reached up to snag my waist, effortlessly helping me down. Then he kept that grip on my waist as he led me towards the raised dais, towards the throne.

There was only one seat and Arokan dropped down into it. Just when I began to suspect that I was meant to stand, he tugged me down onto his *lap*.

My breath hitched when my skirt rose and I wiggled to pull it down. Only his surprised groan made me freeze and I swallowed, my eyes flashing up to his.

"Continue, *kalles*," he rasped in my ear, "if you wish for me to end this feast early."

My cheeks flushed at his meaning as I straightened, feeling the fur cloth covering him settle against the backs of my thighs.

When I didn't move an inch after that, he murmured, "You will eat tonight. No broth. Meat."

My jaw clenched as I eyed the long tables of food, as I watched Dakkari gather around them and pick bite-sized morsels off the platters and pop them into their mouths. Cries of delight rose as they socialized with one another in a language I could not understand.

"No," I said. "You know—"

"The horde will think it an insult if you do not," he said. "You will eat."

My shoulders sagged. It was one thing to refuse food in the privacy of the tent. But if I was going to be by Arokan's side, I couldn't disrespect his people. Not tonight.

"I will send a gift to your village," he said next, making me gasp and turn to look at him. "Three *bveri*. That will be enough meat to feed them for months, if they dry it properly. If you eat from this moment forward, not just tonight, no more fighting me, I will do this."

"Really?" I said softly.

He inclined his head. "*Lysi.*"

Relief so potent that it made tears sting my eyes overwhelmed me. This was a step in the right direction, evidence that the horde king *could* help my village.

"Thank you," I whispered.

He regarded me with those yellow eyes. His tail, which he had tucked to the side when he sat down, came up to wrap around my knee, the gold cuffs lining it chilly against my skin.

Slowly, I relaxed. As relaxed as I possibly could be during a Dakkari marriage celebration with my breasts out, of course. Blowing out a small breath, my gaze darted over the forming crowd, noticing that many had their eyes on us. But just like when we were on the *pyroki*, they averted their eyes whenever I made contact with them.

Other than my *piki,* other than Arokan, I hadn't held anyone's gaze for longer than a couple seconds at camp. Even Lavi didn't look at me for long.

Arokan seemed content to simply watch his people. His features were carefully schooled into an unreadable expression. Though his muscles were loose, his gaze was observant. Always aware...always ready. I wondered if he ever *relaxed*.

Soon, we were approached by a female bearing a serving

platter. She waited at the base of the dais until Arokan inclined his head and then she ascended the steps. She deposited a tray laden with food and drinks, which she perched on the wide arm of the throne.

With a bow, she turned and went back into the throng of the crowd below.

Arokan lifted a goblet made of white bone to my lips. "Drink," he ordered.

I did. Whatever the liquid was burned down the back of my throat and made my eyes water, and I fought valiantly not to hack it back up. I thought I caught his lips curl before he took a long swallow of it himself and returned it to the tray.

Next he lifted a braised piece of meat—*bveri* meat, I assumed, though I didn't know what kind it was—and I opened my lips at his beckoning.

My eyes widened when the flavor of it burst on my tongue. Rich and fatty and so tender that it seemed to melt in my mouth. I'd never had fresh meat before. Years ago, we'd received dried jerky in our rations, sourced from animals residing on other planets, but we'd never hunted on Dakkar in fear of retribution.

Arokan was watching me. Once I swallowed, I was silent for a moment, processing that something could taste like *that*, and then said, "I've never had fresh meat before."

Something flashed in his gaze, his brows and lips pulling downwards.

"You will have fresh meat every day now," was all he replied, though his voice was gruffer than it'd been a moment before.

"When you..." I started. "When you give my village the meat, they won't know how to dry it."

Arokan's jaw clenched. "I will have my *pujerak* give them instructions."

"Your *pujerak*?" I asked.

He tilted his head to one of the far tables. There, I saw the

Dakkari male that had come with Arokan to my village, the messenger who'd first spoken with me in the universal tongue.

"My second-in-command," Arokan replied.

I nodded, biting my lip. He was being...sweet. He was being kind and truthfully, I didn't know how to take it. I felt more at ease with him when we were fighting.

We lapsed into a strange silence as the drums grew louder and louder, as the feast continued. Arokan continued to feed me morsels from the large selection on the tray, in between taking some for himself. But soon, my belly was full of soft, braised meat and simmered roots and tart fruits that made my lips pucker.

Not to mention the fermented drink that made my head swim pleasantly, that made me smile when I watched the Dakkari children darting through the crowds, when I watched the dancing begin.

Soon, I forgot that I was sitting topless in the horde king's lap. I forgot the nerves that had pummeled me all afternoon and evening. For once, I let myself enjoy the night because I'd never had a night like that before.

Arokan was warm underneath me and he shifted his arms tighter when I shivered. The night was growing colder, but I didn't mind. The tray of food was emptied, though some brew still remained in the goblet. Most of the feasting was over by that point and the celebration had turned to revelry. Laughter and voices and drums filled the air.

I don't know how long I sat in Arokan's lap or how long I'd been watching the celebration below in utter fascination. But soon, I felt something begin to shift.

My breath hitched when Arokan lifted some of my hair at the nape of my neck. I felt the tip of his nose drag over my flesh there, soft but purposeful. My spine tingled with the sensation, unexpectedly pleasurable.

He had one hand gripped around my hips and the other

resting on the arm of the throne, his clawed fingers pricking the metal. Suddenly that hand on my hip dipped until his fingers were resting over my sex, just like when we'd been riding on the *pyroki*.

Eyes widened, I shot a glance towards the crowd, but couldn't discern if anyone was watching. The way his legs were positioned, I doubted anyone would be able to see directly, but it was obvious where his hand was.

Those fingers against me twitched and then pressed *firm*. A surprised gasp escaped my throat and I wrapped my hand around his thick wrist, just over his gold cuff, though my grip only encompassed half of it.

When I turned my head to regard him, those eyes were on me. I was frozen again, looking into those eyes, so black in the center that I saw myself in them.

His finger stroked me once, twice.

"*Arokan*," I whispered, panicked, my mind muddled from the fermented drink, my inexperienced body beginning to respond to his expert touches.

The sound of his given name leaving my lips made him growl, made his spine shoot straight. Belatedly, I wondered if I'd made a mistake using it, if I'd crossed a line.

Before I knew it, he was standing from the throne, bringing me with him. He swung me up in his arms and descended the stairs of the dais.

The dancing never stopped, though I felt eyes turning towards us, and the beat of the drums seemed to increase. I felt those beats pulse through me.

He swung us both up onto his *pyroki* with ease once we reached it, which was telling of his strength. To the crowd, he bellowed, "*Kirtva njeti Morakkari!*"

Whatever he said was met with deafening cheers and my lips parted, my chest heaving when I realized what was about to happen. Just then, my eyes met Mirari's in the throng and she nodded at me, smiling.

He urged the *pyroki* into a gallop back through the camp, turning his back on the celebration.

He was guiding us towards the tent.

"It is time, *kalles*," he rasped in my ear, his hand again curling between my legs. "You are my queen now. I will wait no longer."

12

My back hit the furs of the bed.

Heat registered as a fully nude, fully *aroused* Dakkari male lowered himself over me, his head dropping to lick the column of my exposed neck, his tongue hitting the golden collar of the necklace I wore. He hadn't taken it off, had only stripped me of my short skirt the moment we set foot inside the tent with a rough, tearing pull.

I let out a small gasp as Arokan ran one massive palm up my bare leg, spreading it, sinking our naked bodies more closely together until I felt something I'd never felt before: a body pressed against mine, so tightly that it felt like my own.

My eyes fluttered closed, my lips parting when he stroked his hand up my body, over my hip, my waist, up to my breasts, where my nipples were still painted gold. I realized that the fermented drink at the celebration feast had probably been for the best. It had loosened my muscles, helped me relax. While I'd been nervous about this moment, about the inevitable, I wasn't afraid of the pain, of him tearing past my flesh, but I was afraid of how it might...change me. I was afraid that I would like it.

His head rose from the column of my throat, those dark

eyes watching me. His expression was a little wild, a little untamed. Saying his given name had unleashed something within him, something he kept tightly reined in, hidden from his horde.

I shivered, unsure whether I wanted to explore that part of him, that dark, exciting, unfamiliar place.

"*Rei Morakkari*," he murmured, his eyes tracking over my face. They settled on my lips as his fingers trailed back down my body until they reached my sex.

A small whimper left me when he parted my folds, when he stroked me so gently, much more gently than I'd ever thought he was capable of.

"*Rei kassikari*," he rasped.

Arousal pricked me when his fingers shifted over my clit and I bit my lip, holding back a groan.

"*Lysi?*" he asked.

Yes? Was that what he was asking?

"Tell me something first," I managed to get out, though my voice sounded a little breathless.

"*Neffar?*"

"Why?" I asked softly, one question that had been on my mind more than once.

"Why?" he repeated, his brow furrowing. Despite his confusion, his fingers never stopped moving between my legs, never stopped stoking the fire deep inside me that was threatening to break free.

"You could have had any Dakkari female," I said, looking up at him. Mirari had told me as much. "It would have been easier. So why? Why me?"

Arokan let out a sharp breath and dropped his head to my shoulder, pressing his lips there. His surprisingly soft lips. I wondered if the Dakkari kissed, like humans. I wondered what it would be like to kiss him.

Or perhaps that was the fermented drink wondering.

He lifted his head, meeting my gaze, and said, "I heard the courage in your voice before I ever saw your face. A human *kalles* daring to stand against the Dakkari...I was intrigued. I needed to see you. And when I saw your face, your eyes, I knew. Kakkari revealed you to me. I knew you would be my queen. You are strong and you are brave and you were loyal to your kin. That is why."

Whatever I had been expecting...it hadn't been that.

My heart pounded in my chest as I absorbed his words.

"*Lysi?*" he murmured, that low voice caressing my skin like a touch.

This was my new life now. He was my *husband* now, a horde king of the Dakkari. It was unbreakable. It was...done.

I could fight against it and make life harder for myself. Or I could try to assimilate into the horde, to build a new life for myself while continuing to champion my village for aid. I could *help* them, whereas before, it was hopeless.

Perhaps my brother's fire had been a blessing in disguise.

"*Lysi,*" I said softly, meeting his gaze.

Something flickered there at my word, at my affirmation. I felt the shift between us, as palpable as a touch.

He kept his eyes on mine when he ducked his head. When he found my gold-painted nipple and drew it *deep* into his mouth.

I cried out, twisting a little underneath him, as I felt that rough, warm tongue. It felt *good* and I groaned as he flicked my budded nipple, until I felt that small pleasure sizzle in a straight line down my body.

My hands flew to his bulging biceps when he switched to my other breast, when he began speaking in guttural Dakkari, words I didn't understand but words that sounded...reverent. I felt the twisting shift of his muscles beneath my hand, felt the cords of his arms tighten as he continued to stroke his hand between my thighs.

In the distance, I could still hear the drums of the celebration, even that far away. The pulsing rhythm seemed to mimic the way my sex began to throb.

His body was so warm, so hot, like a furnace. His mouth grew ravenous at my breast, tugging and laving, like he was starved for me. When he finally released my nipples, I looked between us, past the heavy plate of my necklace, and saw that he'd cleaned them of the gold. Now they were flushed a dark pink, sensitive and pointed.

"I will spill my seed deep inside your body this night, *Morakkari*," he rasped, his voice dark and gravelly. "You will be heavy with my heirs. You will bear me a horde warrior that will be strong enough to lead, to be *Vorakkar*."

My breath was coming out fast, my chest heaving. Children. I'd never even thought about children before.

But still, I resisted him by saying, "You might be disappointed. It could be a girl."

His lips curled, the sight so shocking that I was momentarily struck dumb.

"She will be treasured. A princess of the horde," he murmured. "But we will have many children. It does not matter if a female comes first."

I gasped when he flipped me in one smooth, quick motion, until I was face-down on the furs. His large palms spanned my hips and he tugged hard, bringing me up onto my hands and knees with him positioned behind me.

"*Ohhh*," I moaned when I felt his tongue lick over my sex, when I felt my belly quiver as it found my throbbing clit. "No, no," I whispered, squeezing my eyes shut.

"*Lysi*," he growled in reply before he returned, using that expert tongue on me. "*Lysi*."

Pleasure was like a sharp blade and I was walking on the edge. It cut me, knowing that I was enjoying this, knowing that even as I protested, I was rocking my hips back at him for more. It cut me because I didn't know why I was still afraid.

"Please," I whispered, but I didn't know if it was directed at Arokan or myself. "Please."

"You are ready, *kalles*," he said. "You ache for me, whether you will admit it to yourself or not."

I perceived him moving behind me, the furs underneath me shifting. His hand, calloused, rough, but warm, ran down the length of my spine. When he didn't move, I summoned the courage to look behind me, directly into his eyes.

"*Rinavi leika,*" he murmured, his tail moving to wrap around one of my thighs, keeping me in place. One of his hands gripped my hips and the other...the other moved up, past my shoulder blades to wrap around the gold collar at my throat.

I inhaled a sharp breath, my eyes widening at the possessive, dominant position.

"*Rinavi leika,*" he repeated, his voice almost...awed. "You are beautiful, *rei Morakkari.*"

I cried out when he thrust into me, his grip on my hips pulling me towards his thick, hot length. Blood rushed in my ears and over it, I heard his bellow of pleasure as his cock slid inside.

Pain pricked me, a sharp, twisting pinch.

"Wait," I whispered, my brows furrowing.

Arokan's eyes met mine. That wild look was present, that untamed emotion from earlier. He growled, a purely animal-istic sound, but did as I asked, though his grip on my throat and my hips tightened, as if worried I would move away.

The pain was fleeting and Arokan kept my gaze throughout it all, half-sheathed inside me. He wanted to fuck me, I saw it in his gaze. He wanted to consume me, to claim me, to make me *his*.

My whole body shivered at that thought as the pain slowly

melted away, only to be replaced by the foreign sensation of fullness.

A moment later, I felt him move, testing me. I felt him retreat from my body, only to drive back in with a forceful thrust.

Lips parting, I couldn't help the gasping moan that tore from my throat.

That was all the permission Arokan needed.

That hand on my throat flexed as he began to fuck me the way I'd imagined a horde king would. Dominant, almost savage thrusts into my waiting sex, as if I was made for his pleasure, as if he owned me. Perhaps he did. Perhaps this was what it felt like to be owned, collared and fucked into frightening pleasure.

Beneath me, my breasts swayed and bobbed with every hard pound of his cock, the heavy plate of my golden necklace jingling in time with his thrusts. My hair fell over my shoulder, tickling my nipples, moving back and forth. Everything was in motion. My arms shook as they held me up, my buttocks clenched, my belly quivered.

"Your cunt is perfect, *kalles*," he growled behind me, punctuating his words with strong thrusts, as if to emphasize his point. "Hot and tight for me. *Vok!*"

"*Ohh!*" I cried out when he picked up his pace even more, the sound of flesh against flesh filling the tent. I felt the sway and slap of his heavy sack against the back of my thighs.

And then I felt something else. That small, rounded bump just above the base of his cock...it began to harden. It began to *vibrate* in pulsing, throbbing beats, in time with his heart.

"*Arokan!*" I whimpered, feeling it press against my puckered, private flesh with every thrust, a wicked, strange sensation that made me *crazed*.

"*Lysi, kalles*," he rasped. "Cry out my name when I fuck you, so you know you owns your body. So you know who owns this cunt."

Oh goddess. His *words* made crazed too.

Squeezing my eyes shut against the rapidly rising pleasure, feeling that hard bump stimulate me, feeling him deep inside, stretching and filling me to the very brim…it was too much.

My spine arched as I reared back my hips to meet his thrusts. I didn't care anymore about what this meant, didn't care that he'd taken me from my village, that he had claimed my body and my life though I barely knew him.

I didn't care because all I wanted to do was *come*.

"*Yes, yes,*" I moaned, my nipples pebbling even tighter, my arms shaking. That hand at my throat pressed and squeezed and after a particularly savage, deep thrust, I began to orgasm. "*Ooh yes!*"

"*Vok!*" Arokan cursed loudly as my sex began to clench around his length and that vibration from his bump only increased, becoming *stronger*. "*Luna!*"

The strongest orgasm of my life consumed me, stretching from one moment to the next.

I hated him. I hated that he alone could make me feel this way, that he alone could control my body this way.

But it didn't take away the fact that I came so hard I saw darkness and stars. I came so hard I was momentarily lost to the world, time completely erased when I resurfaced.

When it was over, I was trembling and my arms collapsed beneath me, though he never ceased his brutal, claiming thrusts into my body.

He was fucking his queen. He was fucking me like a barbaric horde king of the Dakkari and I *hated* that I *loved* it.

With a growl, he pulled out of me and flipped me again until I was flat on my back. He tugged my hips down, maneuvering me so he could easily pound inside me, filling me even as my sex continued to flutter around him.

My brows pulled together, a rough cry tearing from my

throat when that bump pressed into my sensitive clit with every thrust.

Too much, too much! I feared I would come again when I'd only just stopped.

Arokan's yellow gaze was on me. His golden tattoos glittered in the candlelight of the warm tent, the expanse of his broad chest hindered only by the stitched gash I'd sewn up earlier that afternoon.

Flawless, golden flesh, perfectly sculpted into a magnificent male who used that magnificent body against me.

When he ground his hips into me, that vibrating bump made me scream. Like a crazed animal, I dug my fingernails into his flesh, my eyes rolling into the back of my head as I orgasmed for a second time.

I heard his roar of pleasure a moment later, felt his hips drive into me, hard and unyielding. Another foreign sensation overcame me when I felt his seed shoot into me, bathing my inner, flexing walls, filling me up like his cock had. I groaned, my chest heaving, even as I rocked into him for *more*.

Once it was over, Arokan collapsed next to me, a deep sound revving from his chest, a sound I'd never heard before.

Before I knew it, his lips were on mine.

I gasped into his mouth and he used that opportunity to stroke that tongue deep inside, soft and slow and hot.

I guess Dakkari do kiss, I thought, exhausted, unsure of what or even *how* I should feel.

He groaned as I opened for him. Opened for him, just like Mirari had suggested.

As my body calmed, as my breathing slowly returned to normal, as I perceived his seed beginning to leak from between my thighs, he continued to kiss me.

And I responded, dizzy with how gentle he was.

Soon, he pulled away. Looking deep into my eyes, his arm curled under my head, wrapping around the nape of my neck.

With a fierce whisper, he said, "*Rei Morakkari.* You are mine now."

My eyelids fluttered, drunk off pleasure and physical exhaustion and a full belly.

Drunk off *him.*

He had claimed me. Just like I'd always known he would.

And as I fell into a deep sleep, my last thought was: *is there anything left of me that he can claim?*

I didn't think so.

13

When I woke the next morning, my whole body ached in places I never even knew existed.

And for once, Arokan was still in bed beside me.

My head was resting on his shoulder, in virtually the same position I'd fallen asleep in, making me wonder if I'd moved a single inch. He was warm, his eyelids were closed, and his chest was rising and falling in a smooth, soft motion.

Wincing when I moved my legs, I felt a sharp twinge deep inside my body.

It was enough to wake Arokan, who jolted from sleep in an instant, making me tense.

He made that deep, rumbling sound in his chest again and his yellow-rimmed eyes tracked over my face, studying me.

His eyelids lowered slightly and I gasped when his hand moved beneath the furs, moving to cup my sex, his intentions clear.

My breath hitching in alarm, I grabbed his wrist and held it in place. Biting my lip, I whispered, "I'm sore."

He blinked, clarity returning to his gaze, and he sat up in the bed, removing the furs from our bodies, exposing our nudity to the chilly air.

I resisted the urge to cover myself from his seeking eyes, forcing my hands to remain in place, knowing that he'd seen every part of me, that there was no use or purpose for my modesty anymore.

I bit my bottom lip when his finger traced over my sex and inner thighs. When I saw his jaw clench, I looked down and froze as I saw the mess we'd made. Blood and seed coated the furs underneath me and my inner thighs, which were beginning to show the telltale signs of fresh bruises.

Arokan murmured something in Dakkari, his tone sound-ing...angry. Then I jumped when he barked something out towards the entrance of the tent.

He pulled the covers around me before the tent flaps opened to reveal two Dakkari males, once again bringing in the bathing tub and buckets of hot water.

Arokan rose from the bed in his full nudity, rounding towards my side once the males left, leaving a steaming bath in their wake.

I gasped when he gently lifted me into his arms and walked the short distance to the bathing tub, lowering us both inside.

A sigh of unexpected pleasure escaped me when hot water wrapped me in a cocoon of soothing heat, loosening my sore muscles, relieving some of the ache between my thighs.

"Better?" Arokan grunted, shifting me so that I was situated between his legs, until I felt his half-hard cock resting against my lower back.

"Yes," I whispered, surprised by how shy I felt with him that morning. Last night returned to me in vivid flashes of searing pleasure and dominating thrusts. Of Arokan's dark eyes, of his filthy, exciting words that only spurred me on, of his heat and his vibrating bump and the way his hands moved over my body with a familiarity that alarmed me.

The tent smelled like…sex. And after last night, after experiencing the consuming, frightening need and desire I'd felt with him, I was worried that I would never be the same, that I would never look at Arokan the same now that I knew what he was capable of, now that I knew what he was capable of unleashing within me.

Whoever that woman had been last night—that needful, lustful woman who had met his thrusts and wanted *more*—it wasn't me. *She* was a stranger to me, someone I'd just met.

All of my fears had come true. I'd liked it. And now I was changed because of it.

Arokan gently stroked my body, gently washed between my thighs until I was cleaned of the evidence of our mating.

"What happens now?" I whispered, feeling confused and strangely on the verge of tears because of how gentle he was being. I could handle it if he was rough or cold with me, but this Arokan…this male I couldn't handle.

Arokan didn't answer me. He just continued to wash my body, threading his fingers through my hair. Finally, he undid the heavy necklace, massaging the marks it made against my neck, and tossed it to the floor of the tent.

When the water began to cool, he carried me out and dried off my body. He went to the chests on the far wall of the tent, but then hesitated. Instead, he grabbed the pants and tunic I'd made and helped me dress in them.

I was more thankful for that than he probably realized. When I was bathed and dressed in my familiar clothes, I felt like I could breathe again.

"We will get new markings this day," he told me, his voice rumbling out as he pulled on a fresh pair of pants that looked to be made of leather, molding to his thick, muscular thighs. The golden cuffs around his wrists gleamed as he tied the laces.

"Markings?" I asked, eyeing him with trepidation.

He approached me and my breath went a little shallow when

he tilted my chin up to look at him. For a moment, I thought he would kiss me again, like he had last night.

But he didn't. I wasn't sure whether I was disappointed or relieved by that, which disturbed me.

He only looked at me, in a way that made me feel vulnerable and exposed. Like he could see all my darkest thoughts, all my regrets written on my very bones.

Finally, his hands came to grip my wrists. "You will get yours here. You will receive the markings of my line. Of Rath Kitala. For you are of them now and all of our offspring will be of them too."

Realization hit me. My eyes darted to his chest, his arms, tracing the swirling, golden lines, a beautiful pattern over his flesh.

Tattoos.

I felt the pressure of his grip around my wrists and thought that my markings would reflect his golden cuffs. A symbol.

The queen's symbol.

Swallowing the thick lump in my throat, I didn't voice the doubts in my head. What did I know about the Dakkari? Hardly anything. What did I know about being their queen, about being the queen to a horde king?

Nothing at all.

I felt like an imposter already, but receiving the markings would make me feel even more like one. Even more out of my element, further removed from my past life.

Last night, Arokan revealed he thought me strong and brave and loyal. His words had touched something in me, soothed something in me.

I wanted to be strong. But it was more than that because I realized I *had* to be. There was no room for cowardice. Not there. Not in a Dakkari camp.

So, I nodded. I said, "I'm ready."

Arokan seemed pleased with that because he brushed his

fingers across my cheekbone. Then he led me outside, into the fresh air, into the bright sunlight.

That morning was quiet, as if the majority of the camp was sleeping off their fermented drink from the night before. There were two guards stationed at the tent, like usual, who inclined their heads when we emerged, but Arokan kept moving, kept guiding me deeper into the camp.

Any Dakkari that we came upon inclined their heads, keeping their gazes averted, before scuttling off to do their duties for the day. In no time at all, Arokan stopped us in front of a nondescript tent, no different than any of the others around it.

He called out in Dakkari and a long moment later, an older female emerged.

"*Vorakkar*," she greeted, though she seemed put off by the early hour. I watched their exchange with interest, noting that the female didn't shy away from Arokan's gaze, not like other members of the camp.

They spoke quickly in Dakkari, rapid words that floated over my head. I wondered if there would come a time when I would understand the language in its entirety.

Not likely, I thought.

Finally, the older female looked at me. Lips pressed together, she looked me over, from head to toe, before inclining her head and saying, "*Morakkari*. You have come for your markings."

I blinked when she spoke the universal tongue, when she looked me directly in the eyes, her eyes rimmed in green, not yellow. Her dark skin was wrinkled, just like the elders' in my own village, but her hair was still black and shining, plaited and decorated with colorful beads.

"It will be an honor, *Morakkari*," she spoke again, but something in her tone made me question her words. She seemed sharp, cutting.

I realized she wasn't impressed with me, wasn't impressed by Arokan's choice of a queen. Mirari had mentioned those that didn't agree with my being a human among the horde. Was she one of them?

Surprisingly, I found her disinterest in me...refreshing. It was honest. I could handle honest.

"Thank you," I replied because I didn't know what else to say.

"You may call me Hukan," she replied.

I studied her as she studied me. She'd given me her true name. Was it because I was Arokan's queen now? I couldn't help but remember what Mirari had told me. That sometimes Dakkari gave their given names to people they didn't respect, as an insult.

I didn't give mine in return. Partly because I somehow knew Arokan wouldn't approve and partly because I didn't want to. Perhaps the Dakkari were onto something about only giving your name to those you trusted or cared for.

And yet Arokan gave his name to me, I couldn't help but think. I didn't particularly think he trusted me or cared for me beyond simple desire and necessity for a queen.

"Hukan," I repeated.

Her eyes narrowed ever so slightly before she looked at Arokan. He was watching her too, watching me, as if it was all a test. Did he know she disapproved of me?

Probably, I thought. Something about Arokan told me that not much got past him. He was always observing, always aware. It was probably why he made a good horde king, why he was respected.

"Come inside, *Vorakkar. Morakkari*," Hukan said, ushering us inside. Her tent was much smaller than our own, but was comfortable enough with a bed of furs and cushions. Incense burned within, filling the tent with an overpowering earthy fragrance, one that made my eyes tear up.

She led us over to a low table in the center of the tent and I followed Arokan's lead and sat down on the cushions next to him.

Hukan retrieved materials from a chest of drawers and returned to the table, slowly lowering herself down across from us. Her eyes ran over me again. I was so used to the Dakkari averting their gaze that I was surprised how uncomfortable it made me.

"You continue to wear your *vekkiri* clothes," she commented. "You do not think you are Dakkari now?"

I blinked.

Arokan whistled out a low breath. "*Kivale*," he said, though whether it was a name or a warning, I didn't know.

"Your queen should be proud to wear Dakkari adornments," Hukan said and I was stunned at her tone, at the way she looked at Arokan. All the while, she continued to lay out her materials like nothing was wrong. She was criticizing me though we'd just met. "It is a disrespect to you, Arokan. A disrespect to us all."

I sucked in a breath at the sound of his name, disbelief spreading through me. I thought no member of his horde was supposed to know his name, much less speak it.

Except one, I remembered. He said that none knew his name except one.

Who was this female to him?

"Enough," he said, his tone sharp, and Hukan stilled, her outstretched hand freezing over a needle. When I looked over at him, I saw his barely concealed anger. "I do not care what she wears. She is human. She is Dakkari now too. You cross lines in speaking to my queen this way. Even you, *Kivale*."

He was…defending me?

"Forgive me," Hukan finally said after a brief, uncomfortable pause, though she only held Arokan's eyes. "You know I am just an old fool."

Looking down at my pants and tunic, I'd never realized that the way I dressed would reflect poorly not only on me, but on Arokan. I'd never even thought that it could be considered an insult.

"You can ask my queen for forgiveness, *Kivale*," Arokan said, his tone still sharp, like a blade.

Hukan met his eyes, then she looked down at the table, rearranging her needles and pots of gold slowly before she met my gaze.

"Forgive me, *Morakkari*," she said. "I forget my place."

"You gave your opinion," I replied a moment later, because I wanted to keep the peace. "There is nothing to forgive."

She blinked, her lips pressing together.

"I *am* human," I said. "I'm not ashamed that I am and I won't apologize for what makes me feel comfortable."

I sensed Arokan's gaze but I held her eyes. Hukan reminded me of the seamstress I used to work for back at the village. Hard as nails, that woman, and she constantly tested me at every turn with her sharp words and cranky attitude. I was used to criticism, just from people I was familiar with. One thing I did know, however, was that if I didn't stand up for myself from the beginning, I would always be lesser in her eyes.

Hukan looked away first and my fingers twitched, relieved. She looked down at the pots, picked up a clear salve, and asked, "Do you wish to go first, *Vorakkar*?"

I blinked. Arokan would get markings that day too?

Arokan held out one wrist in reply, his irritation still evident. Hukan spread the salve just above his gold cuffs in a thick band, wrapped all the way around, waited a moment, then wiped it away.

Despite the slight tension in the tent, I was soon distracted by the process of tattooing. I watched as Hukan cleaned her needles and then dipped one in the gold, balancing the pot between two fingers with ease. Quickly, she jabbed the needle into Arokan's flesh, re-dipped the needle, jabbed again, re-dipped, jabbed, re-dipped, jabbed. Over and over again until she had an outline of a wide band spanning the space above his cuff.

Though she was incredibly quick and talented with her needle, the process was slow, quiet, and tedious. But there was a mesmerizing beauty about it, a subtle art. It was apparent that Hukan had done this many times before.

Soon, one wrist was done. The tattoo was almost as wide and thick as his cuffs, one solid band of gleaming gold. It was beautiful and it made his skin shimmer in the light.

Arokan's other wrist was done in the same slow, intricate process until the two tattoos were virtually identical.

His eyes met mine and he said, "Now you, *kassikari.*"

I didn't show my hesitation when I reached my wrist across the table. I didn't need to give Hukan any more reason to dislike me. With an almost clinical touch, she repeated the cleaning process, spreading the salve over my wrist.

She dipped the clean needle in the pot, but paused, looking up at Arokan before asking something in Dakkari.

"Rath Kitala," he replied.

"Rath Kitala?" Hukan repeated slowly, her eyes narrowing.

"*Lysi,*" he replied, his brow quirking, as if challenging her, as if daring her to question him.

My own brow furrowed, watching the exchange, confused by it. Hukan's lips pressed together again and then she made the first jab into my wrist, though it was aggressive.

Eyes widening at the sharp pain, I shot a look at Arokan, almost in betrayal. He hadn't even flinched, hadn't moved, during the whole process of his markings. I'd decided that it couldn't hurt *that* badly.

It hurt like a *bitch.* Though, I suspected, after Hukan's second, third, fourth jab, that she was a little rougher with me than she'd been with Arokan. She certainly seemed to put more muscle into it.

Arokan's lips quirked at my outraged expression, but he remained quiet, simply watching me.

Soon, a slim band began to take shape across my wrist. It wasn't solid, like Arokan's, nor was it nearly as wide, but it was the same swirling design as the markings across his biceps, across his chest, across his shoulders.

Soon, she started work on a second band, about half an inch higher than the first, in the same design, though the pattern looked slightly different.

Though tears welled in my eyes at the shooting pain, I blinked them away, not wanting Hukan to see. It felt like I had something to prove to her, so I took pride in the fact that whenever she looked up at me with a searching gaze, my features were expressionless, my eyes dry.

Relief went through me when she released my wrist, wiping away some of the blood that welled and coating the gold in the clear salve.

It was only a momentary reprieve, however, because she gestured impatiently for my other wrist.

So, I gritted my teeth, sent a withering glare over to Arokan, and she began work on the next set of markings.

It seemed like hours later when they were done.

Once she released me, I felt shivery from the pain and my face was probably pale, but I looked down at my wrists, turning them to see every inch.

"They're beautiful," I said softly, looking up at Hukan.

She ignored me, simply cleaned and packed up her materials before redepositing them in her drawers.

Arokan stood and helped me up, placing his hand on the small of my lower back. His heat felt nice.

"*Kivale*," he murmured, inclining his head. "*Kakkira vor.* Thank you for your time."

Then he urged me to the entrance of the tent.

"Let me speak with your *Morakkari* a moment," Hukan said before I stepped outside.

Arokan hesitated, watching her with narrowed, suspicious eyes. He looked at me, then jerked his head and ducked outside, leaving me alone with the older female. I would rather be alone with a hundred *pyroki*, I thought.

"You are not good enough for him," Hukan said simply, her voice quiet and hushed. "He made a mistake in choosing you."

I froze, my back straightening, her words stunningly...*hurtful.*

"Do you dislike me because I'm not Dakkari?" I asked, keeping my voice level and even. "Because I'm human?"

"*Nik,*" she said. "I dislike you because I think you are weak. I think you do not have the spine or the stomach to be a *Morakkari.* Not like his mother."

His mother?

My brow furrowed and I lowered my voice so Arokan would not hear. "You know *nothing* about me."

I sucked in a breath when Hukan reached out to grip my raw wrist, right over the markings she'd just made across my flesh. She squeezed and pain sizzled through me, making me dizzy. "These are the same markings that his mother had. It is a disgrace that they mark you now. He might not see that yet. In time, he will. He will realize how wrong you are for him, for the *horde.*"

I tugged my wrist from her grip with a strong pull, making her stumble. Her gaze flashed up to me in surprise.

"Don't *ever* touch me again," I hissed.

Her jaw clenched, her eyes narrowing, but she wisely held her tongue. Fury rose, hot and quick. I'd never liked bullies and there was no doubt that she was one, despite her age.

"My mother was mauled by one of your wild *pyroki* outside the protection of our village," I told her, holding her gaze, straightening. I stepped forward, so that I was close, so that she would hear me when I whispered, "I killed her myself with a blade to ease her suffering. I was fifteen years old. So don't tell me what I have the spine or the stomach for. You know *nothing* about me."

A sharp breath whistled out from her flat nostrils when I pulled away.

I turned my back without a second glance and stepped out of the tent, away from that cloying incense.

Once outside, I felt like I could breathe again.

14

"Are you well, *Missiki?*" Mirari asked as we walked together through the thick forest spread behind the Dakkari camp. Lavi flanked my other side and Arokan had given me a guard, who trailed behind all three of us. When I'd protested that I didn't need to be watched like a child, he'd only looked at me, grunted, and then turned away to go about his duties for the day. And the guard *still* followed.

My wrists still throbbed from Hukan's markings, the skin surrounding the gold slightly reddened. Mirari told me to keep the salve on them and to wrap them in cloth, which I did.

"Do your markings ache? We should return to camp. I can fetch you the healer," she said.

No, I didn't want to go back. Not yet. Arokan had told me not to venture far when I told him that I needed fresh air, that I couldn't stand another long afternoon trapped in the tent. Surprisingly, he'd relented with little argument. After what Hukan said, I needed to clear my mind.

With a look over my shoulder at the guard, I said softly to Mirari, "A female named Hukan did my markings." I was unsure if I was supposed to say her name out loud, but I was beyond caring. "Who is she?"

Mirari blinked, looking down at the forest path. The forest was overgrown and thick in places, but the path that Mirari led us down seemed maintained, as if Dakkari trekked through it often.

"She did not take to you, I assume," Mirari ventured, her voice hesitant and light.

I was slowly becoming to trust Mirari. She'd never given me a reason not to, despite telling Arokan that I refused to eat when I first arrived at the camp. Though she often told me her purpose was to obey me, she was always honest and didn't shy away from the questions I asked.

I relied on her for information and I was thankful for the things she told me, especially since I understood the Dakkari very little.

"No," I answered her. "She did not."

"She would not," Mirari admitted, with a certainty in her voice that surprised me.

"Why?"

"I do not..." she trailed off, casting a glance behind her shoulder at the guard, who stayed ten paces back. "I do not know if it is my place to say. I would not wish to anger the *Vorakkar.*"

"The *Vorakkar* is not here and I will not tell him," I told her. "Please. I need to know what I'm getting myself into, how to handle her."

Mirari relented, "She is a blood relation to the *Vorakkar.* She is very protective of him."

My lips parted. "How is she related?" A thought occurred to me and I asked, "What does *Kivale* mean?"

Mirari's shoulders sagged. "Hukan was the older sister of the *Vorakkar's* mother. *Kivale* is a term of respect, honoring that blood line."

Hukan was Arokan's aunt.

Damn.

"Hukan is very protective of her line, *Missiki*," Mirari explained. "Her aversion to you is expected. Pay her no mind. She is old. Her years in this life, the tragedies that she has faced within her line, have left her bitter and angry."

What tragedies? I wondered. Did Arokan experience the same tragedies too?

That didn't make me feel any better. She'd known Arokan's given name, which meant that she was close to him. I'd known that. Still, she'd gotten under my skin, she'd managed to hurt me. I told her something that I'd never voiced out loud before.

She thought I was weak, that I wouldn't be able to do my duty when it came to the horde. In a way, I suspected she was right. I was out of my element, thrown into a life I wasn't prepared for. I'd never even *wanted* to be queen to Arokan's horde and I sure as hell didn't ask for it.

But now, it didn't matter. I *was* queen. It was done. Arokan had chosen me for reasons I still didn't understand and his aunt hated me for it.

"Is she the only relation the *Vorakkar* has within the horde?" I asked.

"*Lysi*," Mirari said. "She is the last female of their line. He is the last male. Unless you bear the *Vorakkar* a daughter and a son."

I went quiet, processing her words. I couldn't force Hukan to accept me. She merely tolerated my presence because of Arokan.

Whatever needs to happen will happen, I decided. It was best not to dwell on it.

A cracking branch made me stiffen and our heads jerked towards the sound. But through the density of the forest, I could see nothing and no one.

Memories of my mother rose, though I tried to push them

back. Suddenly, I was fifteen again, alone in the icy forest during the cold season, desperately looking for my mother, a tangy, metallic smell permeating the air. Something had been watching me, something had been following me.

"We should turn back now, *Missiki*," Mirari said, breaking me out of that particular memory. "We have gone far enough."

I nodded, my heartbeat drumming in my chest, and we turned around, heading back towards the camp. I heard another branch snap behind us and we picked up the pace, none of us talking until we reached the edge of the camp again. Even the Dakkari feared the beasts in the wilds, it seemed.

A small burst of relief made me exhale a sharp breath when I saw the busy camp, much busier than it had been that morning. A short distance away, I saw my tent, but the thought of returning filled me with restlessness, so I turned away.

"*Missiki*," Mirari called, questioning.

"Let's walk through camp and see if anything needs to be done," I said in return.

She sputtered, protesting, and hurried her pace to keep up with me, as did Lavi. "*Missiki*, you are *Morakkari* now. You do not help with these things. The *Vorakkar* would be most displeased if—"

"What am I expected to do here?" I asked, stopping to turn towards her. "I need to do *something*."

"I do not know what the *Vorakkar*'s plans are for you but I do not—"

I cut her off by saying, "Well, let me go ask him. Where is he?"

Mirari's gold painted eyelids fluttered in shock.

"What do *Morakkaris* do exactly?" I asked instead when she didn't reply.

"They—they keep the *Vorakkar* pleased, so he can lead effectively."

My eyes bulged and I choked out a small laugh. Then I realized she wasn't joking.

"You can't be serious," I said. "Any female could 'please' him, if that was the case."

"Not any female can provide him heirs," Mirari returned.

My lips pressed together. So was I nothing more than a breeding vessel, a whore with a queen's title?

I thought of his treasure chests lined against the wall of the tent, remembered that they were filled with female adornments and pretty things, chests I assumed were for the females who 'pleased' him.

Something cut me at that thought. Something that confused me. Something that felt an awful lot like jealousy, like possession.

So this is how it is, Luna? You have sex with him once and now you think he's yours?

But he was, wasn't he? By all rights, he was my goddamn *husband*, whether I'd asked for it or not.

"That doesn't work for me," I said, my spine straightening. My eyes went to the guard, still hovering behind Lavi. "Take me to the *Vorakkar*."

The guard's eyes met mine. A scar slashed across his face, across his cheekbone, over the bridge of his nose.

His gaze went to Mirari, though she stayed silent.

Finally, he said in clumsy, unpracticed universal tongue, "He is training now, *Morakkari*."

"Then take me to where he trains."

The guard's jaw clenched but then he inclined his head in a nod. I followed him when he cut a path through the camp, heading in the direction where the celebration had taken place last night.

As we drew nearer and nearer to what I assumed were the training grounds, I heard the ringing clash of blades, of metal on metal, of male grunts, of bodies being flung to the earth.

Nothing prepared me for the sight of what made those sounds, however.

Nor the sight of Arokan fighting with a sword, sweaty, his muscles shifting and flexing, an intense look of savage concentration on his face, as he took on three Dakkari opponents.

Last night, when he'd been driving into my body, he'd worn a similar expression.

I swallowed, feeling a flutter of arousal at the memory of it, which I definitely *didn't* need to be feeling.

The guard halted far enough away from the clearing, giving the males ample space for their training session, and I froze next to him, watching the scene in front of me with morbid fascination.

Arokan quickly side-stepped when an opponent came at him, moving so fast that he was like a blur. He blocked another opponent's blade before it took him in the side and with a bellow, he pushed him back before landing a kick in the center of his chest, making the male *fly* across the clearing.

Throwing out his arm in a graceful arc, he slapped the flat edge of his sword against the third opponent's thigh before ramming his thick fist straight across his nose, making the male's head whip to the side before he landed hard.

I'd never seen anything like it. Never seen something so physically brutal or intense. People in my village weren't warriors, weren't fighters. The majority of them had probably never held a blade in their lives. To see such skill and savagery up close...it was shocking. It reminded me of all the tales we'd been told of the Dakkari since we were young.

Arokan braced, still, eyeing the three males on the ground, waiting. After a moment, when none of them rose, he straightened, some of the tension leaving him, as he barked out something in Dakkari and helped the male nearest him up to a stand, clapping him across the shoulders.

He turned his head to say something to the male and that

was when he caught my eyes. I watched him hesitate, his gaze narrowing ever so slightly, before he called out an order to the two dozen or so males that had also been watching the training session from the sidelines. Four more entered the clearing and began to spar with one another while Arokan made his way towards me, sheathing his sword at his hip.

Arokan nodded at the guard, who seemed to melt away with Mirari and Lavi until it was just the two of us.

"Is something wrong, *kalles*?" he asked, his eyes focused on me.

My heart was still drumming in my chest from that training session. What disturbed me was that my eyes tracked over his flesh, seeing the sweat and dirt, remembering how efficiently he'd dispatched his opponents. What disturbed me the most was that my nipples were pebbled underneath my tunic and despite the soreness of my sex, I was remembering the exquisite feel of his length inside me.

"How long have you been fighting like that?" I found myself asking, trying to distance myself from my body's treacherous demands.

"Since I was strong enough to hold a blade," he answered, cocking his head to the side. "I was trained from a young age."

It showed. I wondered if his father had taught him. If his mother had been a *Morakkari*, it meant that his father had been a *Vorakkar*.

"What is it that you need, *kalles*?" he murmured. The scent of him, his sweat, his musk fogged my brain, made my mouth water.

Blinking, I managed to remember why I'd sought him out.

"Is there anything I can do around camp?" I asked.

He wiped his forearm across his forehead, his fresh gold markings from that morning flashing. Unlike mine, they didn't look reddened or irritated.

"There is no need."

"I *want* to do something," I amended.

He turned the full force of his gaze onto me. "Why?"

I inhaled a short breath and said, "Look, I know how it works. I know that my life, at least for the immediate future, is with you, here." He frowned at that. "Maybe that will change in time, but for now, it would benefit me to learn about this place, about your people. About *you*. And I can't do any of that sitting on my ass in a tent all day."

Something rose from him, wild and quick. He advanced on me, lowered his head ever so slightly, and growled, "Your future is *always* with me, *kalles*. Do not *ever* say otherwise."

My lips parted, not expecting that reaction. "Arokan."

A sharp exhale whistled through his nostrils and he bit out a curse in Dakkari, looking away, past me to his camp.

"That's…" I swallowed, trailing off. "All I meant was that we don't know what the future brings. All I meant was that I'm here now. I'm not going to fight you at every turn anymore. I've accepted that this is the path my life has taken and if that's so, I want to *build* a life here. I need a purpose."

"Your purpose is to stand beside me," he growled, "as my queen."

"As your ornament?" I rasped, frustrated. "As your *trophy*? I'm not going to spend my life like that, Arokan. I can't. It would kill me."

His gaze flashed, his yellow irises contracting.

"I just want a job," I said softly, hesitantly reaching out to touch his forearm. His skin was hot from the sun, from his exertion. "However small it might be. *Anything*."

His gaze went down to my hand resting against him and when he didn't reply, I bit my lip and pulled it away.

In a flash, he caught my hand, keeping that connection.

"Anything?" he repeated, running his calloused thumb across the back of my hand. I'd never known such a simple touch could feel so…arousing. So intimate.

"Y-yes," I replied, my head going a little fuzzy again.

He leaned close, those rapt eyes freezing me into place. Softly, he said, "Then you will aid with the *pyrokis'* care."

My eyes widened and I snatched my hand back, taking a whole step away from him, as if to distance myself from his words. "Arokan, *no*. I can't do that."

"You said anything. You wanted a job, this is the one I task to you," he replied simply.

My breath hitched, my mind flashing to those red-eyed beasts, the same kind of beast that had mauled my mother, that had forced me to end her suffering.

"*Please*, I'll do anything else but—"

"Do you think I have not noticed your aversion to them?" Arokan asked softly.

"I...I..."

"*Pyrokis* are the foundation of all Dakkari hordes," he said. "If you wish to learn more about us, you must first understand *them*. The horde will never truly accept you unless you master your fear and open yourself to these creatures."

I bit my tongue, looking at the ground between us.

"Will you do this?" Arokan asked. "For me? For the horde? For yourself?"

"I don't know if I can," I said softly, but then I looked up at him. Swallowing, I nodded with dread pooling in my belly, and whispered, "But I will try."

He made a sound in the back of his throat, reached out to thread his fingers through my hair. A gasp of surprise left me when he cupped the nape of my neck, tugging me forward, and kissed me right there on the edge of the training grounds, with over two dozen Dakkari horde warriors watching.

Lips parting against him, I clutched his biceps as he took his kiss with the ferocity and thoroughness of a horde king.

"Brave *kalles*," he rasped against me, pulling back. He released me, so quickly that I swayed. "You are—"

Suddenly, alarmed shouts echoed through camp and Arokan's head snapped up, in the direction of the forest.

He jerked his head towards the horde warriors, bellowing out an order in Dakkari, and they all ran towards the back of the camp.

"What's happening?" I cried, as shouts of alarm rang out.

Arokan pushed me into the arms of my assigned guard. "Stay with him, *kalles*. Do not leave his side."

In Dakkari, he said something to the guard, who jerked his head in a nod.

"Wait!" I said, confused and concerned. "What is—"

"Do as I say!" Arokan growled. "I will find you later."

Then he turned his back and sprinted in the direction of the forest, unsheathing his sword as he went.

15

Pacing the confines of the tent, I blew out an impatient, anxious breath for the hundredth time in the last four hours, give or take.

I was worried, frightened, irritated...and I didn't know what else to do, so I simply paced. Back and forth. The scarred guard wouldn't let me outside, though I could tell that night had already fallen. There was still no word about what had happened in the camp prior to Arokan's departure. And if the guard knew, he was keeping a tight lip.

Mirari and Lavi watched me, fidgeting on their cushions. They held blades in their hands, as if they were prepared to fight if something or someone entered the tent.

Earlier, I'd asked them if they knew how to use blades, if they'd been trained to defend themselves.

"*Lysi*," Mirari replied. "All Dakkari know how to fight. We were all trained."

I didn't know how to fight. There had never been a need for it, especially when other work had to be done in the village.

But now, trapped in a tent, after what happened earlier...I couldn't help but wonder what I would do if something came through the entrance and attacked us. I wouldn't know *what* to do.

"What do you think is happening?" I asked again.

"I am sure the *Vorakkar* is handling it, whatever it is," Mirari tried to reassure me.

I'd never been patient, one of my many faults.

"Do you think—"

The tent flap pulled back and Arokan appeared, a stormy, furious expression on his face. He ordered the *piki* to leave and Mirari and Lavi scurried out without a backwards glance, obviously sensing the same mood I was.

Sharp relief made me a little lightheaded but soon, anger took its place. Which probably wasn't the wisest emotion to show, considering Arokan looked...untamed. He looked ready to boil over.

"Where the *hell* have you been?" I cried out. "What happened out there? I've been imagining the worst—*what are you doing?*"

Arokan growled, capturing my hands with his tail in a tight grip when I pushed at his chest, and he tugged down my pants with a rough pull.

Suddenly, I was naked from the waist down, my bare sex and buttocks on display. Then he pushed me down onto the furs, turning me so I was bent over the edge.

My breaths came out in rough pants when I struggled against him, my cheek pressed against the furs, my hair tangling in front of my eyes. "*Arokan*," I hissed. "Right now is not the time for—"

I jerked in shock when he gave my exposed buttocks a slap. Not enough to hurt. Just enough to get my attention, to make me *seethe*.

"*Enough*," he growled. "All I need right now is to be buried in your cunt. Nothing more."

Disbelief and fury and something I didn't want to identify—something that felt an awful lot like *need*—made me buck against him and hiss, "You did not just do that. I'm *not* your damn *pyroki*, Arokan!"

"*Nik*, you are certainly not," he rasped, untying the laces of his pants, pushing the waistband down over his hard cock with a rough jerk. "Kailon is obedient."

I gasped, outraged, and tried to scratch at his arms when his hands came to grip my hips, when they slid under my tunic to cup my breasts. I cried out in frustration when he pinched my nipples softly, a sizzle of arousal running through my belly.

His tail once again captured my wrists, holding them tight behind my back until I couldn't move, not with him keeping me in place.

One of his hands left my breasts and I felt the pad of his finger run down my slit. He found my clit and I made a desperate sound in the back of my throat, my hips bucking. I couldn't tell if I was trying to get away…or trying to press closer.

"Tell me what happened today," I ordered, though, to my mortification, my voice came out breathless.

"I will," he rasped. "*After.*"

"Ugh!"

His finger slid inside me. When that finger curled against my inner walls, I squeezed my eyes shut.

"Damn you," I whispered when my hips moved of their own accord, moving against him, seeking that pleasure I knew he could give me. Maybe this was what I needed…a release. A release of the frustration and worry and anger that had been building and building all afternoon.

Suddenly, his finger retreated and I felt the press of his cock taking its place. Though I bit my lip at the sharp twinge I felt, I didn't cry out as he thrust inside me.

So deep, so hard.

So good.

Stars burst in my vision and I gasped into the furs as he pinched my nipple a little harder.

"*Lysi,*" he hissed and then he pulled out, thrusting back inside with more force.

Then he didn't stop.

He fucked me hard and fast, grunts of pleasure emanating from him, while desperate moans tumbled from me. Every hard, throbbing, hot inch of him stimulated me in places I hadn't even known existed...places that threatened to consume me with pleasure.

He was savage. He was thorough. He knew how to fuck me until I screamed. He knew how to fuck me until I was coming all over his cock.

He bit out a curse. "Already, *kassikari?*" His voice was dark and velvety and absolutely *sinful.* "*Vok,* you need this just like I do. Tell me!"

"*No,*" I bit out in between gasps as my amazing orgasm made every muscle in my body clench tight.

"Stubborn *kalles,*" he grunted, slamming into me *hard.*

It didn't take him long after to orgasm. I moaned into the furs when I felt him shoot his hot seed into me, pulsing and throbbing. His roaring groan of release rang in my ears.

His tail released my hands and it wasn't until just then that I realized he'd been mindful of my fresh, raw markings.

With a purring sound, he dragged me up the bed until I collapsed against him, my head cushioned on his chest, which heaved underneath my cheek. He was flat on his back, with his pants still down to his mid-thighs, his cock resting on his taut abdomen.

When I caught my breath, I pressed my fingernails into his flesh and said, "I hate you."

"*Nik,* you do not," he said next, his voice surprisingly soft. He turned his head to look at me and continued with, "I think you want to. But you do not, *kalles.*"

Arokan stretched his other arm over his head, arching his back a little, and I realized that he no longer looked ready to kill someone. Most of the tension had drained from his body.

I didn't know what the hell had just happened, but he'd fucked a little of my temper right out of me. It should have disturbed me how easily I'd given into him, how much I'd wanted it.

But right then, with my cheek pressed against his chest, with my tunic ridden up to just below my breasts, and his seed leaking from my body…I felt decidedly less disturbed than I should have been.

"What happened this afternoon?" I asked, not wanting to dwell on that thought, needing a distraction.

His muscles tensed. He turned his head to regard me, those yellow-rimmed eyes contracting. "I am not done with you yet."

He wanted…*more*?

Swallowing, I said, "You said you would tell me *after* and this is *after*."

He blew out a breath, reaching out to run a hand through my hair. He grunted, though I couldn't tell if it was in frustration or amusement. "You are right."

Surprise made me raise my brows.

He frowned and said, "We captured a Ghertun scout on the edge of the camp."

I gasped, sitting up to look down at him. "What?"

"He came from the forest. He will not tell us where the rest of his pack is, despite our methods of…persuasion."

I thought back to the movement in the forest we'd heard during the walk we'd taken and I brought a hand to my throat, "I thought there was something or someone in the forest when we went in earlier this afternoon."

Arokan froze. "*Neffar?*"

Had that been a Ghertun? Had he been watching us?

I shivered and said, "We heard branches snapping. I thought

maybe it was a beast of some kind and we turned around. But now…I can't help but wonder if—"

Arokan broke out with a loud curse, pressing a hand to his eyes.

"Arokan," I said gently.

"You will have two guards watching you at all times if I am not with you," he said, his voice hard and unyielding.

My mouth dropped. "That's completely unnecessary. I don't even need *one*."

"Ghertun are *dangerous*. I will *not* risk your safety," he growled, glaring up at me, though his words made my breath catch. "I have seen them do unspeakable things and if there is a scout nearby, then his pack is not far behind."

"You think they mean to attack us?" I asked, freezing. "They mean to attack a whole horde? That's suicide."

"I do not know yet," he replied. For some reason, I had expected him to be tight-lipped about matters like these. It surprised me that he shared the information without hesitation. I was…grateful for that, that he wasn't keeping me in the dark. "It is possible the *tassimara* drew them near. Regardless, we are close enough to *Dothik* that I have to take action before they get too close to the capital."

My heartbeat drummed with dread. "What do you mean to do?"

"Find them before they find us," he answered. "Ghertun scouts usually travel two days ahead of a pack. We have time."

I dragged my knees to my chest and I felt Arokan's hand stroke up my back. We were quiet for a moment before I said, "Thank you for telling me."

"You are *Morakkari*," he replied. "You have a right to know."

Did I? Up until a few days ago, I hadn't even known about the Ghertun's existence, much less the danger that they posed.

Turning my head slightly, I looked down at Arokan, sprawled out beside me.

I could have done a lot worse for myself, I realized suddenly, that knowledge bursting through me. I'd never given thought to joining my life with a man's. Never given much thought to a future with a family, with children, not when my village was struggling, not when there was work to be done, not when Kivan needed me to be strong.

But Arokan was strong. He protected his people at all costs, could show mercy when needed, kindness when it was unexpected.

He hadn't abused me, hadn't hurt me. Instead, he'd made me his queen and answered my questions without hesitation. He'd given me a job that would challenge me, he'd given me guards to protect me, and he'd driven me mad with frightening desire.

He was…not what I had expected.

"I dispatched my *pujerak* to your village this morning," he said quietly.

Hope sprang in my chest. The messenger with the three *bveri*. The deal we'd made last night at the *tassimara*…

"You did?"

He jerked his head in a nod. "He should have already arrived."

I looked away when unexpected tears sprang in my eyes. I didn't want him to see me cry, but the thought that my brother could have fresh meat, actual *food* for the first time…it was something I never thought would happen.

"Thank you," I whispered.

"You honored your promise to me," he said. "I have honored mine."

When I was sure that my tears weren't going to fall, I looked at him, resting my cheek on my knees. It occurred to me that this moment almost felt *comfortable*. That it felt almost natural to sit there and talk to him in that bed.

"When I was younger," I said softly, "a Dakkari horde came to our village. A few males walked through. It was my first time seeing a Dakkari up close. They were just observing us, though their presence put everyone on edge." Arokan grunted. "Then one of them saw one of our villagers. A young woman named Mithelda. He took her, which shocked us all. They left and we never saw her again."

Arokan said carefully, "What are you asking me?"

"Nothing," I said softly. "I just…I wanted you to know that before you even stepped foot inside my village, I had decided that if you had another *use* for me, if the Dakkari did indeed take female war prizes from settlements, that was something I was willing to give you."

Arokan's tail came up and wrapped around my ankle. "Dakkari do not take war prizes, Luna. It is more likely that that male's *Vorakkar* gave him permission to take a *kassikari*. He saw a female he wanted and he bound himself to her, in the old tradition, by capturing her. If he is an honorable horde warrior, I can assure you that this female of yours is safe and well."

I sucked in a breath, staring at him. "What?"

"Horde warriors may only take a *kassikari* with permission," he told me. "Only when he proves himself a valuable and strong warrior to his *Vorakkar*."

"What do you mean by the old tradition?" I asked quietly, my mind racing. He'd said something about that, about claiming me in the old way. What did that mean?

"It is ancient. Perhaps primitive," he said with a small quirk of his lips, which sent my heart racing, "but it speaks to the soul of the Dakkari. We were once a race of warring factions spread across the planet, until we united under one king, though it took many bloody, long wars before then. During that time, warriors would unite their factions together, growing stronger by capturing females from opposite sides to bind themselves together, creating offspring, forming blood ties between the enemy factions that were unbreakable. It created a network across the planet, held together by females and their sacrifices, bridging gaps, gaining alliances. That is the old tradition."

"You..." I trailed off, processing the information. "You always knew, from the beginning, what you intended for me."

"*Lysi*, I told you as much," he replied. "Kakkari revealed you to me. I took you. I bound us."

"Because I'm human?" I couldn't help but ask. "Because you want to forge an alliance between my kind and yours?"

Arokan growled, his hand reaching out to grip my waist, dragging me closer until I was pressed against his side again.

"*Nik*. I took you because I wanted you for myself. I do not care that you are human. That never mattered."

"It should," I whispered. "I told you it would've been easier, easier for your people to accept a queen if she was Dakkari."

"I do not want easy," he murmured. "Nothing worthwhile is ever easy."

My breath hitched and I looked up at him.

"You're being...sweet," I said. "Stop, I don't like it."

Arokan barked out a stunning laugh, which shocked me enough that my jaw fell open.

"Why?" he rasped when he stopped. "Because it reminds you that you do not hate me like you say?"

My belly was fluttering from that laugh and alarm bells went off in my head. Warming his bed, standing beside him as his queen was one thing. Having feelings for him was an entirely different beast.

"You're right," I whispered. "I don't hate you."

That knowledge grated. I *should* hate him. But except for the whole capturing me from my village thing...he'd never given me a reason to hate him.

I gasped when his fingers trailed to my sex, softly stroking between my thighs.

"I would have been more gentle with you last night had I known you were untried," he murmured.

I stiffened as a flush rose to my cheeks. He'd seen the blood coating my thighs that morning. "I didn't think to tell you."

"Even still, you should have."

"It doesn't matter," I said. "It's done now."

Arokan inhaled a slow breath, those eyes watching me, those fingers exploring me. I bit my lip when his thumb brushed my clit. "Do humans have an aversion to mating as they do to nudity?"

I rolled my eyes, though the question embarrassed me. "No."

"Then why were you untried?"

"Because there wasn't any time to think about that," I confessed. "There were men in my village who I think would've had me, if I had shown interest." Arokan stiffened, a growl rising from his chest, though it sounded like he tried to stop it before it emerged. "There was much to be done. I worked all my waking hours, trying to keep us fed. Sex seemed…unimportant compared to that. Food keeps you alive. Sex does not."

Arokan was frowning. His hand paused between my legs and he seemed to be thinking something over.

He went quiet for a long time, long enough for me to grow drowsy from the day, from the sex, from the warmth emanating from his body.

Finally, he said gruffly, "Sleep, *kalles*. Tomorrow will be long."

"Why?" I whispered, my eyelids already half-lowered. Why was he so *warm*? Why did he feel so *good*?

Out of the corner of my eye, I saw his jaw clench.

"Because tomorrow you will stand beside me and do your duty as *Morakkari*."

"What do I need to do?"

"Something I do not think you will like," was all he said.

My eyes closed, lost to the world before I even registered his words, before I even wondered what he meant.

16

Another day, another barely-there outfit.

At least I'm wearing a top this time, I thought, eyeing myself.

"What is this about again?" I asked Mirari as Lavi brushed through my hair. That morning, I had woken to an empty bed, but I hadn't even had time to process what had happened last night between Arokan and me before Mirari and Lavi burst into the tent. It was as if they kept their ears pressed to the hide, listening for any small indication that I'd woken.

The skirt was long, almost touching the tops of my feet, but it had slits up both sides, ending at my upper thighs. The top was sheer, though my breasts were covered in the intricate pattern of gold beads covering the front. The neckline, however, was plunging, leaving my neck and collarbones and valley of my breasts exposed.

"It is not our place to say," Mirari said. She seemed strangely quiet that day.

"It has to do with the Ghertun scout, right?" I asked.

"*Lysi*," Mirari replied.

I blew out a breath, knowing that she wouldn't say any

139

more, and simply sat at the low table as Lavi worked on my hair, twisting it up so it was off my back. It didn't take that long, but not a moment after she was done, I heard the unmistakable sound of Arokan's voice outside the tent as he addressed the guards.

Mirari and Lavi, hearing him too, began to pack up their supplies and when Arokan ducked inside, they inclined their heads in respect and promptly left. I frowned after them, wondering why everyone seemed so somber that day.

Not that I had much time to wonder. Arokan looked fresh from the training grounds and he walked over to the bath that was still set up in the corner from earlier that morning, undressing as he went. I swallowed, watching him unclothe that glorious body, before I forced myself to clear my throat.

Though my bath water had to be cool by that point, Arokan dropped himself in and began to wash quickly.

"What will happen today?" I asked, still seated on the cushion at the table, the remnants of my breakfast laid out before me. I could already tell that I was putting on much-needed weight from the food. Regular meals would do that to anyone.

Arokan glanced over at me, those eyes pinning me in place. My cheeks felt hot as he looked at me. Last night had been... confusing. We'd actually talked without having a fight and it had been oddly comfortable. He'd even *laughed* at one point.

Though that morning, he seemed returned to his *Vorakkar* state—detached, a little cold, though those eyes ran hot when he looked at me.

I watched him scrub his arms and his chest. Finally, he said, "There will be a trial today."

For the scout, I knew.

A trial. That didn't sound so bad.

"You will need to uncover your wrists," he said next, water splashing as he rinsed himself with cupped hands.

I looked down at the wraps around my golden tattoos. Lavi had helped me change them that morning.

"Do they still ache?" he asked once he stood from the tub after the quickest bath in history.

"Not much," I replied, not wanting him to know that they were still tender.

Arokan dried himself off while I kept my gaze averted. He approached, still naked, and he crouched down in front of me, his tail flicking behind him.

Desperately, I tried not to look at his half-hardened cock between his thighs and met his eyes instead. His gaze was on my wrists and he took my hands before gently unwrapping the cloth that shielded the markings from sight.

The swelling was going down at least, though the flesh around the tattoos was still reddened. Arokan got up, retrieved the clear salve from his drawers, and returned. And then, with a surprisingly soft touch, he spread more salve over the healing skin. It felt good and cool. His hands on me felt even better.

"Hukan was rougher than she needed to be," he admitted softly.

My eyes darted up to his, but he wasn't looking at me. I didn't know what to say to that without revealing what Mirari had told me.

"She will be rough with you for a while," he said next, finally meeting my eyes. "Until she knows that you are strong."

"And if I'm not strong enough?" I couldn't help but ask, the insecurities that Hukan had brought up in her tent rising.

"You are," was all he said. "Regardless, I will speak with her."

"Please don't," I whispered, catching his wrist, my hand brushing against his golden cuff. "I can handle it."

Arokan studied me before he finally nodded. "Very well." He stood from his crouched position and my hand fell away from his wrist. "I have something for you."

Curious, I watched him walk over to the chests filled with jewels and gold and—more than likely—night shifts for females.

My lips pressed together when he pulled out a necklace. A beautiful gold chain necklace, and from it hung a pendant. A massive teardrop-shaped, blood-red jewel that twinkled when the light hit it.

I'd never seen anything so beautiful but my mood dampened when I saw it. Because I knew those were the chests meant for his females—past, present, and future lovers. It didn't matter that I was his queen now. A Dakkari horde king would have concubines, without a doubt.

The jealousy surprised me. It was hot and cutting and I didn't have any right to feel it. I *shouldn't* feel it. Shouldn't I be happy that he directed his amorous attentions elsewhere?

I stood slowly and he clasped it easily around my neck. It was as heavy as it looked and I felt that heaviness, that jealousy, settling in the valley of my breasts like a boulder.

"It's beautiful," I said softly, not quite meeting his eyes.

Arokan touched the jewel. I felt the heat of his hand warm it, like it was a living thing, and my breath went shallow.

How many jewels had he given to females, just like this one? Did this necklace belong to another?

Arokan frowned as he studied me but then grunted, turning away, going to dress. Instead of pants, he wore the small furred cloth that covered his genitals, that exposed his thick, muscular thighs. He wrapped his golden belt around his waist and sheathed a dagger and his golden sword in it.

"It is time," he said. "Come."

I followed him out of the tent into the sunlight. It was another beautiful day, though the air felt more chilled than it had yesterday. The cold season was approaching, crawling over the wild lands, and I wondered what the Dakkari did when it came. Did they return to *Dothik*, where they would be more sheltered from the bitter and harsh landscape?

The thoughts were welcome, anything to distract me from the heavy chain around my neck.

Most of the camp was empty, though I heard a low murmur of restless noise coming from the front of the camp, near where the *tassimara* had taken place and where I'd seen Arokan training the day before. Instead of riding his *pyroki*—whose name I now knew was Kailon—Arokan led me through on foot, winding his way around tents I couldn't see past, towards our destination.

We came to where we'd celebrated our *tassimara,* except the only thing that remained was the raised dais. Though instead of one throne, there were now two. Where the tables and the dancing area had been was now cleared of everything but the earth of Dakkar.

The horde was there—males, females, children. They were all kneeling on the earth paces back from the raised dais and they went silent the moment that Arokan and I appeared. Among the crowd, I saw Hukan in the front row, though her eyes narrowed when she saw me. A few rows back, I spotted Mirari and Lavi, who was kneeling next to the horde warrior male I'd seen her with.

But what made my spine straighten, what made my breath hitch and my belly drop, was the being that was kneeling directly in front of the dais, surrounded by four standing guards, each with their swords pointed at him.

The Ghertun scout.

He was bloody and beaten and had a collar around his throat, which was attached to a chain carried by one of the guards.

"Luna," Arokan said, his voice hard but quiet enough that no one would hear him, when I froze.

Jolting, I remembered that the horde's eyes were on us and I followed him up the dais, sitting in the throne he'd gestured for me to take. My throne. Still, I felt like an imposter sitting in it.

Then my eyes went to the Ghertun, since I'd never seen one before.

I thought his skin was a dark gray until I realized it wasn't flesh, but scales. Hard plates of scales that made a whisper-like sound whenever he moved. His eyes were dark, black vertical slits. When he blinked, his eyelids closed from the sides, instead of from top to bottom. His nose was curved, almost like a beak, and his slim lips concealed razor-sharp yellow teeth.

He was watching me too, studying me with his strange, eerie gaze, before Arokan suddenly growled in the universal tongue, "Remove your eyes from my queen before I remove them from your skull, Ghertun."

In a flash, the Ghertun looked down, his shoulders sagging. He made a pitiful sight and my belly tugged, dread beginning to churn in my stomach when I saw how swollen his face was, when I saw his torn clothes, and a gash that separated his scales across his shoulder.

I glanced over at Arokan, my brow furrowed, my lips pulled down into a frown.

"Was he beaten?" I hissed softly.

The horde king—my alien husband—ignored me, though his jaw tightened just enough to reveal he'd heard my question and disapproved of it.

Back to this again, I thought, a flash of hurt tearing through me. Ignoring me in front of the horde.

My spine straightened in my throne, that blood-red pendant shifting on my bosom. Looking down, I saw the markings of my tattoos and they flashed in the sunlight when I clenched my fists.

"I will ask you for the last time, in front of my horde," Arokan said. "Where is your pack?"

"We do not mean you or your queen harm, horde king," the Ghertun suddenly said, his voice like a slither down my spine. "As I have said."

"You think I believe that?" Arokan asked, his tone so quiet that it was chilling. He sounded every bit as dangerous as he looked. Coupled with his fighting ability, which I saw yesterday, it made him just as deadly. "Ghertun do nothing but lie, rape, steal, and kill."

"*Some*," the Ghertun had the nerve to correct and I went still when Arokan growled, his claws digging into the arms of his throne. "Horde king, surely you are not foolish enough to believe we are all like the unsavory of our race?"

Did this Ghertun *have* a death wish?

Again, my gaze jerked to Arokan, though he seemed deceptively…unaffected.

"I would be a fool to take that chance," he countered softly, his voice even and clear. "Even you, Ghertun spy, know that," he mocked.

The Ghertun went quiet. The chains around his neck rattled as he turned to look at me, no doubt reading the seriousness of Arokan's tone. "Horde queen, you are human. You come from an understanding, emotional race—"

"*Do not* address her!" Arokan growled, losing his temper again.

The Ghertun ignored him. "Convince your mate to have mercy on me. I mean no harm."

His words shook me. The pleading in his tone. I remembered, not long ago, that I had the same desperation in my voice when I'd addressed Arokan, when he'd come to take my brother's life.

"*Enough!*" Arokan roared, standing from his throne. "Tell me where your pack is *now*. I am running short on patience, Ghertun."

The Ghertun looked up at my husband, craning his neck to see him, bloodied and weak. Pity rolled in my belly again and I bit my lip when Arokan descended the steps of the dais.

"Does it matter?" the Ghertun asked, though his voice

wavered. "I am dead, regardless of what I tell you. You will slaughter my pack if I say."

Arokan unsheathed his sword and the ringing of it echoed across the clearing.

My breath quickened, my eyes widening. Last night Arokan said I had to do my duty as *Morakkari*, that it would be something I didn't like.

This was an *execution*, not a trial. He'd lied to me. He'd always known what this was. He'd never expected the Ghertun to answer.

But Arokan expected *me* to stay silent and watch. To do my *duty*.

"I am not my father," Arokan said, his voice cold and hard. "I will not make his mistake by taking mercy on a Ghertun spy."

His *father*?

With that, Arokan raised his sword. The Ghertun made a sound, a knowing, small sound.

That sound wrenched something inside me.

Before I knew what I was doing, I stood from my throne and yelled, "*Stop!*"

17

Arokan froze.

A murmur went through the horde.

Though I heard warning bells in my head, I descended the dais, that pendant bobbing on my chest.

"There has to be another way," I said, reaching out to touch Arokan's arm, the arm with which he held the sword.

Slowly, he turned to face me and I knew I'd fucked up from his expression alone. As if the shocked faces of the kneeling Dakkari, as if the guards surrounding the Ghertun exchanging looks or slightly lowering their swords didn't tell me so already.

"*Neffar?*" Arokan hissed at me, turning his back to the Ghertun. He loomed in front of me, so tall and broad that he blocked some of the sunlight, so that I had to crane my neck up to look at him.

"Please, don't do this. An *execution*? For a crime he hasn't committed?" I cried out. "All he is guilty of is being found near the camp. Is that enough to kill him for?"

"You are untainted, *vekkiri*," Arokan said, though his tone was low and dangerous. I flinched. He'd never called me *vekkiri* before, which I now knew meant *human*. "You do not know *anything*."

"But he is—"

"*Enough*," Arokan hissed. "Do not dare to challenge my—"

A cry of surprise tore through one of the guards and before I knew it, I heard the heavy rattle of chains.

Arokan swung back around, pushing me back to protect me with enough force that I fell on my backside, my elbow hitting the ground *hard* when I tried to break my fall.

I watched in horror as the Ghertun scout—who had managed to tear his chains from the guard's grip, though the collar around his neck seemed bloodied for it—swiped out his sharp claws at the nearest Dakkari warrior, raking them down his thigh. The warrior cried out in pain and fell to one knee as dark blood began to well up.

It had all happened so fast that it left the guards momentarily stunned, giving the Ghertun enough time to jump up from his crouched position, so fast he was a blur, and begin to sprint away, back towards the forest.

He didn't make it far.

With a bellow, Arokan slammed the tip of his sword into the long chain that trailed behind the Ghertun, through one of the links. The gold sword rang and vibrated when it caught and the Ghertun gasped out a croaking breath when his neck jerked, choked by the collar, and fell with a heavy thud to the earth on his back.

Frozen, I watched as Arokan tore his sword from the earth, from the chain link, with a growl and stalked towards the scout.

"No, horde king," the Ghertun choked out, his hands flailing in front of him when Arokan loomed close. "I didn't mean to —*please* have mercy on—"

Arokan cut the Ghertun's head away from his shoulders with one smooth, fast arc of his sword, right above the chained collar. It was so cleanly done, so expertly done, that the green blood didn't appear for a few long, shocking moments.

I stared at the decapitated Ghertun, my blood rushing in my ears even as it drained from my face.

Then my gaze trailed from the grotesque head that had rolled across the earth to Arokan, standing just above the still body.

The horde king was looking at *me* with an expression I wasn't sure I wanted to know the meaning of.

Disbelief and horror made my stomach clench as I stared back at him.

That was when I heard the Dakkari warrior—the one who the Ghertun had attacked, because of *me*—groan in pain. I jerked my head over to him, saw that a Dakkari female was hovering over him, trying to stop the bleeding.

I tried to speak, tried to apologize, but the words were lodged in my throat, my tongue glued to the roof of my mouth.

Beyond that sight was the horde. All still kneeling, as shocked about the turn of events as I was. Most were looking at me, still splayed out on the cool earth.

I caught Hukan's gaze. Her lips were pressed together, her expression knowing, like I'd just confirmed all her thoughts about me.

You're an imposter, not fit to be queen, she told me with her eyes. She was almost smug about it.

Arokan approached, sheathing his blade at his hip. Reaching out, he tugged me up into a standing position, though I swayed on my feet and my elbow gave a throb of pain.

He handed me off to one of the guards who hadn't been attacked.

"Take her away," he ordered, then seemed to realize he spoke in the universal tongue. In Dakkari, he repeated his orders and the guard inclined his head, taking my arm and leading me from the clearing.

My breath hitched and I looked back to the injured guard. "Wait, will he be—"

"I will deal with you later," Arokan rasped, his dark eyes on me. Then he turned his back, going to kneel next to the guard on the ground.

Tears burned the backs of my eyes but I looked forward and allowed the guard to lead me back towards the tent.

Now you've really made a mess of things, Luna, I told myself quietly, that heavy blood-red pendant pressing against my chest.

18

Arokan didn't return to the tent until the crescent moon was already high in the sky.

I was sitting, in my pants and tunic, on a floor cushion with my knees pulled up to my chest, listening to the quiet, to the gentle flicker of the candle flames, when he ducked inside.

My gaze darted to him and I inhaled a slow breath. All day I'd prepared for this, but it still didn't prepare me for the shame I felt when I saw his expression.

The afternoon and evening had not calmed his ire towards me. It showed, plain as day. I thought of his strength, how easily he'd killed the Ghertun, and for the first time since he'd taken me from my village…I wondered if he would hurt me too.

Whatever he would do to me…I could take, I thought, steeling my spine though I didn't quite meet his gaze fully.

"How is the warrior?" I asked softly. It was a question I'd thought constantly since I left the clearing. He'd been hurt because of me, because I'd distracted Arokan by questioning his decision, because I'd prolonged an execution that had always been inevitable.

"He will heal," Arokan said, his voice terse.

Relief went through me, though it was slight. "Can I...can I see him?"

"*Nik*," Arokan growled immediately. "You cannot."

My heart raced and I swallowed the thick lump in my throat.

Long moments passed. I waited. And waited.

Finally, I couldn't take the silence anymore. With all the courage I could muster, I looked up at Arokan, who was standing before me.

"I'm sorry," I said, my tone clear, though my voice shook slightly. "I—I never could have imagined that...that..."

"Division breeds uncertainty and fear," Arokan said. "Do not ever question me in front of the horde again, *Morakkari*. Do not ever question me in front of my warriors or our enemies, *Morakkari*."

I flinched. His soft words somehow seemed worse than if he were yelling at me at the top of his lungs. I almost wished he would. But I realized he probably didn't want the horde to hear.

This was a private matter. And I had made it public by challenging him in front of his people.

Division breeds uncertainty and fear.

He meant division between us. This was between *us*.

"I'm sorry," I said again. "But I wasn't prepared for an execution. You said it was a trial. I thought I could save his—"

"It is not about what *you* want, Luna," Arokan growled. "It is about what keeps the horde safe. *My* decision ensured that."

"Then we were already divided before we ever set foot onto that dais," I said quietly. "Why didn't you tell me? You didn't think I could handle it? You kept me in the dark when you knew what would happen, when *you* and *only you* had already decided his fate."

"Do not turn this around on me, *kalles*," he said softly.

That reminded me of something. "You called me *vekkiri* earlier," I said. "Why?"

"To remind you," he growled.

"Of what? My lowly place in this universe?"

"That until recently, you said you did not know of the Ghertun's existence," Arokan said and I froze. "To remind you that while you were behind the walls of your village, safe, the Dakkari were losing many to their savagery and carnage. You do not know what they are capable of."

Safe.

Maybe we had been safe, but we'd also been starving and filled with fear that at any moment, the Dakkari would come for us all.

"Is that what happened?" I whispered, looking up at him. "Today, you said your father made a mistake by showing mercy to a Ghertun."

It was the wrong thing to say, at perhaps the worst possible time. I should have bitten my tongue.

Arokan's shoulders bunched. I watched, in horrified fascination, as his temper rose, as anguish and regret and anger all flashed over his features, before he managed to rein them back in. It made me realize how much he kept on a tight leash inside. It made me realize how much control he possessed.

"*Lysi,*" he rasped, his eyes staring daggers into my own. "A much similar situation. My father found the scout. At his trial, my father granted him mercy and let him go. Three days later, in the dead of night, that scout led his pack to my father's horde."

My breathing went tight, fearing that I already knew what had happened.

"Half of the warriors were out patrolling, which they knew because they had been watching us. They caught us unaware. We were outnumbered."

"Arokan," I whispered.

"Three of them slaughtered my father in his bed before anyone knew they had infiltrated the camp. Afterwards, they raped my mother and then killed her too. It was her screams that alerted the guards, that began the full-fledged attack on the horde."

Horror made me clasp my hand over my mouth as nausea rolled in my belly.

"I was young at the time. I was sleeping in Hukan's tent that night, near the front of the camp, the furthest away. My mother's screams woke me. They still haunt me. Even though I fought against her, Hukan got me out, got a group of females and children out, and we rode until we happened upon another horde, whose *Vorakkar* tracked down the pack and killed them all in retribution. A *Vorakkar* who killed that scout, which is what my father should have done from the beginning, without hesitation, without pity or sympathy."

Stunned silence filled the tent. I couldn't begin to imagine what he'd witnessed, the brutality and horror of such an attack. His mother, his father...

Tears pooled in my eyes, but I didn't look away from him.

"I..." I croaked. "Arokan, I'm sorry. I didn't know."

"I have been *Vorakkar* long enough to know not to take chances with the safety of the horde," he said next. "Which is something that you need to realize, Luna. I do not have to ask you to approve my decisions when it comes to them. I will do *whatever* it takes to keep my people safe. Even if it means killing a being who *could* be innocent, whose pack *might* be innocent. By leaving the Dead Lands, those Ghertun have already signed their fate, that spy signed his fate. Would you truly risk the lives of the horde to save one Ghertun? Knowing what you do now, would you ask me to be merciful again?"

The answer rang clear in my mind.

"No," I whispered.

"Would you kill him yourself if you had to?" Arokan asked next, that cold voice unyielding.

The question caught me off guard. "I—I wouldn't know how."

Arokan looked away, his jaw ticking, his hands on his hips.

"Tomorrow," he said, "you will start your day tending to the *pyroki*. You will walk among the horde, you will keep your head high. You will wear what your *piki* dress you in without complaint. You will show the horde that you remain strong, regardless of what happened today."

I swallowed, looking down at my lap.

"You are *Morakkari* now, Luna. Despite what I called you today, you are Dakkari now," Arokan rasped. I looked up at him as he said, "Act like it."

I nodded.

Arokan went to his drawers before undressing. I looked at him out of the corner of my eye, seeing the scars lining his back. Not for the first time, I wondered how he'd received them.

"Arokan," I whispered.

The horde king paused, turning his head to look at me.

"I really am sorry," I said. "I know I made a mess of things today but...I'm trying."

"I know, *kalles*," he replied a moment later before pulling on pants made from hide, concealing his nudity. My eyebrows furrowed when I saw him sheath his dagger in the belt.

"Where are you going?"

"To hunt the Ghertun pack," he replied. "I sent scouts ahead. We might have caught their trail."

My lips parted. "You'll kill them all?"

He turned to look at me again, studying me. "I will not return until we do. They are too close to us, too close to *Dothik*."

I blew out a sharp exhale. After a moment, I nodded, rising from the cushion, my legs numb from sitting for so long.

"Be careful," I told him. And I meant it. A week ago, I

would've been praying that he never came back so that I could return to my village, our bargain forfeit. "Please."

Now…it made me worried that he was leaving again.

I was too emotionally exhausted to figure out why. I didn't care why. I knew what I felt and I wanted him to be safe.

He was still disappointed in me. I could see it in his gaze, but he reached out his hand, cupping my cheek, before he murmured, "Stay close to your guards while I am gone, *kalles*."

With that, he turned his back and ducked through the entrance of the tent without so much as a goodbye.

And I stood, in that empty tent, feeling like I failed as I watched him go.

19

Mirari watched me from outside the open pen enclosure with something akin to horror on her face.

"*Missiki*, please," she begged for the hundredth time. "This is not fitting for you. Not for a *Morakkari*."

I huffed and blew a strand away from my face. Though the air was cool, I felt a drop of sweat run down my back, and my arms trembled slightly as I hefted yet another pile of *pyroki* shit with my shovel and threw it into what I called the Shit Corner.

A young Dakkari boy—whose given name was Jriva—was elbow-deep in the Shit Corner, sifting through the *pyroki* excrement. Though he didn't speak the universal tongue, Mirari had translated for him when he said that they used the shit as fuel and to enrich their soil in *Dothik* and throughout other outposts around Dakkar. He told me his job was important, that he took great pride in it.

The boy seemed happy with my presence. He was no older than ten and had told Mirari to tell me that one day he would be a horde warrior. He would prove himself to the *Vorakkar*—to my husband—with his strength and protect the horde and his family.

He'd beamed up at me as he said it, as Mirari translated, though he was surrounded by *pyroki* filth. I couldn't help but admire his tenacity, for someone so young. He reminded me a lot of Kivan, which had struck a chord of longing and loneliness inside me.

Mirari was fisting her hands on her dress. "Careful of your slippers, *Missiki*," she called. "They were just crafted, especially for you."

It didn't matter. I was obeying the *Vorakkar*. That morning, I'd allowed myself to be dressed in another skimpy outfit and then I'd walked myself over to the *pyroki* pen with my chin held high, though I felt the eyes of the horde on me.

After much reflection yesterday and a long night in an empty bed, I'd come to realize that Arokan had been right. I was a queen now and I needed to act like it. I needed to integrate myself into horde life and win over his people.

If that meant getting dirty in *pyroki* shit and humbling myself before the horde, I would do it. Arokan told me I was Dakkari now. And, despite what Mirari said, I wasn't above doing dirty work just because my husband was the *Vorakkar*. I'd worked hard all my life. I wasn't about to stop now.

So, in response to Mirari's concern, I kicked off the sandals and threw them over the low gates of the enclosure, right next to her.

Her shoulders sagged. "That is not what I meant, *Missiki*. Now look at your feet!"

Unlike Mirari, Lavi seemed positively gleeful watching me. Her eyes twinkled with delight and amusement as she stood next to Mirari.

Casting a glance over my shoulder, I blew out another breath, eyeing a *pyroki*, which had ventured close to me. Those red eyes watched me and it tossed its neck, stamping its four feet on the earth, when I shoveled yet another pile into the corner.

Somehow, I'd managed to forget how absolutely terrifying they were, how massive they were. And while my hands had been shaking on the shovel for the first hour I'd been in the pen with them, they were now steady. Mostly, they ignored me, which gave me confidence.

Many of the *pyroki* were gone. Arokan had taken out half of the horde warriors with him to hunt down the Ghertun pack and their *pyroki* had gone with them.

An elderly male, who hadn't given me his name, was in charge of the pen. He looked over at Jriva and me from the troughs he was filling with fresh water, his eyes assessing our progress. Unlike Jriva, he spoke the universal tongue and when I told him that I wanted a job at the pen, he'd told me to clean it out, despite Mirari's immediate protests.

"If the *Morakkari* wishes to work with the *pyroki*, then she must start where I did," he'd replied to Mirari, his tone unyielding and strong.

He'd expected me to balk and turn away. He'd expected me to leave, I saw that in his dismissive gaze. Despite my title, I didn't have his respect. I didn't have the respect of many of the horde after yesterday's events.

So, he was surprised when I tied back my freshly washed and brushed hair and asked for a shovel. He handed me one hesitantly and I steeled my spine and I went to work.

"If the *Vorakkar* sees you doing this," Mirari said again, "he will not be pleased."

"Mirari," I hissed. "Enough."

Wisely, she closed her mouth, but she still eyed the large piles of excrement that I had to shovel. It would take me most of the afternoon.

Her shoulders sagged and then she walked to the entrance of the pen, snagging another shovel from where they were lined up against the enclosure.

"What are you doing?" I asked, straightening.

"I cannot allow you to work here all afternoon," Mirari said, tucking her long skirt up into her waistband, leaving her long legs exposed. "I will help."

"Mirari, you don't have to do that. This is my task."

"I am your *piki*," she simply replied, scrunching her nose when she stepped into the pen.

A little bloom of affection and gratitude for her opened in my chest as I watched her shovel a nearby pile. I shook my head, unable to keep the small smile from my face at her look of disgust.

Lavi seemed even more thrilled to watch Mirari, who bit out something in Dakkari at her when she saw the other *piki* grinning. Whatever she said made Lavi's smile die and she, too, after a moment's hesitation, slouched into the pen to help.

Jriva laughed in his Shit Corner as the three of us shoveled and any passing Dakkari looked at us in bewilderment, even lingering to watch before continuing on their way.

Once most of the pen was cleared, the *pyroki* master came over and dismissed us.

"I'll be back tomorrow," I informed him, wiping my forearm over my brow.

The news seemed to displease him but he didn't argue with me. Instead he said, "*Lysi, Morakkari.*"

We walked the short distance back to my tent, my two assigned guards trailing behind us, and I wiped my feet at the entrance before turning to the *piki*. "You can go for the day and wash and rest. If I need you, I'll send for you."

Mirari shook her head and said, "We will help you wash."

"I can bathe myself," I told her, reaching out to touch her shoulder. "Go."

Hesitantly, Mirari inclined her head, addressed Lavi in Dakkari, and then turned and left.

My bath from that morning was still inside the tent, though the water was cool. I undressed and slid inside, sighing. The cold water actually felt good after sweating in that pen and I scrubbed myself thoroughly before stepping out and dressing in my pants and tunic.

Not a moment afterwards, one of the guards called out, "*Morakkari.*"

"*Lysi?*" I called out, frowning.

The tent flap pushed in, but it wasn't my scarred guard that came through the entrance.

It was Hukan.

I straightened, still frowning. What was she doing here?

"*Morakkari,*" she greeted, her tone careful. "I have come to check on your markings."

I blinked, my eyes straying to my uncovered wrists. I didn't trust that was why she'd come, but I knew I couldn't turn her away. She was Arokan's family, had very likely saved his life when he was a boy.

I nodded and she approached, reaching out her hands to clasp my wrists, peering down at them closely, turning me this way and that way.

"Human flesh is delicate, I see," she commented.

My lips pressed together but I wisely stayed silent.

She glanced up at me, the green ring of her eyes contracting as she studied me. Arokan didn't look anything like her, except for the black color of their hair. Arokan's skin was darker, more golden, and his features were broad and masculine.

"It was foolish what you did yesterday," she murmured.

I gritted my teeth and tugged my wrists from her grip. "I already know that. I knew that the moment I saw your face in the crowd," I admitted to her.

"I do not particularly care for you," Hukan said.

I huffed out a laugh. "I hadn't guessed."

"However, Arokan does, for whatever reason," she continued, her lips twisting in an expression of distaste.

I looked at her, surprised. "Why did you come here, Hukan?

ZOEY DRAVEN

Really? And don't say to check my markings because we both know that's a lie."

"I came to give you advice."

Shaking my head, I said, "Arokan already spoke to me about what—"

"You have a big heart," she said, which made my brow furrow in further surprise. However, the way she said it made it seem like an insult, not a compliment. "You wished to save his life. But that big heart will not win over any Dakkari, especially in regard to a Ghertun."

Inhaling a sharp breath, I said, "Arokan told me what happened. To his father and his mother. Your sister."

Hukan's eyes flashed.

"I'm sorry," I said. "And you're right, what I did yesterday was foolish. I understand that now. A guard was injured because of me and I may have lost the respect of the horde."

"You were not born to lead," she said, twisting that knife in my chest. "Arokan was. He was born for this. He must make the ugly decisions that no one else wants to make. He needs a strong queen at his side, who brings strength, not failure, to the horde."

"I realize that," I said slowly, holding her gaze.

"I can help you get back to your village."

My breath left me. Stunned, I whispered, "What?"

"I can arrange a guide for you, to take you there," Hukan said, her jawline as hard as stone. "You will only drag him down. The best decision is for you to leave and never come back."

Disbelief and anger made my tongue knot.

"You must leave right now though," Hukan continued. "I can distract the guards. You can meet my guide in the forest. You can be back in your village this very night."

"Get out," I rasped.

"*Neffar?*" Hukan asked, surprised. "I am offering you what

you want. Take it. You can leave before Arokan returns from the hunt."

"I said get out," I repeated, my tone low.

Her eyes narrowed.

"I don't care what you think of me," I said. "But one thing you should know is that I *never* go back on my word. I promised myself to Arokan and it's a promise I intend to keep. For the rest of my life."

Hukan's expression darkened.

"Leave now," I said. "Don't speak to me again unless absolutely necessary and I won't tell Arokan about this, about how you planned to betray him by sneaking me away."

"One day," Hukan hissed, "he will *ask* me to send you away. When that day comes, I will rejoice."

I bit my tongue, trying to keep my temper in check, and watched her spin and leave the tent without another word.

I brought a shaking hand up to my lips, anger enveloping me, though I tried to see reason. She was his blood relation. She was only trying to do what she thought was best for him.

But that didn't matter.

I was his *wife*, his *queen*.

Act like it, Arokan had told me. He'd told me I was strong. He hadn't even hesitated when I'd voiced my insecurities that I wasn't strong *enough*.

But I was also human. Hukan accused me of having a big heart, but I wouldn't be ashamed of that. I wouldn't let her get to me.

So I didn't care if I had to shovel *pyroki* shit for the rest of my life. I would do it.

Marching over to the tent's entrance, I stepped outside into the late afternoon sunlight and looked at the scarred guard, who I knew spoke the universal tongue. I didn't ask. A queen didn't ask.

Instead, I demanded, "Take me to the warrior who was injured yesterday."

20

The tent was dark when I stepped inside after the guard announced my presence. Guilt hit me in the stomach when I saw the injured warrior sprawled out on his bed. A female was tending to him, his mate, I realized, and that guilt doubled.

"Hello," I greeted, hoping that at least one of them spoke the universal tongue. "May I come in?"

The female nodded and relief went through me. *"Morakkari,"* she greeted, inclining her head, standing from beside the bed.

The warrior was eyeing me in surprise. His right thigh was bandaged all the way to his knee. It was elevated on cushions and I pressed my lips together, my shoulders sagging.

"I…" I trailed off. Incense was burning in the tent, similar to the kind that had been burning in Hukan's, though not quite as potent. The female had been grinding up herbs in a pestle, probably for her mate's wound, to decrease the risk of infection. Clearing my throat, I met the warrior's eyes and said, "I wanted to apologize."

The female made a sound in the back of her throat, but the warrior kept my gaze.

"It was my fault you were injured," I said. "I made a mistake. I have come to ask your forgiveness."

Both of their gazes were wide and the female blinked rapidly, processing my words.

The warrior averted his eyes—which I took as a good sign—as he said, "*Morakkari*, you do not need to apologize."

"I do," I said simply. "And don't say I don't need to because of the *Vorakkar*. I *want* to apologize, for putting you in danger. The *Vorakkar* made the right decision. I see that now. And I'm so grateful that no one else was hurt due to my foolishness. Please, warrior, accept my apology."

Arokan might be upset to know that I'd come there, after he told me I couldn't see the warrior. But I didn't care. It was what I should've done first thing that morning.

The warrior didn't hesitate. For a brief flash, he met my gaze and then looked away. "I do, *Morakkari*. Thank you for honoring our *voliki* with your presence."

His acceptance didn't make all the guilt go away, but I felt slightly better now that I'd come.

"Thank you," I said. "*Kakkira vor*."

Words that Mirari had taught me. They meant 'thank you' in Dakkari, or at least I hoped they did. By the small, albeit warm, smile the female gave me, I hoped I didn't butcher the words.

"I'll let you rest," I said softly with a smile at both of them. "But if you don't mind, I'd like to check in on you later. I can bring you your meals."

I turned then but the warrior called out, "*Morakkari*." I looked at him. "There is talk throughout the horde that you worked in the *pyroki* enclosure this morning."

"I did," I said hesitantly.

"The *mrikro*, the *pyroki* master," he started, and I assumed he meant the grumpy elderly Dakkari, "enjoys *hji*. It is a fruit. You can acquire it from one of the merchants near the front of the camp. It will...soften him towards you."

Bribery. The warrior was telling me to bribe the *mrikro* grump into giving me a better job, one that didn't include shoveling shit.

I grinned and laughed slightly. "*Hji*, huh?" I nodded, already forming a plan for the morning. "Thank you, warrior. I'll keep that in mind."

<hr />

AROKAN RETURNED in the middle of the night. I'd been tossing and turning, thinking of the story he'd told me about his father and mother, about the Ghertun.

So, when I heard the clattering of hooves across the earth and hushed Dakkari voices, I sat up in bed, clutching the furs to my chest. Soon, I heard heavy footsteps approach the tent and my breath hitched when Arokan ducked inside, looking tired, but unharmed.

Relief trickled through me. His eyes burned into mine but he didn't say anything. Instead, he extinguished the sole candle I'd let burn, undressed until he was nude, and then climbed into bed beside me.

He smelled like salt and the earth and pure Dakkari male. Greedily, I dragged him into my lungs as I settled back down onto the furs.

Arokan gripped the back of my neck, pulling me towards him before running the tip of his nose along the column of my throat. My breath hitched, desire building at the small touch.

"Did you find them?" I whispered into the darkness, finding the familiar, glowing yellow of his ringed eyes.

"*Lysi*," was all he said, his voice floating over the flesh of my neck. He ran his tongue there next and my hands trembled underneath the furs.

"Were any of the warriors hurt?"

"*Nik.*"

His scent muddled my thoughts as his hand trailed down. I could feel him hard against my body. I was quickly learning that Dakkari males had a healthy need for regular sex and just remembering that consuming need made my belly quiver.

I stayed as still as possible, torn between reaching for him and simply lying there, frightened by the potent desire I felt for my captor husband.

Never in a million years did I think I would want him this way. The thought hadn't crossed my mind when I made that initial bargain.

He felt me tense when his fingers reached my sex, when he gently ran his thumb along my slit. He stilled and pulled back, peering down at me with those observant, watchful eyes.

Whatever he saw made his jaw tick and with a rough sound, he pulled his hand away, settling back against the cushions.

"Sleep, *kalles*," he ordered and then promptly shut his eyes. "*Veekor.*"

Confusion, frustration, and perhaps even relief flooded through me.

I bit my lip, still able to feel the heat of his hand between my thighs, the warmth of his tongue ghosting across my neck. Squirming, I blew out a quiet breath and then hesitantly settled back into my cushion, facing away from him.

What was that about? I wondered.

Closing my eyes, I listened to his steady breathing, trying to calm my racing thoughts and my burning body.

And I fell into another restless sleep, wondering why he'd stopped…and realizing that I hadn't wanted him to.

21

The *pyroki* master was happily munching on his *hji* fruit that I'd brought him from the market stalls that morning. While I wasn't shoveling shit anymore, the task he'd given me wasn't much better and it terrified me more.

I had to groom the *pyrokis* that had returned with their horde riders late last night. Except for my husband's, of course. No, the *pyroki* master seemed to think that taking care of Kailon was solely his responsibility and one he took great pride in.

Kailon had eyed me carefully as the master demonstrated what I was to do for the rest of the morning. My heart had fluttered madly in my chest, thinking that any moment, the black-scaled, red-eyed beast could tear off a chunk of me...just like a *pyroki* had done to my mother. My hands had trembled. I could feel rivulets of sweat stream down my back. I thought I would throw up my morning meal as I stood as close to Kailon as I dared.

The beast was just like my husband in a way. Big, intimidating, powerful. It had eyes like steel and didn't seem impressed with me *at all*.

The master gave me a stiff-bristled brush and led me over to a *pyroki*, which stamped its feet and made a hair-raising sound at my approach.

"Do not fear them," the master ordered me, giving me a frown. "They sense it. They will take advantage of it."

It was impossible for me not to fear them. That fear felt imbedded within me as I thought about what Arokan had said. That if I didn't understand and accept the *pyroki*, I would never win over the horde. I wondered if it was possible when I felt this ball of fear lodged in my gut. I knew I would *always* have it.

Mirari and Lavi watched me from outside the pen. Mirari had apparently deemed grooming not as undignified as shoveling shit and hadn't offered her help that day, not that I wanted it.

I had to do this. Not only for Arokan, but for myself.

Then the master left me with the *pyroki*, sauntering back to oversee Jriva, who still had the Shit Corner duty.

The brush felt like it weighed a hundred pounds in my palm as I slowly approached the beast. It made that awful groaning sound in its throat again and I took a deep breath, carefully catching the reins in my grip as the master had showed me, to keep the head steady.

I sensed movement out of the corner of my eye. When I turned my head, I saw Arokan, walking with the messenger and another Dakkari male. I hadn't seen him since he came to bed last night, but our eyes connected and he stopped, breaking off his conversation to watch me.

He crossed his arms over his massive, golden chest and waited. The two other males noticed and watched me as well. Arokan cocked his head to the side as if saying 'get on with it already.'

My jaw clenched. He was testing me, wanting to see if I would actually do it.

Indignation rose, briefly overlapping my fear. I set my

shoulders back and tugged the *pyroki's* head towards me with a pull of the reins, holding him steady. When he struggled, my muscles strained but I held him tight, fighting the panic as much as the creature.

Then I brought the brush down, running it across the scales, scraping off a speck of dried blood, trying not to think whose blood it was. Ghertun or Dakkari or *pyroki*.

The *pyroki* struggled again, making my breath hitch in fright and surprise, but I held him firm and whispered, "*Stop.* I'm not hurting you."

The *pyroki* seemed surprised to hear my voice, stilling for a moment, tilting its head to the side.

"Trust me, you can do a whole lot of damage to me, more than I could ever hurt you."

The *pyroki* blew out a harsh breath through its slitted nostrils, blowing snot to the ground.

"Gross," I whispered without malice, my hand still trembling as I scrubbed the brush across its scales.

So, because it seemed to help, I continued to talk quietly to the beast as I brushed off the evidence of a battle. I told him about my village, about how low the temperature was that day, about Arokan being almost as grumpy as the *pyroki*, about Mirari and Lavi.

Hell, it helped *me*. It kept my mind off the fact that this beast towered over me, could easily crush me with its weight or kill me with a single snap of its powerful jaws. Talking to the *pyroki* somehow made the task at hand easier.

When I was finished scrubbing at the scales, I stepped back, dropping the reins. My feet carried me until there was a healthy distance between us and the *pyroki* eyed me before tossing its neck and then sauntering over to the trough of meat.

I squealed when I felt a cold nose brush the back of my neck and I wheeled around to see another *pyroki* had snuck up behind me. A curious one, a *pyroki* not claimed by a horde warrior, considering it had no golden paint flanking its hide.

I brought up my hands to it as I backed away again, this time going all the way to the fence of the enclosure. The *pyroki* followed and every step it took ricocheted my heartbeat.

"All right," I said to it. "That is close enough."

"He will not harm you, *kalles*," came Arokan's voice, right behind me.

I whipped my head around to see that he'd come up to the fence, was draping his arms over the metal, his tail flicking behind him.

"You don't know that," I said. "They are unpredictable."

"*Nik*, they are not."

I bit my tongue, turning my face to the side when it nudged against me, sniffing my cheek.

"*Arokan*," I hissed, sliding closer towards him.

He caught me through the fence, holding me in place, even though I struggled to escape.

In my ear, he rasped, "You just groomed a *pyroki*, Luna. You can handle this one. Just stay still and let him explore your scent."

"Why is he doing this?" I hissed again.

"He is curious."

I pushed further back into Arokan, just moments from climbing over the fence, but he held me still. It took me a moment to realize that I'd turned to him for safety. It took me a moment to realize that he must truly think I was safe, or else he would never let the *pyroki* near me.

That knowledge made me blow out a breath, made me try to relax as I kept still and let the beast sniff me.

Something cold and wet and slimy touched my cheek and I realized it was the snot from his nose. Gross.

But after a few long moments, the *pyroki* finally lost interest and slowly backed away, trotting over to another *pyroki*, who he smelled too.

A deep sigh of relief left me, but it didn't last for long. Soon, Kailon came over, sensing that his master was near. Unlike the other *pyroki*, Kailon didn't take an interest in me, only had eyes for Arokan and seemed to marginally tolerate my presence.

"Why do you fear them so much?" Arokan asked softly, reaching out his hand to stroke Kailon's neck.

I looked into the *pyroki's* red eyes, remembering that red peering at me in the ice forest on that cold night—

"A *pyroki* killed my mother," I told him, the words tumbling out of me, and I couldn't look away from Kailon.

Arokan's arms tensed around me.

Or, rather, I killed my mother because a *pyroki* had mauled her in such a vicious way that there was no hope left for her.

"So, you see, I will always fear them," I told him softly, "because I know what they are capable of. I've seen it."

"*Kalles*—"

"Don't," I whispered. "Please."

Arokan took my hand and pressed it to Kailon's snout, though my whole body tensed.

"I am sorry about your mother, Luna," he said in my ear. "But know this...Kailon is loyal to me. Kailon has saved my life many times. Now, he is as much yours as he is mine. He will serve you if you ask him, he will be bound to you if you ask him. He will never harm you so you never have to fear him. They are intelligent creatures, sometimes more intelligent than we are."

Kailon's scales felt cool beneath my hand, but Arokan's hand felt hot.

"I know you fear them. I feel your body shaking, feel your heart thundering in your chest," he whispered, but I never took my eyes away from Kailon's. "You make me proud, *kassikari*."

My breath hitched, surprise washing through me.

"You fear them, but you are here. That should make you proud too," he told me.

He was being kind again. And just like last time, I didn't know if I liked it. Because it made me feel things I shouldn't.

Finally, I turned my head to look directly into Arokan's eyes. They were so black that I saw my reflection in them, that I saw Kailon's reflection in them.

I thought about what Hukan said—that I would never be strong enough to stand at Arokan's side—and I thought about what she'd offered me to leave him—my old life.

I thought about telling him about Hukan's betrayal, but I kept my mouth shut on that subject. She was still his family and I would need to tread lightly.

"Stop being nice," I whispered.

His grin made my belly warm. "I forget that you do not like it, *kalles*."

He released me then and I let my hand glide away from Kailon's snout. Arokan said something in Dakkari—a command —and his *pyroki* obeyed, wandering off to eat.

When I felt like I could breathe again, I realized that many eyes were on us. The *pyroki* master, Mirari and Lavi, the two guards assigned to me, the two Dakkari males who'd been speaking with Arokan, in addition to members of the horde that had been wandering by at the time.

My cheeks flamed, wondering if they'd seen my fear, hoping they hadn't.

When I looked at Arokan, he was back in *Vorakkar* mode, looking down at me with his stoic expression, so unlike the teasing warmth of his voice a moment before.

You make me proud, kassikari, he'd said.

I nodded up at him and whispered, "Thank you."

He inclined his head and a moment later, he turned and left.

I watched him go, watched him return to the Dakkari males, and they resumed onward towards wherever they'd been going. I bit my lip, swallowing, before turning back to the pen.

The *pyroki* master called out, "You have many to groom still, *Morakkari*, before the sun falls!"

I sighed, set my sights on the next *pyroki*—one that seemed more docile and quiet than the rest—and slowly made my approach.

It was going to be a long day.

I WAS SQUIRMING in the bathing tub as my husband petted my body at his leisure.

For once, he'd finished with his duties around camp early and had come to wait for me at the *pyroki* enclosure around dusk, seemingly content to watch me interact with the creatures. Afterwards, he'd led me to our tent, where a hot bath and a hot meal had already been waiting.

I'd scarfed down the dinner in record time, ravenous after my long afternoon with the *pyroki*, and then he'd promptly stripped me and carried me into the tub with him.

And after a thorough washing of us both, Arokan now seemed content to simply run his clawed fingers up and down my body, touching me in places that made my sex quiver, but doing nothing more.

Though he was hard and aching against my backside, he simply caressed me. *Teased* me.

And I bit my lip through it all, not wanting to give into him, not wanting him to know that I *wanted* something more.

Frustration and my arousal grew hand-in-hand and I made a small sound in my throat when he threaded his fingers through my hair, my eyelids fluttering at how good it felt, at how gentle he was being.

But I kept still, though he was slowly driving me to

madness. A part of me was wondering why he hadn't wedged himself inside me already, right there in the bathing tub. I was wet for him, aroused, though I would never admit it.

I felt him take a deep breath, his chest rising against my back, and his wandering hand slowed to a stop, resting on my hip.

My eyes flew open, waiting. But he did nothing and I swallowed the frustrated sound rising in my throat.

"I am told you visited the injured warrior and his *kassikari*. That you returned a second time and brought them a meal while I was gone," Arokan said softly.

I stiffened. He'd told me I couldn't see the warrior, but I'd done it anyways. Was he angry?

"I needed to see him for myself. To apologize for what happened," I replied.

"A *Morakkari* does not apologize."

"This one does," I told him.

Arokan huffed out a sharp breath. "And why did you go to the stalls for *hji*?"

I turned to look at him over my shoulder. "You're keeping tabs on me?"

"Your guards report to me."

I pressed my lips together and said, "Because the warrior said that the *pyroki* master enjoys *hji*. And since I'm sure my guards already told you, I did not want to shovel *pyroki* shit for the rest of my life, which I did yesterday."

Arokan grunted, but didn't reply.

"Maybe I shouldn't have," I mused. "I think I liked yesterday better, shit and all."

"You did well today," Arokan rasped. "It will get easier."

I didn't know if that would happen.

But what he said next made me still.

"Tell me what happened, *kalles*. How your mother got attacked by a *pyroki*."

Even though my mother was dead, some part of me still feared for her. She'd been trying to hunt, after all, outside the village walls. If a Dakkari had come upon her then, she would've been killed on sight.

"Tell me, Luna," he said softly, as though sensing my hesitation.

"It was during the cold season," I said. "Our rations were low. The Uranian Federation couldn't get a supply drop to us because of the weather. We were all hungry."

His hand tensed at my hip.

"My mother was desperate. My brother was barely ten at the time, a child, and he cried and cried all day and all night. She went beyond the walls. She took a blade and I was scared that a Dakkari might find her. So I followed after her.

"I don't know what she was trying to do. She'd never killed anything before in her life. But like I said, she was desperate. She would do anything for us. So, she ventured into the ice forest nearest our village. I trailed behind her because, even though I was afraid for her, I was also hungry. I kept hoping that maybe she *would* find something. Anything, so that we could eat. I should have stopped her."

That fact hurt most of all. That my own selfishness and my own desperation got her killed.

"I remember seeing red eyes through the trees and before I knew it, she was screaming. A *pyroki* was on her, attacking her, biting her stomach and her arms...and I ran into the clearing, not even thinking. It bolted when it saw me, but the damage was done."

"Luna," Arokan murmured, turning my face so he could see me. His lips were pulled down into a frown, but his eyes were soft.

I swallowed, blinking back tears as I looked at him. "It was awful," I whispered. "I was in shock and she was still alive, but in a tremendous amount of pain. There was blood, so much blood. Black on that ice. And I kept thinking the *pyroki* would return. But my mother saw me and told me to protect Kivan. Always. I promised her that I would.

"Then she handed me the blade. It was slippery with her blood," I said, though I wasn't even sure I was talking to Arokan anymore. "She asked me to...to...and I did. I had to. I didn't want her to suffer and I knew she was beyond help. But—" my lip trembled as I admitted, "I fear I made it worse. I was clumsy with the blade, didn't know how to use it and I—I—"

"*Kalles*, look at me," Arokan said gently. My eyes found his and I'd never felt more vulnerable and exposed, sitting there in the bathing tub with him, with only the light from the candles illuminating our eyes as I spilled my darkest memory. "You were brave. Not many would have done that, but you were brave and you loved her enough to want to end her pain. Do not be ashamed of that."

"But I am," I said. "I'd never felt weaker."

"How old were you?"

"Fifteen."

He made a sound in his throat, his eyes closing for a brief moment. "Not more than a child yourself."

"I was old enough," I whispered. "And if I'd been strong enough to call her back, if I hadn't wanted to *eat*, she would still be alive. It was my fault."

Arokan ran his hand down my wet hair, fresh from washing. He was quiet for a moment and then said softly, "*Pyrokis* give birth in the cold season and the wild ones build their nests in the ice forests across Dakkar."

My brow furrowed. "What?" I whispered.

"They are fierce creatures when their young are threatened. I am certain that was why your mother was attacked. She accidentally came across a wild *pyroki* nest and the mother was defending what she believed was a threat to her offspring. Just like your mother, she was desperate to save her young."

I squeezed my eyes shut as that knowledge sunk in.

"They are not normally vicious creatures," he said gently. "But they form strong attachments to their offspring and protect them at any cost, just like humans, just like Dakkari. Your mother's death was a tragedy, *kalles*. She was in the wrong place at the wrong moment. Do not *ever* think that it was your fault, Luna."

A part of me would always know the truth. That I could've prevented her death. Nothing would change that. I had internalized it so deep, that guilt, that I had thrown myself into doing what I'd promised her: protecting Kivan. I had forgotten myself in doing so. I had worked long hours and slept little. I had snuck portions of my food into his so he wouldn't go as hungry. I had defended him against the village, to Polin when he'd wanted to exile him to another settlement for another one of his mishaps.

I had bargained with a horde king to save his life, although right then, that didn't feel like a hardship. Not when I was fed, clean, and protected. Not when Arokan's warmth felt like a luxury. Not when his deep voice sent shivers down my spine and he touched me like I was a gift.

He was strong and brave and he made the decisions that no one else wanted to make, just like Hukan said.

I admired him for that, though it also frightened me.

I remembered feeling weak after my mother died. I remembered being afraid. I never wanted to feel that way again.

"Arokan," I said softly, remembering what Mirari had said about the Dakkari females.

"*Lysi?*"

I took a deep breath and asked, "Will you teach me how to fight? How to wield a blade? How to be strong?"

He cocked his head ever so slightly, studying me, his lips still pulled down into a frown.

"Knowing how to fight with a blade does not make you strong, *kalles*," he said, his tone gentle.

"Before you left, you asked me if I would kill the Ghertun scout myself if he threatened the horde," I said. "And that scared me because I haven't touched a blade since...since my mother. I'd never needed to, back at my village. I stayed inside the walls and lived." I licked my lips. "But I'm not in the village anymore. I'm *here* and this is my life now. And if you think there's a possibility that I will have to protect myself or the horde one day, then I'm asking you to teach me how."

"*I* will protect you, *kalles*," he said.

"I know," I whispered. And I did. I knew he would protect me at all costs, though I didn't understand why. "But if you're not around? What then? It couldn't hurt for me to know some basics. My *piki* told me that Dakkari females know how to fight. Why shouldn't I?"

He blew out a rough breath, considered my words for a long, tense moment.

Finally, he nodded and I felt relieved.

"I will teach you," he said. "We will begin tomorrow."

"Thank you," I whispered.

"Simply because you are my queen," he said, "does not mean I will go easy on you, *kalles*. You wish to learn? You will. Just like all other Dakkari do. With blood and sweat and fatigue. *Lysi?*"

His words sent a chill down my spine, but I set my jaw and whispered, "*Lysi.*"

But I couldn't help but wonder what I'd gotten myself into.

22

"Again," Arokan commanded roughly.

I was panting and my legs and arms were shaking from the seeming *hours* of exercise that Arokan was putting me through.

When he said he wouldn't be easy on me, he'd meant it.

I'd asked for this, however, so I would take whatever he gave me. I wouldn't complain. I would *learn*.

I got back into position across from him, about arm's length away. His expression was unreadable as his hand flashed towards me. My stomach dropped and I ducked, the underused muscles in my thighs straining from the repetitive motions.

I popped back up, sweat dripping down my back, just as his other hand whipped out towards me, so fast it was a blur. It was too late. I'd been too slow and his hand connected against my shoulder, not hard enough to throw me off my feet, but hard enough to sting.

Making a sound of frustration in my throat, I prepared for his next strike and managed to block it with my forearm, though there would be a bruise there in the morning.

"Good," he praised. "Again."

It was dark already. My day—which had started in the *pyroki* enclosure—had been long. I was exhausted and aching and hungry...but I felt strangely calm. The exercises Arokan had made me run through made me focus, made all other thoughts and worries drift from my mind until I was centered on nothing but *him*. My opponent. My husband.

Though we'd been training since before the sun set, he hadn't given me a blade or a sword or even a small dagger. No weapons, he'd told me, until I strengthened my body, until my muscles reacted instinctively, until I would know how to use them.

So, I got into position again, trying to ignore the warriors and any passing members of the horde that had gathered to watch. I even saw Lavi watching, with her warrior, though I'd dismissed her before I finished in the *pyroki* enclosure.

When Arokan ran through the set again, I didn't block a single strike, though I managed to shuffle away and pivot on the last one.

"You grow weak," he commented and I hated that he didn't sound out of breath at all, while I was dragging air into my lungs like it was water and I was dehydrated. "Your movements grow loose. We are done for tonight."

"One more," I said, hating that word. Weak. Pulling in a long drag of air, I exhaled slowly, looking at him. "Just one more."

He nodded.

That set, I managed to block two of his six strikes.

"Enough," he said, coming to me once it was done. "We will start again tomorrow."

I nodded, everything aching. I would pay for this in the morning.

His voice softened as he bent his head low. "You did well, *kalles*."

Looking up at him, I gave him a small, tired smile. "You're just saying that so I don't suffocate you in your sleep."

He huffed out an amused breath, shaking his head. "Come. You *need* sleep."

My body might have been tired, but my mind felt energized. Still, I didn't argue as he led us back to our tent, our *voliki*, as the Dakkari called it.

Our tent, I mused. When had it become *our* tent to me and not *his*?

Once inside, a hot, fresh bathing tub and a meal was waiting for us, just like the night before. Arokan brought the food tray close to the tub and then promptly stripped my sweaty clothes off and then his own.

And just like the night before, when he led me into the hot water that felt sublime against my aching muscles, when I settled between his strong thighs and let him wash me, I felt his thick cock hard and aroused, pressing into my spine. And just like the night before...he did nothing about it.

It confused me. It frustrated me. Because I was beginning to suspect that I *liked* sex with him, though it had been rough and consuming and...magnificent.

We hadn't had sex since before the Ghertun scout had been executed. Considering that when Arokan had first brought me to the camp, he'd hardly been able to keep his hands off me those first few days...I was beginning to wonder if he was already losing interest in me.

Even as I wondered that, I kept still as he washed me.

"Turn," he ordered gruffly.

My breath hitched and I hesitantly did as he said, wondering if he would initiate something, my belly fluttering in antic-ipation.

His eyes met mine as I straddled his thighs in the bath, the water sloshing around.

A brief look down revealed his hardened cock, the engorged head bobbing out of the water, against his abdomen. I saw the glimmer of the golden tattoos around it, one at the base, one just below the head.

"Wash me," he murmured, handing me the cloth he'd been using, still lathered with soap.

I took it, biting my lip, and pushed the damp ends of my hair over my shoulder.

Arokan's eyes dragged down to my jutting nipples, his eyelids going heavy. As I leaned forward and ran the washcloth over his shoulders, he ducked his head and caught one nipple in his mouth. I sucked in a surprised breath, my hand pausing as pleasure tingled down my spine, as he laved his hot tongue over it, flicking the hardened bud back and forth.

I steadied myself on his broad shoulders, my sex spasming and clenching as arousal arrowed down my body.

After a moment's hesitation, I resumed washing him, scrubbing his skin perhaps a little more roughly, especially when he switched nipples.

And he continued on like that. I bit my lip to keep from moaning as he teased me, as he suckled me to madness, all while I continued to wash him, trying to act like what he was doing wasn't making me lose my goddamn mind.

So, I washed wherever I could reach—his back, his arms, his chest, his abdomen—until I couldn't avoid his cock any longer.

He grunted when I ran the cloth over his length, but I only made a few short passes before I moved onto his thighs.

Arokan made another sound but then he pulled back from my nipples and leaned against the back of the tub. His cock was still jutting from the water, impossible not to see, but his expression was hardened, his mouth set in a straight line, his jaw clenched.

Again, frustration rose as I washed his thighs. He'd stopped after teasing me again. Just like last night. My nipples felt tender, sensitive. My sex ached as much as my muscles did from the training session.

He watched me carefully—I could feel those eyes on me—before he reached over to the food tray and popped a chunk of braised meat into his mouth.

Disbelief ran through me, though I hid it well. He'd stopped and now he was eating. Was he truly not going to initiate anything that night?

I blew out a shaky breath and tried to distract myself with the task at hand. I finished quickly and by the time I was done, my mind felt a little less foggy. Once I was done washing him, once I'd draped the washing cloth over the lip of the bathing tub, he offered a piece of braised meat to me.

Without hesitation, I took it. Already, I was used to the taste, the energy that the fresh food gave me. I'd been with Arokan, with the horde, for less than two weeks, but already, I could feel my body changing. I was gaining much-needed weight. My hips were softening, my rib bones weren't as prominent as they had been before. I didn't feel completely depleted of energy any longer. I could actually feel something that resembled *strength* building in me.

I couldn't even remember the taste of the Uranian Federation rations. That made me feel guilty, as it probably always would. Though I knew that Arokan had fresh *bveri* meat delivered to my village, it would only be a matter of time before it ran out.

Arokan reached out, the water trickling from his elbow, and he pressed his thumb against the line that had formed between my brows.

"What worries you?" he murmured, his voice deep and quiet and calm, as if a moment before, he hadn't been kissing my nipples.

I hesitated in telling him, which he noticed. But after a moment, I said, "I was just thinking about my village."

He exhaled a sharp breath, his hand falling away. He turned

his head and plucked more food from the tray, feeding some to me and then eating some himself.

"Do I treat you well?" he asked after an awkward silence.

The question made me blink in surprise. "Yes, Arokan," I said softly and it was true. "You do."

He'd never mistreated me. He'd treated me better and with more respect than I could have ever imagined. It had taken me off guard at first, especially considering I'd grown up hearing how merciless and ruthless the Dakkari were.

But I was learning that not all stories and rumors were true. Sometimes, the truth was quite the opposite.

"But you will always remain loyal to your village," he said next, as if it were obvious. "Not to the horde. Not to me."

Warning bells went off in my head at his tone. He sounded...disappointed.

"That's not fair, Arokan," I whispered.

His eyes studied me. "Tell me how."

"I know, deep in my heart, that I will probably never see my village again. My brother," I said. His lips pressed together. "I made you a promise. One I will keep. In a way, my loyalty *is* to you."

"And if I released you from your promise?" he questioned quietly next. My brow furrowed, my lips parting. "What would you do? Would you stay or would you leave?"

My mind raced. What was he doing?

"I..." I trailed off. I thought about it. If Arokan allowed me to return to my brother, would I go? "I don't know," I whispered, truthful.

His jaw ticked and he looked away.

My chest ached at his expression and I reached out before I knew what I was doing, pressing my palm against his cheek. I'd never touched his face before, but it was surprisingly soft, save for the small battle scars that marred it every so often.

He met my eyes as I said softly, "My village is a place.

Though I was born in that village, though I was raised there, it is not my home. My *family* is my home, my brother is my home. Despite everything he's done, I still love him. Despite everything I've given up for him, I still love him. You cannot ask me to choose. Because I cannot and I will not."

Arokan looked at me, his eyes darting back and forth between mine. He reached up to touch my hand and my lips parted, remembering what Mirari said, that perhaps a *Vorakkar* needed softness, needed warmth most of all. My heart twinged in my chest, surprising affection enveloping me.

"You are right, *rei Morakkari*," he murmured, surprising me. *My Queen.* "I should not have asked."

My heart beat in my chest as I stared into his eyes.

Then he asked, "You were born on Dakkar?"

I blinked. "Yes. Does that surprise you?"

"It does," he admitted. "It seems like not long ago the old king accepted the settlements."

"Accepted?" I questioned, a small, sardonic smile playing over my lips.

He inhaled a breath. "Forced through the Uranian Federation's bribery," he amended.

I relaxed, shaking my head. "That sounds more like it. I always wondered, considering our presence was never...accepted."

"Dakkari are set in tradition," he explained after a brief moment of silence between us. "Those in the capital are most opposed. They do not see what the hordes see. The *Dothikkar* does not even see."

"And what is that?"

"Your struggle," he answered.

My brow furrowed.

"Admittedly," he continued, "even I did not know the extent of it until you told me how low your food supply was. We have always assumed that the Uranian Federation treated their refugees well, that they ensured they had enough rations and water and supplies."

"In the beginning," I said softly, "they did. When I was young, right around when my brother was born, there was plenty of food. But it's dwindled over the years. And we were not allowed to hunt or to gather our own food to fill that loss."

"Those are the *Dothikkar*'s orders," he told me, his expression grim. "We follow them because it is his will."

I shook my head. "You punish those that try to feed their families," I said softly. "How is that right? Your land is bountiful. Your game roams free and is plentiful. What is the harm?"

Arokan's jaw ticked. "Humans and other settlements have long proven that they cannot follow our traditions. They destroy and burn our land—Kakkari. This is unacceptable."

"Only because they need to be taught," I argued gently. "We have been here for decades now. I was born here but even I know little of the land, how to plant in your soil successfully, how to hunt your game so as not to diminish the population. These things only require *knowledge* and knowledge is free."

"It is never free," he corrected softly.

"You said your *pujerak* told my village how to dry *bveri* meat when you sent him there," I said. "That is knowledge. And because of it, it will keep my village fed for far longer than any of our rations have."

"That came at a price," he said. "You paid it. It was an exchange."

"My only payment was agreeing to eat. That was hardly a price," I said.

"Nevertheless, it wasn't free. Eating gives you strength. That strength is useful to the horde...to me."

My face heated at his implication.

"What if the villages make payment to you in some way?" I asked next. "In exchange for the rights to hunt, to grow crops."

"That is not my decision. That is the *Dothikkar*'s decision alone," he said, his tone warning me that I would get no further that night. But I would keep trying. I owed it to my village, to my *race*, to keep trying.

I changed the subject, perhaps not very tactfully, but I found I enjoyed speaking with him, even if we argued.

"Were you born in the capital?" I questioned. "Or within a horde?"

"In *Dothik*," he answered.

"Is that why you know the universal tongue so well?" I asked next, remembering that Mirari said that most in *Dothik* were taught the common language.

"*Lysi*," he answered. "My father believed that it would be useful, though I detested learning it. He was right. It is quite useful to me now."

I let out a small laugh. "You might like me better if you didn't know what I was saying."

His grin was small but it sent a thrill through me. "I do not know. I enjoy your sharp tongue."

"Do you miss *Dothik*?" I asked, trying to distract myself from the warmth building in my belly at his words.

"*Nik*," he said immediately, which surprised me. Then again, I knew very little of the city. "It is a grand place. There are more luxuries and comforts than here in the wild lands, but I would never give up my horde for all of them. The spirit of the Dakkari is to roam, to follow the land wherever it leads us. That is freedom. It is what calls to me, to us all. Those in *Dothik*… they have forgotten that. The *Dothikkar* has forgotten that."

Arokan of Rath Kitala…I could never imagine him any place other than in the wild lands, on the back of his *pyroki*, with a sword at his side, fighting for the safety of his horde.

Hukan had been right once again. Arokan had been born for this. He had been born to be a *Vorakkar*.

Panic infused my veins right then. I was beginning to suspect that my heart was being claimed, a little bit at a time, by the horde king whose naked lap I was straddling in that bathing tub.

He was unlike anything I'd ever imagined. And that scared me.

"Like you said," he murmured, brushing his fingers against my hair, "*Dothik* is a place. My horde is my home."

23

"Oh, *Missiki*," Mirari murmured, squirming in discomfort. "I do not...I do not know if I can..."

My cheeks burned and I kept my voice quiet as I asked her advice, so even the guards outside our tent wouldn't hear. "Please. He hasn't...he hasn't, erm, *approached* me in some time. I don't know what to do."

It had been four days since that night in the bathing tub when he'd told me about *Dothik*. Four days and three nights and Arokan *still* hadn't touched me. Of course, he *touched* me during our baths before bed. He stroked my body and touched me in places that made me bite my lip and try to hold back a moan. But anything more, even when we lay in bed at night, was nonexistent.

And I was slowly losing my mind because of it.

My body felt like a stranger's once again. I was almost constantly aroused because of his teasings, my body *needing* release. My skin felt sensitive to the touch. I'd woken up that morning in an empty bed with my hand between my legs and I'd been so tempted to release some tension myself. But Mirari and Lavi had entered shortly after and I'd sighed in frustration and let them dress me for the day instead.

But now, as Lavi finished braiding my hair, I wanted to know what Mirari thought.

"Is it…is this strange?" I asked, worried about her reply. My eyes went over to the chests that lined the tent wall and my belly burned. It wasn't the first time I wondered if Arokan was releasing his own tension elsewhere. And that thought *cut deep*. It made jealousy swarm my veins.

The only thing that didn't make me completely lose it was that I didn't know when he'd have the *time* to seek out another female. He went about his duties during the day with his *pujerak* and his advisors and at dusk, he collected me from the enclosure and we trained together until long after nightfall. After which, we retired to our tent.

Mirari lowered her voice and said, "It is, *Missiki*. I am sorry to say. Dakkari males are very…very needful."

My stomach dropped, my eyes closing. I knew it. I knew something was wrong.

"It all makes sense now," she said softly.

"What do you mean?"

"It is rumored that as of late, the *Vorakkar* has been especially short with his warriors. Frustrated. Rarely does he show his temper, but I am told it's been rather apparent lately."

My brows rose, surprised. With me, Arokan didn't seem any different, though there had been something in his gaze that confused me. A tightness.

But everything had been normal between us. We spent a good deal of time together, especially at night, so wouldn't I notice if something was wrong?

"I don't know what to do," I confessed, looking into her eyes. Mirari and Lavi—though she only spoke a handful of words in the universal tongue now—had become my friends. I trusted them. And I trusted Mirari to tell me the truth. I knew she would, had never held back before, despite her being my *piki*.

"Does he ever make his interest clear?" she asked softly, though she still seemed a little uncomfortable with the subject.

I furrowed my brow. "Sometimes I think so. He, um, touches me at night. I always think he will initiate something, but he always pulls away shortly afterwards."

Mirari blinked. "Why do *you* not initiate then?"

"What?"

Mirari shook her head. "*Missiki*, do you ever touch him too? Do you seem receptive to him? What do you do when he makes his interest clear?"

"I..." I trailed off. I looked down at my lap, at the golden marks across my wrists. They were fully healed now and beautiful. "I just...wait."

Mirari sucked in a sharp inhale. "*Missiki...*"

"Is that bad?" I asked, looking up at her. "It's bad, isn't it? Ugh, I don't know what I'm doing. I've never had to think about this before."

"Never?" she asked skeptically.

My cheeks flamed again. "No. I was inexperienced before the *Vorakkar*."

"Oh, I see," Mirari said gently. "In that case, *Missiki*, you need to take initiative. Males need to know that you desire them as much as they desire you. If you do nothing when he touches you, he must think that you do not want his advances."

"But..." I whispered, dread pooling in my stomach. "But I do."

"Then it is not a problem," Mirari said, smiling, relaxing at my admission. "Just communicate with your body that you wish for him to continue."

"I don't know how," I confessed again.

The other times we'd had sex, had I touched him, been receptive to him?

The night he'd come to me after I refused to eat, I'd been still and unresponsive. He'd touched and kissed my body but it was only after my stomach growled that he stopped. Or had it also been because I was simply lying there, scared and nervous? I remembered he'd kept looking up at me. Had that been to gauge whether I was enjoying it? Had he stopped because he thought I *wasn't*, not only because I was hungry?

Then the night of our *tassimara*...I think I *had* been responsive. The fermented drink from the celebration had helped relax me. I'd enjoyed what we did, after the initial pain.

The second time we'd had sex, I'd been angry, but that anger had turned to passion, to need. I'd screamed into the furs so loudly with the pleasure he'd wrung from me.

Was that what this was about? Arokan believed that I wasn't receptive to him anymore?

I blew out a breath. I'd given him no indication that I was. I'd let him stroke my body, let him suckle and kiss my nipples without so much as a word or a sound or a touch of reciprocation. Of course, he would think that.

Damn.

I was a fool. An inexperienced fool who desired her horde king husband but didn't know how to show him.

"How..." I trailed off, meeting Mirari's eyes again. "How can I show him that I want him?"

"Many ways," Mirari replied, seemingly over her initial embarrassment. "Males are easy. They do not need much. Just give into your instincts as a female. Do not hide your sounds or your movements. Let him see your enjoyment. Be open to him, like I told you before."

Easier said than done. I'd grown up in a village where sex was hidden, hardly discussed. I was relying on those same instincts to hide what I felt whenever Arokan touched me.

"You train together at night, do you not?" Mirari asked next.

"Yes," I answered. "Why?"

"Fighting can be...exciting. Primal. The *Vorakkar* would never hurt you, though he pushes you hard. You can use that to your advantage. Think of your training sessions as foreplay."

I laughed even though I wanted to hide. "There are so many of the horde watching."

"So?" Mirari asked. "It is only you and him. Ignore the others."

Lavi spoke, probably frustrated that Mirari wasn't translating the conversation like she normally did. Mirari looked at me for permission and I nodded. Then I listened as Mirari told Lavi all my troubles with the *Vorakkar* in Dakkari.

Lavi waved her hand in response, glancing at me. She said something that made Mirari chuckle.

"What did she say?" I asked, biting my lip.

"Lavi said that you should just suck his cock," she laughed. "*That* will tell him everything he needs to know and make him worship the ground you walk on. Like I said, males are simple like that."

I WAS MAKING a mess of this 'foreplay' business.

Cursing Mirari for ever planting the idea, I gripped the small blade in my hand and arced out my arm the way Arokan taught me.

"You are pushing your hips too far back," Arokan grumbled from behind me, watching my form.

I blew a strand of hair out of my eyes as his hands came to my hips, pushing them forward. The sweet ache of my muscles almost made me groan. I'd been constantly sore ever since our training sessions began earlier in the week. But I liked it. It meant my body was growing stronger, rebuilding itself.

"You are unfocused tonight," he rasped. "Perhaps we should end early. I have been pushing you too hard."

I was just about to protest, but then thought that retiring to the tent early might not be such a bad idea. Because I'd decided earlier that tonight was the night. I couldn't take the sexual frustration anymore and I didn't think Arokan could either.

Ever since Mirari had told me about his short temper, I'd looked for signs of it. While he never raised his voice to me, he was definitely tense about something. His shoulders were bunched, his brows lowered into a dark expression, his fists clenching every so often.

My horde king was wound tight because of me.

"Yes," I said, looking over my shoulder at him, dropping my arm. "Let's end early."

He nodded, stepping back. "I have a matter to attend to," he said. "Go eat and rest. I might return late."

I frowned, but he had already turned away.

"*Vorakkar,*" I called out before I realized it, catching sight of a small group that had formed to watch us practice.

He stopped, looked back.

I opened my mouth, but no words came out.

"Never mind," I said, shaking my head. What was I going to say with a group watching? That I wanted him to come back with me so we could fuck each other senseless?

I was at that point though. I'd never particularly thought about sex, or needed it. Back at my village, I would masturbate whenever the need arose, but nothing more. Even *that* had been difficult to find time for, considering how filled my days had been with work.

Now, I felt like I would scream with the frustration of it.

Arokan turned back towards the front of the camp and I lost sight of him between the tents. I couldn't help but wonder where he was going...and so late.

When I returned to the *voliki*, I ate and bathed myself, but even the tub seemed too big without Arokan in it. I had grown so used to spending the nights with him that now it seemed strange, like the time was stretched. It was different. I didn't think I liked it.

As I waited, my thoughts ran wild. Insecurity reared its ugly head and I couldn't help but wonder, for the hundredth time, if Arokan was assuaging his lusts elsewhere.

I didn't think I could handle that if it were true. Over the short amount of time we'd been together, I'd grown to care for him. There had been a point, early on, when I hadn't cared. I'd *hoped* he was visiting other females.

Now, that possibility made my hands shake, made my heart palpitate in my chest.

I didn't want him touching anyone else. I didn't want him using that magnificent body on anyone else. I didn't want him kissing or gently stroking or warming anyone else but *me*.

He was *mine*. Mine alone. And it amazed me how intensely that feeling rose in my chest and held, how that feeling took shape and hardened like stone.

Unable to wait any longer, I stalked out the tent entrance, surprising my two guards.

I needed to see for myself where he was, who he was with.

"I need some fresh air," I told them. *"Lo navi kikkira anr."*

Though they initially tried to protest, I began to walk through camp, threading my way in the direction Arokan had gone.

Maybe I was being crazy, but I blamed it on the frustration. I just needed to know to finally stop these treacherous thoughts once and for all.

I walked between tents, keeping an ear out for his voice. And I heard quite a lot. I'd never really walked between the *volikis* at night, but it suddenly occurred to me how easy it was to hear families or couples or warriors inside. And every time I heard a female moan, or cry out in pleasure, my heart froze because I wondered who was giving it to her.

I don't know how many tents I passed where couples were

having sex. It only drove in what I already knew: that the Dakkari liked sex, liked having it regularly, and that Arokan and I were *not* having it.

And strangely enough, it brought me close to tears. Perhaps it was the frustration, perhaps it was how much I'd grown to like Arokan, how my belly warmed and fluttered whenever he was around, whenever I heard his voice, or perhaps it was simply close to my bleeding time. I didn't know.

Regardless, I was on the verge of having some sort of emotional breakdown when I finally heard his voice.

It was coming from a tent set a little farther away from the others. A larger one, the same size as ours. A single guard was posted out front and as I approached, his brow furrowed.

I heard Arokan's voice again. He was speaking in Dakkari. It sounded like he was asking a question, but his voice was low and deep.

Then I heard the light voice of a female and my stomach lurched.

Before I knew what I was doing, I was striding towards the *voliki*. The guard tried to stop me but I wouldn't be deterred.

All I could think was that Arokan was *mine* and he was with another female that night.

So, before the guard caught hold of me, I pushed the flaps of the tent entrance back with a forceful slap and lunged inside, bracing myself for whatever I would find.

24

Stunned silence filled the tent at my unexpected appearance.

Arokan straightened from the table he was standing over, his brows pulled down, the first to recover. *"Rei Morakkari,* is something wrong?"

My lips parted and I stared wide-eyed at the group of eight other Dakkari standing in the large tent. Arokan, six Dakkari males—four of them warriors, then his *pujerak,* then another elderly male—and two older females, Hukan included.

Profound relief, mixed with shame and mortification, made me stutter, "I—I—no, I just—"

It was a meeting. All were standing around a drawn out map of what I assumed was Dakkar. They had been discussing something before I'd barged in.

Fool, fool, fool, my mind whispered, over and over again.

Hukan's eyes burned into mine but I looked away, towards my husband. He came closer, concern obvious on his face. He must've thought something was wrong. I was close to tears and I'd come to find him.

"No," I said, clearing my throat, hardly able to meet his gaze. "I apologize for interrupting. Everything is fine. Excuse me."

"*Kalles*—" he called, but I was already backing out from the tent, my proverbial tail firmly tucked between my legs.

Once outside, I walked as fast as I could back to our tent, praying that he didn't come after me. I didn't think I could face him now, not after that, not after I tried to spy on him.

Luck wasn't on my side. I'd only made it about halfway back when I heard his heavy footsteps, when I heard him call out, "*Morakkari*."

I didn't turn. I walked faster because I was a coward and I was too embarrassed to tell him everything going on in my head.

He didn't press the issue, fortunately, and simply kept up with me—not that it was difficult on his end—until we made it back to our tent. He spoke with the guards outside, probably dismissing them for the night, before he entered, his gaze finding mine.

"Luna," he said slowly, looking at me like I'd lost my mind. "What is—"

"I'm sorry," I burst out, turning to face him, my hands shaking at my sides. "I'm sorry. It was so foolish. I didn't mean to—to do that. But then I did. And Hukan was there and you thought that something was wrong."

His brow furrowed, his expression perplexed. It was the most confused I'd ever seen him...and for good reason. I was acting like I was mad in the head.

Maybe I was.

But I didn't know when it had changed between us. I didn't know when my feelings had started to develop into something more, but it was driving me insane.

"*Kalles*," he said, still frowning, but he approached me, placing his heavy hands on my shoulders. "Calm down. Tell me what is wrong."

"Nothing," I said, closing my eyes for a brief moment. "I mean, something is wrong, but it's not..." I took a deep breath. "Now I'm just embarrassed. I feel foolish."

"Why?" he asked quietly, trying to understand.

I realized there was no way out of this. I needed to be honest, though it frightened me.

I looked up at him, my heart thrumming in my chest, and licked my lips before I confessed, "Because I thought you were with another female."

Arokan stilled. His frown deepened and he watched me carefully as he asked, "Why would you think that, *kassikari?*"

I wondered if he used that word on purpose. *Kassikari*. Mate.

My eyes fluttered to the chests lining the wall and his gaze followed there.

"Because I've always assumed," I began, "that there were others. Why else would you have those trinkets? Those necklaces...the night dresses you've given me?"

Until that moment, I'd never seen the range of my husband's anger. Of course, he'd been upset, he'd argued with me, we'd bickered. The worst I'd ever seen until that moment was after I almost foiled the Ghertun's execution, when I got the warrior hurt, when Arokan had told me about his parents.

Even then, it wasn't like the controlled fury that flared his nostrils now. He stalked over to the three chests lining the walls. He opened the lid of one, brought it over to where I stood, and dumped its contents at my feet.

Shocked, I watched the contents tumble out, glittering and beautiful. Strands of jewels and polished, shining stones... intricately crafted figurines of a *pyroki*, of two figures I assumed were Dakkari deities, of other animals roaming Dakkar...golden hair pins with ruby-colored crystals...rings and baubles and silk cloths...shimmering sheer dresses and fur scarves...

"Arokan—"

Arokan brought the second chest and tumbled out its contents…and then he brought the last and did the same.

I was standing before a small mountain of riches, of beautiful things I'd never even seen before.

Slowly, I took my eyes from the pile of wealth to look at him hesitantly, wondering what I would find in his eyes.

He was staring me down, his jaw clenched, the empty chests tossed carelessly behind him.

"I do not know what infuriates me more," he said softly, slowly, the yellow of his eyes appearing golden in his anger. "That my queen believes these gifts belong to others or that she was indifferent when she believed I was straying from our furs."

"Arokan," I breathed, my eyes wide. "I was not—"

"This," he said, cutting me off with a clipped tone, gesturing to the pile in front of me, "is a *deviri*."

Hesitantly, I whispered, "And what does that mean?"

"It is an offering to my chosen mate. A gift to my bride."

Shock made my head swim.

"W-what?"

His anger was still palpable as he explained, "I have been collecting these trinkets for you since before I was a *Vorakkar*. Before I was even a horde warrior. Some jewels were my mother's. Others I acquired from *Dothik*, from outposts spread across Dakkar, from merchants and stalls and traders that come from all across the universe."

"Arokan," I breathed, frozen, my heart thumping so loudly in my chest.

"You think they belong to others? They do not. They belong to you and only you, Luna. From the moment I saw you in your village, they have belonged to *you*."

I'd *really* fucked up this time.

"I'm sorry," I whispered. "I—I didn't know."

"*Nik*, it is obvious you did not," he scowled.

A weight released off my shoulders as I studied him. There

were no others, I realized with relief. He was angry that I thought he had 'strayed from our furs,' as he'd put it. Now, I realized he hadn't. He wouldn't.

I had a lot of explaining to do.

Carefully stepping over the *huge* mountain of gifts, I hesitantly pressed my palms to his bare chest, feeling his heat beneath them.

He still wore a scowl and his anger was still evident as I looked up at him.

"I'm sorry," I whispered. "Arokan, I really didn't know. Please forgive me. I never meant to…to insult you."

Which was what I'd done. Perhaps without realizing it, since I didn't know what the chests were, what they represented. But I'd also questioned his loyalty, his fidelity, because I didn't know whether the Dakkari were monogamous like humans tended to be.

"Dakkari…" I started hesitantly. "They only take one mate?"

His expression darkened. "Do humans take multiple? Is this something I need to consider in my future with you? Because I will *never* allow you to take another, or so much as *touch* another male. Know this, *Morakkari*. Absolutely not. You will ensure his death if you do."

I blinked. "No," I breathed. "No, Arokan, we only take one mate." I groaned, closing my eyes. "This is a mess. A complete mess I've made."

I needed to explain this, as clearly as I possibly could, even if it revealed my jealousy. Because there was no way around it. Not now.

"At first," I started, "I didn't care if you had others."

He growled, looking away, irritated.

I turned his face so he looked back at me. "You can't blame me for that. I was a virgin, taken from my home, everything was new. I was scared and uncertain. As long as my brother was safe, I didn't care. So when you gave me that night dress from one of the chests, I just thought it belonged to another. I thought nothing more of it.

"But then, it changed. Something changed. Maybe it was after the *tassimara* or even before then, I don't know. All I know is that when you gave me that necklace before the Ghertun's trial...I could hardly look at it because I thought it—I thought it was someone else's."

"It was," he said, his voice sharp. "It was my mother's. The way you reacted to it...I simply thought you did not like it."

I pressed my lips together. "It was beautiful. But it made me...it made me jealous. So jealous I felt like I couldn't breathe."

Arokan blinked and he made a sound in his throat, some of the rage in his eyes lessening.

"Then whenever I even *looked* at those chests, I couldn't help but feel jealous. Truthfully, until just now, I've hated them. I've hated the sight of them."

"*Kalles—*"

My voice shook with nerves as I said, "Then we stopped having sex."

Arokan stilled.

Meeting his eyes, though my face was burning with mortification, I admitted, "I thought you were going to other females because you certainly weren't coming to me."

"*Vok*, Luna..." he hissed, disbelief flashing over his expression. But at least it wasn't anger. I hoped he was beginning to realize why I'd acted so foolishly this night.

I bit my lip and then whispered, "So tonight, I couldn't take it anymore. It was stupid and jealous, but I went out to see if—"

"You seemed indifferent whenever I touched you," he growled. "I watched you carefully, looking for some indication. You never gave me one. Despite what you may think of me, I am not a beast. I will not force you if you are not willing."

"I know," I groaned softly, squeezing my eyes shut. "I know. Until today, I didn't even realize that was how you were perceiving it. I am inexperienced in matters like these. But...I liked when you touched me, Arokan. I just didn't know how to show you."

He froze. Underneath my hand, I felt the muscles in his chest flex.

"*Neffar?*" he growled.

His eyes were glowing golden now, but not in fury. In something else entirely.

I remembered my talk with Mirari and Lavi that morning. Determination shot through me. That and pent-up frustration and desire despite the mess I'd made that night. I *definitely* had some lost ground to make up.

With that thought, I brought my hands—trembling—to laces of his hides.

His breath hitched. "What are you doing, *kalles?*"

Nervous adrenaline and need rushed under my skin as I carefully tugged him to sit on the edge of the bed.

Arokan looked stunned as I dropped to my knees in front of him, reaching into his hides for his thickening, hot cock.

"I'm taking some much-needed advice from a very wise female," I told him, eager and anxious and determined.

Though I had no idea what I was doing, I ducked my head and wrapped my lips around his pulsing cock.

His resounding bellow was—probably—heard all around camp.

25

"*Vok, kalles!*" Arokan rasped, his eyes darkening, his thighs spreading. His voice was hoarse from his bellow.

I looked up at him as I opened my mouth wider, trying to take him deeper. But it was next to impossible to take more than a few inches. He was too thick.

So, instead, I focused on his throbbing head, pulling back for air before leaning forward again to suck softly on the sensitive flesh.

I hoped I was doing this right. I knew next to nothing about pleasuring a male, but judging by the way Arokan's chest heaved, how a tumble of groans and growls rose in his throat, how his eyes never left me...I figured I was doing something right.

What I didn't expect was how aroused this would make me.

Nonetheless, I felt my sex gush, especially when he reached his hand down to gather up my hair when it fell in my face. He gripped it gently, helping to guide me in a steady rhythm over his cock.

I moaned around his length and he whispered something in Dakkari, his eyes closing for a brief moment. My eyes found the rigid bump just above the base of his shaft and I saw it harden. Intrigued, I reached forward and brushed my fingers over it, feeling it begin to vibrate at the stimulation.

Arokan exhaled a sharp breath, his head falling back in pleasure, the strong tendons in his throat stretching. A thrill went through me. I liked this. I liked seeing him this way, I liked that I was doing this to him.

"Does that feel good?" I whispered, pressing the bump.

"*Vok, lysi,*" he hissed, his voice broken.

Pleased, flushed with excitement and arousal, I returned to sucking the head of his cock. Soon, however, my jaw began to ache. I pulled back to catch my breath, continuing to stroke him with my fist. Then, curious, I leaned forward and licked the vibrating bump, laving it with my tongue, remembering the press of it against my clit when he fucked me those first times.

That made him roar with pleasure. Then, I felt the grip in my hair tighten, felt him pull my head back, exposing my throat.

I met his gaze with half-lidded, glazed-over eyes and reddened lips.

"Enough, *rei Morakkari,*" he rasped, his breathing ragged. With one quick maneuver, he pulled me from between his legs and back onto the bed. "You will make me come before I am ready."

Then he stood from the bed, his engorged cock bobbing. He didn't bother to kick off his pants, he simply tugged mine down and tossed them to the floor, baring my lower half.

He cursed and took my legs in his grip, pulling them wide. "Look at how pink and wet your cunt is for me, *kalles.*"

I bit my lip, wiggling my hips, trying to inch closer to him. "Please, Arokan," I whispered. "*Please.*"

With a rough growl, he positioned his cock at my entrance and he thrust inside me with one stiff, teeth-chattering, *sublime* motion. He let out a deep, deep groan that I felt reverberate in my own body.

"*Oh yes!*" I moaned, my eyes squeezing shut. A little pain twinged deep inside, but I didn't care. I just needed to get used to his size again. It felt *good*, that pain.

"There is *nothing* better than your cunt, *kalles*," he rasped, wrapping his arm underneath my hips, pulling me down over him with more leverage and power.

Then he didn't stop. He gave me a single moment to adjust to him and then he *couldn't* stop. He pounded into me with deep, hard thrusts that made stars burst into my vision.

Our *voliki* was filled with primal, erotic sounds. The sounds of sex and mating. Of flesh slapping against flesh, of moans and groans and cries, and whispered words and savage curses.

It was perfect. He was perfect.

Arokan caught my wrists in between it all. He looked at the gold markings and then he threaded our hands together so our tattoos touched and aligned.

Dazed, my lips parted, I looked up at him, on the verge of coming. Any moment now, he would send me over the edge.

His hands squeezed mine and he leaned down low over my body. With his marked flesh against mine, with his cock buried deep inside me, he murmured, "We are one, *kassikari*."

My breath hitched and then he caught my lips in a fierce kiss, growling deep in his throat. I returned it with enthusiasm and fervor.

And it didn't take long until that kiss, his touch, sent me over the edge.

My scream was muffled against his lips and I turned my head instead to bite his shoulder, unfathomable pleasure tearing through my body.

I think he liked that because he roared, his thrusts deepening, growing rough and savage. Then I felt his seed spill into me, felt his body tremble and jerk, as he came undone.

Afterwards, I lay underneath him in a warm haze, disbelieving that anything could feel so good.

Arokan lifted his head, though I still felt his cock pulsing inside me. His heavy-lidded gaze sought mine and I tilted my head up in invitation. He took my lips and I disentangled our hands so I could wrap them around his massive shoulders.

Closing my eyes, I smiled, drugged on sex and Arokan. *Finally*, some of the tension that had been building and building over the past week left, though it was by no means gone.

Arokan seemed to feel the same way because when he pulled his head back to look down at me, his eyes burned with need and he rasped, "I am not done with you, *Morakkari*."

"Good," I whispered back. "I'm not done with you either, *Vorakkar*."

APPARENTLY, Arokan still wasn't done with me *hours* later when I had to beg him for a reprieve.

"J-just a little while," I gasped, still feeling my sex flutter with the last two orgasms he'd wrung from me. "I just need to rest."

He growled but acquiesced, dragging my limp, thoroughly pleasured body up the bed, tucking me into his side.

I blew out a shuddering breath, still panting from the exertion. I'd been unprepared for this, unprepared for the full force of his desire and need.

But I had loved every single moment of it.

His seed leaked from between my legs. I didn't know how many times he'd come inside me, but the evidence was all over the furs. They would need to be washed thoroughly in the morning, but I was too exhausted to care that night.

Apparently, my horde king had been holding back. *A lot.* I'd always assumed that the Dakkari had a healthy drive for sex, but I didn't know just how *much* they needed it.

His hand stroked over my body gently, his tail wrapping around my thigh, holding me against his side. My fingers traced over the slim, flexible appendage, and the tip twitched at my touch.

I smiled, stretching a bit. I would be doubly sore in the morning. Not just from the training, but from the marathon of sex.

"Did I hurt you?" he finally asked, his voice guttural and rough yet quiet.

"No," I whispered, looking up at him. "You didn't. I feel good."

His lips twitched at that word, his brow quirking as if to say 'only good?' I liked this side of Arokan too. All the tension had left his body, leaving him relaxed and loose.

"I heard you've been somewhat of a terror to your warriors lately," I commented.

He grunted and he angled a look down at me. "Keeping tabs on me?" he asked, repeating words I'd once said to him.

Surprised, I couldn't help but chuckle. "I have my sources," I said, unwilling to give up Mirari's name.

"My warriors have nothing to fear from me in the morning," he rasped, stroking that large palm down my back, settling over my buttocks and squeezing, making my breath hitch. "I will be as docile as a newborn *bveri.*"

I grinned.

"What else have your sources said about me?" he asked.

Damn.

"Not much," I said.

"Tell me," he murmured.

I bit my lip but then said, "I know that Hukan was your mother's sister."

He grunted again. "*Lysi.*"

"I know that you and Hukan are the last of your line," I said, watching him.

"Until you gift me young, we are," he murmured. "But Rath Kitala will flourish once more. I know it."

My breath hitched. *Until*, not *if*. As if it was a certain thing. And perhaps after tonight, if my cycle was correctly aligned…it *was* a certain thing.

That should frighten me, shouldn't it?

"How do you know we're even…compatible in that way?" I whispered.

His tail twitched. "You think I am the first Dakkari to take a human as a mate?"

I thought of Mithelda, of what Arokan had said about her capture from my village.

But what he was implying made me pay attention. "There are children *already*?" I asked, my heart speeding up in my chest. "Dakkari-human children?"

"*Lysi*," he confirmed.

Disbelief went through me.

"Not in my horde, obviously," he continued. "In others."

I couldn't believe what he was saying. "You've seen them?" I asked in awe.

He nodded. "They are young. Healthy. Strong. So, *lysi, kalles*, I *know* you will bear me children."

I blew out a breath then nibbled on my lip as I felt more of his seed leak from my body.

He tilted my chin up so I met his eyes. "What do you think of, *kalles*?"

Softly, I confessed, "Truthfully, I've never given much thought to children. It never seemed possible for me."

"Do you desire them?" he questioned, his eyes rapt.

The answer came to me easily, which was surprising in itself.

"Yes," I whispered.

The knowledge pleased my husband. I could see that plainly. He leaned forward to capture my lips and I let out a small sigh, his kiss fogging my mind.

"We will make it so," he murmured against me. "If we have not already."

I blushed, despite everything that had happened that night, and he pulled back to study me, seemingly amused.

My eyes strayed to his shoulder, where I saw one of his scars curve around from his back. I reached forward to trace the raised line. Though I could not see his back, I knew that the majority of his flesh was covered in scars, as if he'd been whipped.

Before, I'd never been courageous enough to ask, but right then, I felt the question tumble out before I could stop it. "What happened?"

He caught my hand, pressing his lips to the center of my palm before they trailed over my wrist, kissing my golden markings.

He took his time answering me, but finally he said, "A *Vorakkar* must be strong for his horde. He must be able to withstand pain and suffering in order to lead them best and he must not let pain and suffering break him."

My brow furrowed. "I don't understand."

"All *Vorakkars* wear these scars, *kalles*," he told me. "It is the final test, the test chosen and carried out by the *Dothikkar*."

My eyes widened in realization. "He…your king did this?"

The pain he must have withstood. The agony. How long had he been whipped? Shock and disbelief and horror rolled through me.

"I chose this," he corrected, taking my face in his hands. "I have always known my purpose was this. I have always known I would be a *Vorakkar*. It was inevitable. It was but a fleeting moment in my life, a necessary step in order to achieve something more. I would do it again without hesitation."

I understood what he was saying. One sacrifice to achieve everything he'd wanted.

But…

"It's barbaric," I protested.

"It is the old way, the old tradition."

There seemed to be a lot of those, I couldn't help but think.

"How many tests did you have to go through?" I asked.

"As many as were necessary," he told me. Something told me he didn't want me to know the exact number and I wasn't entirely sure I wanted to know.

I blew out a breath. "We'd been told that there are six horde kings across Dakkar, which includes you. Is that true? There are five other *Vorakkars?*"

"Six," he corrected. "And the *Dothikkar* is currently in the process of selecting a seventh."

"So many," I commented softly.

Arokan ran his hand back up my bare spine until he cupped the nape of my neck, holding me still as he said, "The Ghertun grow bold. We simply need more horde warriors to patrol the wild lands, to keep them in line."

Concern touched my brow. "It's that worrisome?"

"*Lysi*, I will not lie to you," he confessed. "They reproduce very quickly, which means their numbers grow quickly."

"Is that what you were meeting about tonight?" I couldn't help but ask.

"Partly," he answered. "Mostly, the *bveri* are beginning to migrate south. Soon, it will be time to leave this area, to follow them. We will journey for a new encampment during the next moon cycle."

The knowledge sent a thread of panic through me. South. Further away from my brother. Would I ever see him again?

Not only that, but I felt like I'd just begun to settle there. Now, he was telling me we were to pack up and leave, to start fresh elsewhere.

This is the horde life, I told myself. *The Dakkari way*.

"How do you feel about that, *kalles?*" he asked me softly, studying me.

"It seems overwhelming," I said honestly. Then I sighed, touching the solid muscles of his chest, tracing the golden markings of his skin. "But I'll enjoy seeing more of Dakkar. Though I was born here, I've seen very little of my home planet."

He made a sound deep in his throat and his arms came around me, pulling me more tightly into his body.

I felt warm and safe in his arms. And I knew, without a doubt, that I'd given up yet another piece of my heart to him that night. How much more could he take before there was nothing left?

"I will show it all to you, Luna," he murmured. "I promise."

26

"Are you frustrated, *kalles?*" Arokan growled, his voice rough and wild, spurring on my emotion.

I was frustrated *and* tired *and* sore beyond belief.

"*Yes,*" I hissed back, the weight of the dagger still unfamiliar in my hand. It was perfectly balanced. The handle was made of *bveri* bone, strong and solid, and the blade was of light yet lethal Dakkari steel. Expertly crafted, or so Arokan had told me.

Arokan rushed me out of nowhere and I was unprepared, distracted by his words. I gasped and he grabbed my throat, to tell me that I'd let my guard down, that if he were an enemy, that would have been a kill shot. I would be dead.

The Dakkari didn't mess around. Not with training. They'd been raised warriors, even the females, and everything that Arokan taught me demonstrated that.

He was hard on me because he wanted me to learn quickly. He wanted to make me stronger.

My husband squeezed my throat lightly, not enough to hurt, but enough to get my attention. My breathing went tight because I remembered when he'd done something similar between the furs, when he'd pinned me down and mounted me from behind.

Great. Now I was frustrated, tired, sore, *and* aroused.

"Get angry," he growled, his body pressed against mine. "Feel that emotion and then let it go. Emotion will get you killed if you let it."

My eyes narrowed and I pushed him away, my muscles straining.

"Again," I said, panting with exertion.

His mouth tightened but he jerked his head in a nod.

It was a calm, peaceful night, though it was late. Arokan had finished with his duties later than usual, but he'd asked if I still wanted to train that night once he returned.

I'd wanted to, but instead of going to the training ground, he'd led me into the forest, much to my confusion.

I'd been nervous, considering the last time I'd been there, the Ghertun scout had most likely been watching my every move. But I trusted Arokan. He wouldn't bring me there unless he believed it was safe.

"Use the environment," he'd told me. "Anything can be a weapon if you use it correctly."

With that in mind, I rushed him first that time. I'd been frightened to accidentally cut him with the blade or injure him in some way, but quickly, my fears had been alleviated. Arokan was much too skilled as a warrior to be seriously harmed by a novice like me. And when I *had* managed a shallow cut early on, he'd simply looked down at it and grunted, "*Good.* Very good, *kalles.*"

I'd been much too pleased by his praise to admit I'd cut him on accident.

He quickly side-stepped my rush, his arm swiping out to disarm me of my blade. It thudded softly onto the forest floor, but there was no time to reach for it.

Before I knew it, he dove for me and I hit the ground hard,

the air in my lungs whooshing out of me. He straddled his thighs around my hips, keeping me pinned as his hands pressed down on my shoulders. And though I struggled to catch my breath, I never stopped struggling underneath him.

Out of the corner of my eye, I saw the dagger. It was close. I reached for it when he leaned down over me, my fingertips brushing the handle.

"Not quick enough, *kalles*," he murmured. He bent his head close, his eyes flickering down to my lips.

There. I'd dragged the blade close enough with the edge of my middle finger and I snagged it quickly.

"You want a kiss for your victory, *Vorakkar?*" I whispered, quirking my brows.

His eyes flashed, desire firing in his gaze, and he lowered his lips, intent to claim just that.

But right before his lips touched mine, I whipped the dagger's edge up to his throat, hovering just above his flesh.

Every muscle in his body tightened. His nostrils flared wide as he looked down at me in surprise.

Grinning, breathing hard, I whispered, "Maybe *I* get the victory kiss this time."

Arokan growled. "Then take it, *kalles*."

My grip on the blade loosened and I dragged him down, my free hand threading through his thick hair as I took his lips in an almost angry kiss. I poured all my frustration, all my need into that kiss.

He met me head on, devouring me until my head spun, sucking on my tongue in a way where I felt it between my legs. I grew hot and wet for him in no time at all. The blade fell from my hand to the ground beside me and Arokan repositioned himself so I could spread my legs wide.

With a grunt, while I scrambled to untie the laces of his hide pants, he pushed up the short skirt I'd allowed Mirari and Lavi to dress me in that morning—and I thanked all the deities in the universe for that fortunate decision right then.

I gasped when he slid inside me with a rough thrust, my fingers gripping his shoulders as his head came to rest against the column of my neck.

It was rough and fast and primal. It was exactly what we both needed, to release the tension that had been building for the better part of an hour, ever since we started the training session.

And when I came, I bit into his shoulder to conceal my scream, lest the guards come running. Arokan, on the other hand, couldn't hide his roar of pleasure and it echoed around the forest, ringing in my ears, as he emptied himself inside me.

Afterwards, I laughed, lying in his arms as we recovered.

"*Neffar?*" he asked, his tone husky and lazy and content. That orgasm had stolen all the fight right out of him.

It was amazing what sex could do, how it made me feel. The past few days with Arokan had been...spectacular. Consuming. I'd felt like I was in this happy daze as I walked around camp, as if nothing could dampen my mood, not even my duty at the *pyroki* enclosure or whenever I happened to catch sight of Hukan's glares.

"I was just wondering if the guards heard," I teased, pressing my cheek against his shoulder.

Arokan grunted. "They have heard worse around camp. I assure you."

I shook my head, still grinning. Looking up, I saw a million stars twinkling through the canopy of the forest. The dark, black trees towered overhead and if I was with anyone but Arokan, I might have found them eerie and frightening. But right then, they were beautiful against the even more beautiful backdrop of the inky sky.

I sighed in contentment, feeling his arm tighten around me,

and I squirmed closer when a cool breeze chilled the sweat from our activities on my skin.

"You did well tonight," he praised softly. "You reminded me of something. That until the very last moment, there is always an opportunity to change your fate."

"That was lucky," I commented, my cheeks heating.

"*Nik*, do not dismiss it, Luna," he told me. "You distracted me. You did not give up. And you waited until the opportune moment, luring me into a more comprising, vulnerable position so that my throat would be easier to cut."

My belly fluttered. Though we were discussing a kill strike, one might think he was baring his entire soul to me given how breathless I felt.

"You feel comfortable with the blade?" he asked me next, quietly.

Because of my mother, he meant.

He remembered that and it touched me that he thought to ask.

"It'll take some getting used to," I admitted to him. "But it was better than I thought it would be."

He turned his head to look at me and I found myself looking directly into his eyes, our faces only inches apart.

"Do you have a father?" he asked.

"What?" I asked, laughing a little at how surprising the question was, how unexpected.

"You never speak of one. You only speak of your mother."

"You think I just sprang out of the ground?" I teased. "A little gift from Kakkari?"

He growled, leaning forward to nip my fingers in frustration. I chuckled, my belly swarming again.

He elaborated his question by commenting, "I had heard that the old Earth colonies, before they were destroyed, had the ability to create offspring without a father. Just a mother."

"Oh," I said. "Yes, but it was long ago. And for your information, I was created the old-fashioned way."

He shook his head, grumbling something in Dakkari at my teasings.

I sobered a little.

"My father died a long time ago," I told him. "Even before my brother was born. He got sick and it took him quickly. I was four at the time, so I hardly remember him. Mostly, I just have these vague impressions or memories. My mother never wanted to talk about him. I think she never stopped mourning him and not remembering made it easier to move on."

I used to think about my father a lot when I was little, how different life at the village might have been. When my mother was alive, she struggled to have her voice heard. As a female, with two small children, the village council, Polin included, had never taken her seriously. It had always angered me, watching her get dismissed.

"What were your parents like?" I asked, curious. "Were you happy as a child before…before the *pyroki* attack?"

"*Lysi*," he murmured. "I was."

I nodded, glad.

"Dakkari are not shy about showing their offspring their affection," he told me. "They showed me every moment. My mother was gentle, yet strong. My father was everything I wanted to be. He would train me himself, even in *Dothik*. He wanted me to be strong because he told me that one day, I would need to protect my mother, my queen, and my daughters."

My breath hitched and emotion welled in my chest at his words.

"He could be hard," he continued. "But his lessons, not only during trainings, have directed my life. The memory of them have led me to this. I have felt both of their presences, their guiding hands, in every action I have taken. For that, I am grateful." He met my gaze again. "I felt them when I saw you. Their force and Kakkari's force led me to you. They knew that I needed you."

My lips parted, my heart throbbing.

He was just...so wonderful.

Overwhelmed, I didn't know what to say, so I simply leaned forward and gave him a soft kiss. He breathed me in deep and shifted, so I lay more comfortably in his arms.

When we pulled apart, I whispered, almost shyly, "I'm glad they did. I'm glad they led you to me."

Because it was becoming obvious to me that I was falling in love with my horde king. I'd fought it at first, but the past few days had only intensified my budding feelings, had only proven to me that somehow, some way, I'd been given a gift.

A precious gift. One I had never expected.

But Arokan was real. He was right there, pressed against me, whispering sweet things that made my spine tingle.

He was offering me everything.

Yet, I was holding back.

Why?

Was it because of my brother and his uncertain future? Was it because nothing in my life had gone as planned or because Arokan seemed too good to be true and I distrusted that? Was it my doubts and fears and insecurities about leading the horde that continued to plague my every step?

It was everything.

And until the answers to those questions became clear, I couldn't give him everything in return.

I just hoped it wouldn't destroy us both in the process.

27

"Lysi," Arokan growled, his hands gripping my hips. "*Rin nekanevexi rei kakkiva, rei Morakkari!*"

You ride my cock so well, my Queen, he'd said. Dakkari words I knew like the back of my hand now.

I gasped, feeling my horde king's large palms slide up my bare torso, and I groaned deep in my throat as his fingers pinched my nipples, making my hips snap over him *harder*.

"Arokan," I moaned.

Building, building, building...

Too much, too much!

Then I was destroyed, falling into a powerful orgasm that made me scream, that made me buck my hips over my husband's thick cock faster, without rhythm, gripping his chest to anchor myself as I came apart.

Through my ringing ears, I heard his roar of pleasure and then felt his seed flood into me, filling me.

Arms trembling, I collapsed over his heaving chest, pressing my cheek into the warm flesh, hearing his heartbeat drum in my ears as he continued to come inside me.

Once it was done, once reality began to return, I peeked up at him, my thighs still straddling wide over his hips.

It had been two weeks since that night in the forest. Two weeks that had flown by, yet seemed like they'd stretched into months. Two weeks of settling into my life in the horde, two weeks of long, satisfying days, and two weeks of even longer, even more satisfying nights with my husband.

"You've created a monster," I whispered to him.

Grinning in satisfaction, Arokan stretched his arms over his head and my eyes went a little unfocused as I watched his muscles pull and flex. He *knew* what that did to me.

He groaned when my inner walls tightened around him and he agreed with, "I have."

A spot of morning sun shone down onto the furs next to him through the venting hole at the top of our *voliki*. Mirari and Lavi no longer entered at the first signs of my waking, considering most mornings Arokan still remained with me. And waking with my horde king was almost as satisfying as drifting into sleep beside him.

"Today will be long," he murmured, scrubbing a hand over his face. "Hopefully one of the scouting parties will return."

The moon cycle was almost over and that meant it was time to leave this place. The *bveri*, our main source of meat, lessened by the day, as the hunting parties reported to Arokan. We would follow them south and make a new home, a new camp elsewhere.

Arokan had sent out a few scouting parties of horde warriors ahead to scope out possible sites. The journey would take at least three days of traveling with the entire horde and it would be slow-going.

And while some of my dread at leaving had lessened over the weeks, there was a sadness that would always remain. I would be journeying farther away from my brother and the possibility of ever seeing him again seemed slim to none.

A couple weeks ago, I had lightly broached the topic with Arokan, asking if there was any chance I could at least visit him before we left the area, to make sure he was all right. Arokan had studied me for long moments, but finally said, with a grave expression, that he couldn't spare the warriors to take me. Not right then. Not when they were making preparations to leave and when they were coming across more Ghertun during patrols than normal. It wasn't safe.

He wouldn't risk it. I'd understood, of course I had. But it hadn't stopped the overwhelming feeling of disappointment. I'd never brought it up again.

"Any day now," I commented softly, looking up at him, my fingers tracing the golden markings across his chest.

Once a scouting party returned with a viable camp location, we would pack up and leave.

"*Lysi*," he murmured, his eyes warm and dark as he looked at me. Belly fluttering, I gave him a small smile. "*Bnuru tei lilji rini, kalles.*"

Give me your lips, female.

Leaning up, I pressed them to his and my head spun pleasantly as he deepened it, taking my mouth in a warm, thorough kiss.

When I pulled away, I whispered, dazed, "I love how you do that."

"You love many things I do, *kalles*," he teased, brushing his lips across my cheekbone, my nose.

I pushed at his shoulder, half-rolling my eyes, and then I climbed off him, knowing that we both had to begin our days, even though I'd rather spend it *all* between the furs with him.

I'd gone from frightened indifference to being a little bit obsessed with my alien husband. Now it was the depth of my feelings for him that frightened me. Every single day, those feelings only continued to grow and flourish.

"The *mrikro* is expecting me," I told him, turning from him to wash his seed from between my legs and dress in my tunic and pants. "He wants me to assist in training one of the *pyroki*."

Arokan rose from our bed, snagging me around the waist before I could slip through the tent's entrance. I looked up at him towering over me in question.

"What is it?" I asked softly.

He looked on the verge of saying something, his tail flicking behind him. But then he released me and said, "Nothing, *kalles*. I will come find you later."

I nodded. Then with one last, lingering look at him, I left.

———

THE *MRIKRO* HAD a unique way of punishing me. He knew that though my fear of the *pyrokis* had lessened slightly over the weeks I'd been working for him, it was by no means gone. That fear, which had been instilled in me for over ten years now, would *always* be there.

However, I'd come to learn much about *pyrokis* in the last few weeks. I knew that fearing them wasn't necessarily a bad thing because it also made me respect them. It made me respect their strength, their surprising emotional intelligence.

It was because of that fear that I never let my guard down around them either. They were intelligent creatures and they would take advantage if I was weak with them.

So, later that afternoon, though my heart was pounding in my chest and I wanted to shrink away, I stood my ground as a fully grown, misbehaving *pyroki* charged right for me.

I felt the ground vibrate, heard the alarmed gasps of Mirari and Lavi, who were always watching me from the fence enclosure.

The *mrikro* yelled, "Do not cower, *Morakkari!*"

I stared into the blood-red eyes of the *pyroki* as I felt a strange calm come over me. Closer and closer he came, but he tossed his neck when he saw I wasn't moving out of the way.

I was braced, my thighs in a slight squatting position, my arms slightly outstretched, a position that Arokan had showed me over our weeks of training. A default position for defense, which allowed for quick movements.

I was ready. I felt ready and I certainly wouldn't let this annoyed *pyroki* get the best of me. I was a damn *queen* for Kakkari's sake.

Only five feet away, the *pyroki* finally realized I wasn't going to move. At the last moment, he veered to the side ever so slightly, hitting me hard enough in the side to steal my breath. But he didn't knock me off my feet, not like the other times I'd had this battle with him.

I figured it was progress.

Inhaling lungfuls of air, trying to replenish my supply, I looked over my shoulder at the *pyroki*, who was trotting close the training enclosure fence, as if celebrating his near victory.

The *mrikro* approached. "Good, *Morakkari*," he praised. "He is beginning to recognize his defeat. It should take another week."

"At least he didn't knock me on my ass this time," I commented, brushing my hands on my pants, finally catching my breath.

"Take him back with the rest," the *mrikro* ordered. "Jriva will brush him down."

I nodded and, steeling my spine, approached the stubborn *pyroki*, still prancing away. I snagged his reins with a quick tug, though he shook his head. But I noticed, as I led him out of the training enclosure, he didn't give as much of a fight as he usually did.

As I walked him back to the larger enclosure, I stopped, spying a cloud of dust billowing in the distance. My stomach dropped a little, though I was also relieved. A scouting party was returning, though they weren't coming from the south.

Would they report back to Arokan with favorable news? Would the entire horde pack up and leave as early as tomorrow morning?

I'd never done well with change. I liked my routines and whenever we left this place, everything would change, at least for a little while.

But this is my life now, this is my duty to the horde, I thought quietly.

I tugged gently on the *pyroki's* reins and led him back to the larger enclosure. Once there, I made sure he got his place at one of the feeding troughs and hesitantly stroked his flank before I left him.

Kailon came up to nudge me before I left the enclosure. Slowly but surely, Arokan's beast had warmed up to me and I spread my palm over his snout.

"Hi handsome," I whispered, giving the creature a soft smile and a pat. Arokan had a special bond with Kailon and because of that, I felt surprisingly comfortable around his *pyroki*. Arokan had assured me that Kailon would never harm me...and I trusted my husband. I believed him.

I spent some time with Kailon, stroking over his scales, and chatting happily with Jriva, the young boy who had finally been promoted from the Shit Corner to groomer.

However, we were interrupted when I heard, *"Morakkari."*

I turned to see one of my guards at the fence enclosure.

"Lysi?" I asked, straightening.

"The *Vorakkar* requests your presence," he said, tilting his head towards the front of the camp, where Arokan often held his meetings with his chosen council.

I nodded, saying goodbye to Jriva, and followed my guard through the camp. I nodded and smiled at members who greeted me and soon, my guard brought me to the large tent I'd barged into when I thought Arokan was with another female.

"He waits inside," the guard said, taking post outside the entrance.

I nodded, eyeing the group of *pyrokis* that had carried their warriors in the scouting party. They must've returned already, though they'd been a long distance away when I'd first seen them.

Their riders must be inside, I thought.

Arokan just probably wanted to inform me that we would be leaving soon, to prepare me for what was to come.

So, with a deep breath, I ducked into the tent.

As my eyes adjusted to the darkened space, I gave a small smile when I saw Arokan, warmth infusing my chest as it always did. He was regarding me with a careful expression, studying me, in *Vorakkar* mode, as I liked to refer to it.

Five warriors were also in the tent, looking tired from their journey, though they inclined their heads in respect when I entered.

"What is it?" I asked Arokan. "Have you found—"

Shock made me freeze when Arokan stepped aside, revealing someone behind him, someone I had not seen when I first entered.

A hundred different emotions raced through my body when I saw someone I never thought I'd see again.

"Kivan," I breathed.

28

Kivan was there, standing next to Arokan.
My brother.

"H-how?" I breathed, feeling my legs tremble with the overwhelming emotions of relief and love and happiness.

Kivan gave me a tired, hesitant smile. He was dirty, his clothes worn. He looked as though he'd lost weight, his face gaunt.

"Kivan," I murmured, tears springing into my eyes before I rushed my brother and wrapped my arms around him. Though he was five years younger than I was, he still dwarfed me.

"Hi, Luna," he whispered in my ear, bending low so that his cold cheek was pressed against mine. "Are you all right?"

"Yes," I said, still stunned, hardly daring to believe that this moment was real. "Yes. Are *you*?"

I pulled back to study him more and my chest tightened as I did. The weeks and weeks I'd been gone had not been good to him. He'd suffered. Not just physically. I saw the strain in his eyes.

My eyes went to Arokan, who was standing a respectful distance away. In a low voice, I heard him dismiss the horde warriors who, I realized, had brought my brother here. That was why they hadn't come from the south.

Arokan had tasked them with this, despite the risk it posed.

With that knowledge, I felt perhaps the last part of my heart binding itself to him. Affection and respect and love filled my breast.

He'd done this for me.

His yellow-rimmed eyes came to me once the warriors departed, when it was just the three of us in the tent.

"I have offered your brother a place in this horde," Arokan told me.

My lips parted, my eyes widening.

"He knows my terms," my husband said, his expression still careful. "He has not yet told me he will accept my offer, but perhaps after speaking with you, *rei Morakkari*, he will. I will leave you to speak."

I caught my husband's arm before he ducked out of the tent. I squeezed his forearm, holding his gaze, as I whispered, "Thank you."

He inclined his head. I knew there would be much to discuss with him later, but right now, I needed to make sure my brother was all right.

"There will be guards posted outside," Arokan told me, though it was perhaps more for my brother's ears than mine. My horde king didn't trust my brother. Not yet.

Hopefully in time, he would.

I nodded and then he left, leaving me alone with Kivan.

I immediately embraced my brother again before cupping his face in my hands, inspecting him.

"I can't believe you're here," I whispered, tears tracking down my cheeks.

He frowned, reaching out to trace them. "I've never seen you cry before, Luna."

I laughed, though it sounded slightly hysterical. "I'm happy.

So happy that you're here. I've thought about you so much. You're always on my mind."

"You're always on mine," Kivan said, though his shoulders dropped. He closed his eyes for a long moment and then said, his tone grave, "Luna, I'm so sorry. You're here because of me. I can't tell you how sorry—"

"Shhh, Kivan," I tried to soothe, frowning. "It's okay. I'm fine."

"But that Dakkari—the horde king!" Kivan said, his voice hushed. "He—he—"

"He is..." I trailed off with a small smile, not quite knowing how to explain Arokan of Rath Kitala.

He was the strongest, most honorable male I'd ever met. He was everything a leader should be, needed to be, and more.

Finally, I said, "He's not what you think, Kivan. He's good to me. *More* than good to me."

His expression told me he didn't believe me. "Luna," he urged quietly. "You're confused. You don't know these Dakkari. They—"

I was surprised by how defensive I felt, how quick I was when I argued, "No, *you* don't know them, Kivan. You have no idea who they are. But I've lived among them for over six weeks now. They have accepted me as their own."

Well, with the exception of one, I thought, thinking of Hukan.

Kivan looked at me, seemingly surprised by my tone. "Luna...I—"

"I've been treated well," I continued. "I've been fed, I've been protected, I've been safe. I've *lived* here," I whispered, "and not simply *survived* here. There's a difference and I didn't realize that until the *Vorakkar* brought me to his horde."

"You...you *like* being here?" Kivan asked, disbelief in his tone.

"Yes," I answered immediately. "So much so that whenever I've thought about the village, about you, I've felt guilty."

Kivan blinked.

With a deep breath, I said, "The horde king...he means more to me than you realize, Kivan."

"What?" he asked in disbelief. "You cannot mean that."

"I do," I answered. "He's my husband."

My brother's eyes bulged almost comically and he seemed at a loss for words, his mouth gaping open, making his cheekbones seem even more hollowed.

"When he took me from the village, he said he always knew I would be his queen," I told him. "That was my purpose and what he wanted from me. And I'm not going to lie, I rebelled against it for a long time, struggled with it as I adjusted to my new life. But eventually, I realized that my feelings for him grew every day. He's honorable and kind, but hard when he needs to be. He's a better male than I could have ever thought. He's protected me and *strengthened* me and cared for me. Now, I'm proud to be at his side. I'm proud to be queen of this horde."

Kivan processed my words with a grim expression. He swallowed. "This is hard for me to take in, Luna."

"It will take time," I said. "Just like it did for me. What matters is that you're here now. I asked my husband if I could see you again and here you are. You're here because of him."

"When the horde riders came to our village yesterday," Kivan said, "I wasn't sure what to expect. They had brought food—*meat,* actual meat—with them last time, which surprised us all. We weren't sure if they had come to collect some form of payment. Instead, they asked for me. They told me I could see you if I went with them."

I smiled, pushing back a long strand of hair that covered his eyes. He needed a hair trim, which was something I'd always done for him.

"The *Vorakkar* sent that food to the village," I told him.

"Why?" he asked, suspicious.

"Because I refused to eat when I first arrived," I told him, a little embarrassed about that fact now. How far would I have really gotten, not eating? "I felt guilty about having food when I knew you were hungry."

His expression softened. "Luna…"

"So he made me a deal. If I ate, he would make sure the village ate too."

Kivan blinked and then looked down.

"He said he offered you a place here," I whispered, tilting his chin up so he could look at me. "Please tell me you'll accept."

Kivan's nostrils flared.

"You'll be safe. You'll always have food in your belly. You won't have to live in fear anymore."

"And what about the rest of the village?" Kivan asked.

I sobered. But then I asked, "After I left, did they treat you well? Did Polin?"

"That doesn't matter," he murmured. "It was my fault."

My lips pressed together. "You were an outcast, weren't you?"

He didn't reply, but his shoulders sagged.

"Kivan," I whispered, biting my lip. He must have been scared. He'd lost me and then he'd lost the respect of the village, what remained of it, at least. They'd turned their backs on him.

"Would you go back with me?" he asked, his tone serious.

My brow furrowed. "Why would you want to go back, after how they treated you?"

His mouth opened and closed. Finally, he said, "Because it's home. Once you are back, everything will be normal again. You'll see. So, will you?"

I looked at him, my chest tightening. Because Arokan had asked me this once. He'd asked if I would choose my brother and the village over the horde, over him. And I'd told him that he couldn't ask me that, that it wasn't fair.

233

But right then, I had my answer.

"No," I whispered.

He sucked in a breath.

I looked at the notch in his throat, my heart heavy, before meeting the familiar color of his eyes. It was strange looking into them after so long. I was so used to the dark eyes of the Dakkari that human eyes now seemed...alien.

"My home is here now," I said. "Kivan, I—before I came here, I never realized how much I struggled. For us...for you."

"Luna..." he said, shock making him freeze.

"And it wasn't your fault," I said, rushing to get the words out. "It was my own guilt. When Mother died, I didn't tell you everything."

"What didn't you tell me?"

I took in a deep breath and said quietly, "After she was attacked, she was still alive. Her second to last request was that I protect you like she would've. And then her last request...it was to end her suffering."

Kivan's face paled.

"I did," I whispered. "But because of it, I've held onto so much guilt and self-loathing over the years. I threw myself into doing what she asked of me, into taking care of you. And now, I can see that I may have stopped taking care of myself in the process."

It hurt to say these things out loud because I knew they hurt Kivan, I could see it in his face. But I wanted to be honest with him, for once.

"Luna," he breathed. "I'm sorry. I'm so sorry. I never realized...that I, that you—"

He broke off, words failing him.

"I love you, Kivan," I told him, reaching out to take his hand, squeezing. "But I've learned to love myself too. And I can't go back. My place is here, with him. My home is here. I hope that you'll consider making it yours too."

I FOUND Arokan in our tent a little while later.

Though it had been a long, hard conversation, I had left Kivan in the tent with posted guards and ordered a bathing tub brought in and a hot meal. After he rested, I would visit him again. Despite what his answer was—whether he would return to the village or stay—I wanted to spend as much time with him as possible.

But right then, I needed to see my husband. I wanted to.

I went to him, pressing my face to his wide, warm chest, breathing him in. His arms came around me, pressing me to him. He didn't speak, as if he knew I needed time to process what had happened.

Finally, I pulled back to look up at him. Whispering, I said, "You're good to me. I don't tell you nearly as much as I should, but you are, Arokan. Thank you. Thank you."

His eyes softened. He brushed his fingers through my hair, careful of his claws. "My only wish is your happiness, *kalles*."

"I am happy," I told him, giving him a soft smile. "Now, even more so."

"He has agreed then?" Arokan asked in a low tone. "To remain with the horde?"

"He hasn't given me his answer," I said. "But we talked. I told him many things that I should have told him a long time ago... and I feel lighter for it. I think he will accept your offer, once his mind processes everything that's happened."

Arokan nodded.

"He asked me to go back with him," I admitted.

Arokan's jaw ticked. "I figured he might."

"I thought about when you asked me if I would choose to leave or stay if I had the choice," I said softly.

"I remember."

"I told him no."

The yellow rim of his eyes contracted. *"Lysi?"* he said softly, his voice steady.

"I just knew," I said, giving him a smile as I reached up to touch his jaw. "While I love my brother, I also know that I cannot betray the horde. I wouldn't leave them. More importantly, I wouldn't leave *you*."

Arokan blew out a long exhale through his nostrils and he bent low so he could touch our foreheads together.

"Lysi?" he rasped.

I smiled. *"Lysi."*

We were quiet for a long while and then he murmured, "Knowing you, *kalles*, I worry that you feel guilt for this."

I shook my head because he knew me well.

And while I did, I recognized that was the Old Luna.

The New Luna, however, said, "I'm learning to give myself permission to be happy. Guilt was a large part of my life. It fueled a lot of my decisions. But I've paid my dues, I did what my mother asked of me. Now I just want to be free to make the choices I want to make without fear."

"You will," he murmured, gripping my chin gently to meet my eyes. "I know you will, *kalles*."

I grinned and then pressed my lips to his in a soft, thorough kiss.

When I pulled back, I accused, "You've been keeping this secret from me."

"I was not sure he would come," Arokan confessed. "But he did. I offered him a place here for *you*, Luna. Only for you."

"I know," I whispered, my heart drumming in my chest. If I'd ever doubted Arokan's feelings for me, those doubts were gone now.

"It was fortunate timing that he arrived today," my horde king said next, his tone strange.

"Why?" I asked.

"Because while you were with your brother, the scouting

parties returned. They found a viable camp with plenty of resources."

It was time, I realized. Time to leave.

"Regardless of what your brother's decision is, *kalles*," Arokan said, "we will leave at first light in two days."

29

The morning we were set to leave, the entire camp woke when it was still dark out to begin dismantling the camp. The majority of the day before, I'd worked on packing up the items I'd collected over the past six weeks—the various articles of clothing I'd made, little trinkets from the market that had been gifted to me by the vendors, my store of dried *hji* fruit that I obsessed over, the golden dagger that Arokan had crafted for me after our training session in the forest.

Including my *deviri,* I had a total of five chests that I'd packed, not including the chests I packed with my Arokan's belongings.

Then the morning came, dark and cool. I watched as the domed *voliki* were dismantled with stunning efficiency and ease. I watched as the *pyroki* enclosures were taken apart, their metal bars and troughs packed onto one of the numerous carts that emerged. Since my help was denied with the tents, I assisted the *mrikro,* ensuring the *pyrokis* were calm and tethered until our departure, while my brother watched me from the sidelines.

That morning, I was stunned how quickly the camp

changed, going from a lively, populated place to a barren, empty patch of land.

When the sun rose, we were ready to leave. The sky turned from an inky black to a blush pink. But apparently we weren't to leave yet. The horde gathered, over a hundred members, warriors, females, children. I stood by Arokan's side as he led a prayer of thanks to Kakkari, as an elderly Dakkari male dug handfuls of a golden granular substance from a sack and spread it over the earth where the camp had once been.

It was a calming experience, a goodbye, a thanks to the land that had provided for us during our time there.

Then, it was time to move on, to leave.

My eyes met my brother's from across the empty clearing. The night before we left, my brother had told me he would stay with me. He wouldn't leave me. I had been relieved and gladdened by the news, but it didn't stop me from warning him not to do anything foolish. My husband would only be so merciful and if my brother did anything to jeopardize the horde, his punishment would be swift.

It would take time for my brother to adjust. I knew that. I was simply glad he would give the horde a chance. I was glad he would be safe, he would be fed, and he would be with me.

Arokan turned to me, breaking my gaze. I looked up at him, aware that my brother still studied us.

"We begin again, *rei Morakkari*," he told me softly.

"I'm ready," I replied.

"ARE YOU WELL, *MISSIKI?*" Mirari asked, crouching over me, an alarmed look in her gaze.

When she'd seen me pull my *pyroki* to a sudden halt and jump off its back to dart into the covering of the forest we passed, she'd cried out and immediately followed.

"I'm fine," I said, wiping my mouth once I was finished emptying my stomach of my morning meal.

"Here," she said, taking a cloth from her travel satchel, and I thanked her, taking it to clean up.

I heard the quick vibrations of a *pyroki* approaching fast and I looked up to see Arokan. He'd been riding towards the front of the horde that morning and I'd fallen back a little to ride next to my brother and my *piki*. He must've heard Mirari's alarmed cry and came racing towards us.

"*Kalles*," he rasped, swinging off Kailon with ease to come to me. "What is wrong?"

Concern was etched into his features and I felt bad for alarming him so much. "Nothing," I replied. "The dried meat this morning just didn't agree with me. I feel much better now."

He nodded hesitantly, but then said, "Come ride with me for the next stretch. *Lysi?*"

I nodded and he helped me up onto Kailon's back before he swung behind me. Once Mirari was back on her *pyroki* and she'd tethered the one I'd been riding to her, the horde continued forward again.

"Luna," my brother called when we passed. "What happened?"

Arokan stiffened behind me, no doubt because my brother had announced my name to the horde members within earshot. I didn't mind, but I knew the Dakkari were particular about given names, so I would speak with my brother about it the next time we were alone.

"I'm fine," I assured him. "I'll ride with you in a bit, all right?"

He nodded and watched us as we passed, Arokan guiding Kailon back to the front of the horde. On the way, I caught Hukan's glare. I simply acknowledged her with an incline of my head—a sign of respect, just because she was related to my husband—but then looked away. She'd ignored me for the better part of the past few weeks and I intended to do the same.

I didn't think she would ever accept me into the horde and I didn't want to waste energy on a lost cause.

It was the second day of travel already. From sunup to sundown, we rode at a slow pace towards our destination. The night before, we'd camped in a small, empty clearing, laying down nothing more than pallets and furs while the warriors took shifts in watching over us. I set up my pallet by Mirari and my brother. Lavi slept near her warrior, who one day I hoped she would bind herself to, once Arokan gave him permission to take a *kassikari*.

It wasn't the most comfortable, but Arokan had come to me once his shift was over and his warmth had helped lull me into a deep sleep.

Traveling with the horde was different than I'd expected. I'd expected long, drawn out days stretching from minute to minute, a sore backside from riding on a *pyroki* for the majority of that time, and restlessness.

And to some extent, those things were a reality. But I didn't expect to enjoy it, not as much as I did.

"Are you sore?" Arokan asked me, one arm wrapping around my middle from behind as his other hand held onto Kailon's reins.

From the *pyrokis*, he meant.

"It's not as bad as before," I told him. My time in the *pyroki* enclosure had helped build up my inner thighs and buttocks against their hard scales. "My brother is suffering though."

Arokan said, "We can provide padding if he wishes."

I shook my head, smiling. "He won't take it. He's almost as stubborn as you are."

He grunted behind me, leaning forward to nip my earlobe in warning. My smile died, my breath hitching, because he *knew* how sensitive my ears were.

We hadn't had sex since the night before we left camp.

Going from having sex multiple times a day to nothing as we traveled with the horde was difficult.

"I miss you," I whispered to him, turning my head to look back at him.

He growled, "Soon, *kassikari*. I promise."

Time couldn't pass fast enough.

WHEN WE TOOK A BREAK NEXT, I switched back to my own *pyroki* and rode beside my *piki* and my brother towards the back of the horde train.

"How do you feel?" I asked Kivan. "Are you sure you do not want the padding?"

Just like I knew he would, he scowled and said, "No, I don't need the padding."

Biting back a smile, I watched his expression pull lightly as he adjusted on the *pyroki*.

"Regretting your decision to stay?" I couldn't help but tease.

He shot me a look. "I will remain wherever you are, Luna," he said, "even if it means I have to ride on these damn beasts for the rest of my life."

I laughed, but caught Mirari's chiding look out of the corner of my eye.

"Brother," I said, looking at him. "There's something you should be aware of."

"What?" he asked, frowning, adjusting again on the *pyroki*.

"The Dakkari are particular about names. About who knows them," I tried to explain.

"What does *that* mean?"

"It means you should not use her given name for anyone's ears," Mirari chimed in, her tone clipped, her frown disapproving. "It is disrespectful to the *Morakkari*."

Kivan's jaw dropped as he looked from Mirari to me and back again.

"You're joking, right?" he asked. "She's my *sister*."

"Then address her as such," Mirari argued. "You embarrass the horde and the *Vorakkar* when you use her given name."

Kivan scowled at her. "You should mind your own—"

"Enough," I cut in, sighing. Mirari and Kivan had butted heads often during our travels, even before we'd left the camp. I didn't know why, but it was getting tiresome.

"Luna, this is ridiculous," Kivan argued.

Mirari's eyes bulged in irritation and I said, before she could, "My *piki* is right, Brother. It is the Dakkari way. You must respect them."

"But *our* way is calling someone by their name," Kivan protested, anger flushing his cheeks. "We are not Dakkari, so why does it matter?"

"I don't want to argue," I said, trying to keep calm. "But you live with the horde now. You will respect them, do you understand? You may call me by my name when we are alone, but if we are not, then you will not use it."

Kivan looked at me, his jaw clenching in frustration.

"Yes?" I said, needing to hear it.

"Fine," Kivan said, looking towards the landscape to the left of us. Tall, peaked mountains rose from the earth, more and more as we traveled south.

I sighed, exchanging a look with Mirari, before we all dropped into an uncomfortable silence. Finally, I said softly, "Are you upset with me now?"

Kivan shook his head, meeting my eyes. "No. It's just...it's different. Not just about the names. About you. About seeing you with *him*. About this all."

I nodded, understanding what he was saying. "Sometimes different is good," I said gently.

"I haven't decided that yet," he replied, stubborn as always.

Mirari made a sound in the back of her throat, like a scoff, and my brother scowled at her. They were like two petulant children with one another and I shook my head, rolling my eyes.

"What is so terrible for you?" Mirari demanded. "You are protected. You are fed. You are not dressed in those dirty rags you came in. You have your family, the *Morakkari*. That is the most important thing of all. Family. Yet, you complain like a spoiled youth, over and over again."

Kivan gritted his teeth and turned away.

I cast a look at Mirari, surprised by her venom, the anger in her voice. Even Lavi, who only caught some words she recognized, looked at her with a furrowed brow.

Mirari looked down, seeming to realize that she'd gone too far. Everything she said was—to a certain extent—true, but Kivan needed time. Just like I'd needed.

"Forgive me, *Missiki*," she said softly. "I did not mean..."

"Perhaps it is my brother who you should apologize to," I said, my tone gentle. "Not me."

Her shoulders sagged and she looked at my brother. Even though it looked like the last thing in the world she wanted to do, she forced herself to say, "Forgive me, *nevretam*. It is not my place to criticize you."

Kivan looked at her, though he too seemed embarrassed by her apology.

"It is just that," Mirari continued, looking up at me and then Lavi and then settling on my brother, "you should be grateful just to be with your family. You should not take that for granted. It is a gift."

Kivan's brow furrowed, sitting up straighter in his seat at her tone.

"I do not have family, you see. I have never known them, " Mirari confessed and my heart clenched at the sadness I heard in her voice. "I was grateful when the *Vorakkar* accepted me into his horde, though I did not have a line, though I was simply an orphan from *Dothik*. I worked hard to show him I belonged and then he gave me the great honor of serving the *Morakkari*, though I was an outsider before."

I frowned, reaching over to squeeze her hand, our *pyrokis* bumping together. I didn't know. I didn't know that she'd been an orphan. She'd never spoken of it.

It must be why she disliked my brother. Though he had suffered as well back in the village, he'd come into the horde with Arokan's approval, but he had rebelled against it, had shown his displeasure readily, when Mirari had seen her acceptance into the horde as a fortunate blessing.

"So you see," she continued, holding my brother's gaze, "though you may not understand now, better things await you, if only you try to accept them."

I could see Kivan processing her words. Something in his gaze changed and I knew that Mirari confessing she'd been an outsider struck something within him. He'd been an outsider too, even before I'd left.

"You are right," he finally said softly, blowing out a breath. "I should be more grateful. I have been treated well and I have been reunited with my sister. Perhaps I should be the one asking for your forgiveness."

Mirari blinked and then looked away. If I didn't know any better, I'd say she was embarrassed, though I didn't know why.

"Perhaps," Mirari said lightly.

Even still, I looked at my brother, saw him looking at Mirari with a peculiar expression, as if he was just seeing her for the first time. Hope and pride made me smile. *Perhaps* Mirari's words would be a turning point for him, something for him to think about. When my brother met my eyes, I nodded at him, pleased with what he'd said.

Then I spied something behind him, in the forest we were riding next to.

My breath hitched and the color must've drained from my face because Mirari asked, "*Missiki*, are you going to be sick again?"

The being darted behind a tree when I spotted him, but I would recognize the sheen of his grey scales, the unmistakable curve of his razor-sharp teeth anywhere.

A Ghertun.

A *scout*.

He'd been watching us.

30

"You are certain, *kalles?*" Arokan asked, his expression serious, his eyes rapt on me.

When I'd urged my *pyroki* into a run towards the head of the horde, when I'd told my worried husband in a hushed, urgent voice about the Ghertun I'd seen, he'd immediately stopped travel and quickly ordered his warriors out into the forest to search for him.

Now, I was standing next to him, behind the line of warriors that acted like a barrier between the forest and the horde as we debated what to do. The search party had returned and told Arokan they saw no sign of a Ghertun, or even the *tracks* of one, which I said was impossible.

"Yes," I said, holding his gaze. "I *saw* him. He hid when I spotted him. Right there!"

Arokan's eyes went above my head, his eyes surveying how large the forest was. I could practically *see* his mind working and then his *pujerak*, his second-in-command, approached us.

"Your orders, *Vorakkar?*" he asked, looking between us.

Arokan was silent, still thinking it over. Finally, he shook his head, looking at me and then his *pujerak* before he said, "We cannot risk splitting up the horde. The forest is large. If we cannot even track the scout, it will be impossible to locate his pack. I will not send half the warriors away when we may need them, in case of an ambush."

The *pujerak* inclined his head.

Arokan continued. "We are a day's travel away from the new camp. We keep the horde together, keep the warriors alert, and we send a scouting party out once we settle. *Lysi?*"

"*Lysi, Vorakkar,*" the *pujerak* said. Then he walked away, relaying Arokan's orders to the rest of the horde warriors.

Arokan turned to me and I whispered, "I know what I saw, Arokan. He was there."

"I believe you, *kalles,*" he murmured, reaching out to touch the golden markings around my wrist. His eyes went to the forest again and then he looked back at me. "You will ride with me until we reach the camp. No exceptions. Tell your brother and your *piki* they may be near you as well."

I nodded, rubbing my arms when I looked back at the forest. A feeling of unease settled over me. How long had the Ghertun been tracking us before I'd seen him? He could have been watching us for *miles.*

"Luna," he murmured softly, reaching out to cup the nape of my neck. I turned my eyes to him. "I will always protect you. You have nothing to fear."

I gave him a small smile. I nodded and said, "I know."

He tilted his chin towards where my brother, Mirari, and Lavi were standing, speaking quietly. "Go tell them to ride up front. Hurry back. Kailon awaits."

NEEDLESS TO SAY, I didn't get much sleep that night, especially since Arokan didn't join me on the pallet. He stayed up through the night with the warrior watch and I only saw him again at sunrise, when we left our temporary camp for the last and final day of journey.

Shortly, we moved away from the large forest, leaving it behind—and the Ghertun with it, much to my relief—and I noticed that the landscape began to change again, going from empty stretches of land and forests to more mountainous regions of tall hills and low valleys.

"There is a small Dakkari outpost not far from here," Arokan murmured down to me. "It is called *Juniri*. We enter the southlands now."

Everything was new to me. I'd only ever been outside the walls of my village once and one time only. Now, I was covering miles and miles of strange, foreign land with my Dakkari horde king. And I felt like the world had opened to me. I felt free.

Looking at my brother's expression as he gazed around told me he felt at least an inkling of what I felt.

Arokan called for a break in travel mid-morning, so the horde could rest for a brief while and take their second meals before we made the final push towards the new camp. We stopped at the base of a tall, jutting mountain, the ground covered in a type of red dirt that stained my feet when I slid down from Kailon's back.

Just in time too, I couldn't help but think, biting my lip and taking a deep breath. Nausea had been roiling through my belly all morning, but I'd managed to keep it at bay, so as not to alarm Arokan or stop the horde's travels. But I didn't think I could keep it in any longer.

So, I dismissed myself shortly after we stopped, claiming to Arokan that I needed to empty my bladder, and Mirari and Lavi came with me, a guard trailing not far behind. Once the guard gave me privacy, I found a secluded spot, out of eyesight of the horde, and heaved what remained of my evening meal the night before into the red dirt. I hadn't eaten that morning, still too nervous about the Ghertun, so unless my nausea was some kind of virus…I thought that it might be caused by something else entirely.

"*Missiki*," Mirari said quietly, coming to crouch beside me, a fresh cloth already out of her travel satchel.

I counted the weeks in my head. When women had gotten pregnant in my village—though that occurrence was rare since there weren't many young females—it had always taken more than a couple months from the time of conception for morning sickness to begin. It was entirely too soon for mine to begin unless…

Unless Dakkari females had a different pregnancy term than humans.

I took the cloth from Mirari, wiping my mouth, before looking up at her. Lavi was hovering nearby too and Mirari said something to her. Lavi nodded and disappeared.

"No," I whispered. "I don't want Arokan to worry. Not now."

"I sent her for water," Mirari assured me. Relieved, I blew out a breath before another wave of nausea hit me and I threw up again. Mirari soothed me as best as she could and when Lavi returned, she had me take a cooling sip from the cup, which helped.

Not once did I experience my bleeding time when I'd been with Arokan. My cycle had been relatively unpredictable at the village, due to a low supply of food and a high supply of stress. I hadn't thought anything of it, but now, I was beginning to suspect that perhaps my horde king had gotten me pregnant that very first time, the night of our *tassimara*.

When I looked into Mirari and Lavi's eyes, I knew they suspected what I did.

"Should I send for the healer?" Mirari asked quietly.

"No," I said. "The guard will report to Arokan. Besides, I'm not even sure. It's only been a couple mornings of this."

Mirari watched me and then said, "The healer carries special

Dakkari herbs and mixes for this purpose, *Missiki*. You wish to be sure?"

"She can tell me if...if I'm pregnant?" I whispered, shocked. "*How?*"

Mirari nodded and then looked at the cup of water. "I can be discreet. Relieve yourself in here and I will have her test it with her herbs."

My cheeks burned. "You want my *urine?*"

"How else can you test for a baby, *Missiki?*" Mirari asked, confused, frowning.

I blinked. Humans had always...waited.

"All right," I said, taking the cup. Mirari nodded and gave me a little privacy as I did my best to pee in the small cup.

Once I was done, she took it from me. We emerged from behind the mountain once I was sure the worst of the nausea had passed.

We rejoined the camp shortly after and Arokan reached out for me when I found him sitting with his *pujerak*, a few warriors...and my brother, much to my surprise. My horde king settled me in his lap and I smiled at him when he fed me some dried *bveri* meat, though I worried my stomach would rebel.

Out of the corner of my eye, I saw Mirari leave and go seek out the healer, a middle aged, heavy-set, no-nonsense female I'd seen multiple times around camp. I watched them speak briefly as I bit my lip, only half-listening to Arokan speak with the *pujerak* as they ate.

The healer's eyes connected with mine, even from a distance. I inclined my head in a brief, subtle nod and she blinked, dropping her gaze in respect, before she took the cup from Mirari, said something to her, and left.

I closed my eyes briefly in relief.

I might be pregnant, I thought silently to myself, testing that possibility, feeling a warm glow that rose from the thought that both frightened and excited me.

However, I didn't want to get my hopes up. Not yet.

Not until I knew for certain.

Only then would I tell Arokan.

31

"You'll probably need more furs once the cold season comes," I commented, helping Kivan with the last touches in his tent. "But the *Vorakkar* says that the weather is milder in the southlands, so perhaps these will suffice."

"It's more than we ever had in the village," Kivan commented, staring around at the small space. "I've never seen so many furs in my life."

"That's true," I murmured softly, looking around.

The *voliki* was small, but it was the same size as the unmated warriors' tents, just enough for one. Warm and cozy.

"What now?" Kivan asked after a brief moment of silence.

A loaded question. We had reached the new camp yesterday afternoon, right on schedule, and by nightfall, *all* of the tents had already been erected. The golden barrels that held the fire for cooking meat so it wouldn't scorch the earth were rolled out and lit, giving the camp a warm glow. And as the sky blackened, the horde continued to work. The *pyroki* enclosure was put together and I helped fill the troughs with food and water. I saw Arokan only briefly as he helped erect the training grounds.

The camp had almost the same layout as the previous one. The back of the camp—which included our tent—butted up to a tall hill. And while it had made me nervous, next to that tall hill was a thick forest, unlike any forest I'd ever seen. Instead of trees, it was made up of black vines that crawled up sharp, jutting rocks. The vines crisscrossed overhead, growing between the rocks that acted like trunks until the forest seemed like nothing more than a black mass of darkness and chaos.

Arokan said there was a stream inside, which would provide access to fresh water. Though I worried about Ghertun, still spooked from the earlier encounter, Arokan assured me that there would be a plethora of patrols to keep it clear.

But right then Kivan was looking at me with a wary expression. Now that we'd begun to settle into our new camp and the journey was over, Kivan was nervous about what his purpose would be.

"I'll bring it up to the *Vorakkar*," I assured him. "I work with the *pyroki* during the day, but there is plenty around camp to do. We will find you a job."

Kivan nodded. It was getting late. Already the second day of being at the new camp was fading away and I still had to visit the healer. It was something I'd been putting off all day, once Mirari told me that morning that she wished to speak with me, that she had completed her tests.

I didn't know why I was avoiding the meeting. I hadn't experienced any more nausea since we'd been journeying and I didn't want to hear that I'd gotten my hopes up for nothing. Ever since it became a possibility that I could be pregnant...it was all I'd thought about. I *wanted* a baby, I realized. The intense longing for one surprised me, considering I had never given children much thought before.

But I did. I wanted to be pregnant. I wanted to give Arokan children, a son or a daughter.

"I have something I need to do," I told my brother, knowing

I couldn't put off the meeting any longer. Better to get it over with and move on. "Rest. And put that salve on your thighs. It helps with the *pyroki* burn. Trust me."

Kivan looked up at me and nodded, already reaching for the pot of clear healing salve I'd brought him.

I smiled at him, reaching up to ruffle his clean hair. "I'll see you tomorrow, Kivan."

Once I ducked outside the tent, I looked at one of my two guards—the one that spoke the universal tongue—and asked him, "Will you take me to the healer's tent?"

Thankfully, he didn't ask why, but simply led me to her. In no time at all, as the sky darkened into a beautiful indigo, I stood in front of her home and the guard called out, announcing my presence and my desire to speak to her. I knew Arokan would look for me soon, so I needed to be quick. I knew the guards would report to him that I'd come there, but I would tell him my reasons if he asked. I would be honest with him.

Once the healer gave me permission to enter, I stepped inside and was immediately assaulted with the intense smell of burning herbs and the heat from the small fire she had going in her own personal barrel.

"*Morakkari*," she greeted, inclining her head, standing from the low table she was seated at. I'd interrupted her evening meal, I realized.

I mirrored her actions. I didn't actually know if she spoke the universal tongue, but I greeted her with, "Healer, my *piki* said you requested me."

"*Lysi*," she replied and I was thankful I wouldn't need the guard to translate our conversation. "My herbs revealed to me that you are pregnant with the *Vorakkar's* child."

I reached out to grip a tall chest to keep from falling over.

"*Morakkari*," the healer exclaimed, rushing to sit me down at the low table.

I blinked, falling onto the cushion in disbelief. "A little warning next time would be great," I breathed as she immediately thrust a small cup of hot tea into my shaking hands.

I stared into the dark liquid as her words began to penetrate.

"I'm..." I whispered. "I'm pregnant?"

"*Lysi, Morakkari,*" she replied, taking a seat across from me. "Drink. It is good for the young."

"How can you be certain?" I asked.

Her brow furrowed, her head cocking to the side. "The tea? It is a blend I make myself."

"No. *Nik.* About the pregnancy. You are certain?" I clarified, hope beginning to spring in my chest, though I desperately tried to keep it reined in. "I haven't had any morning sickness the last two days. I thought..."

"My herbs have never told me an untruth, *Morakkari,*" the female said, "and I have done this for many, many years."

"But I'm human," I pointed out. "Not Dakkari. Maybe the test doesn't work for me."

"Your child is Dakkari," she said gently.

I looked down at my belly, my breath hitching.

A child.

A baby.

Excitement, fear, hope all swarmed within me and I looked back up at the healer.

"I'm pregnant?" I said, just to clarify one last time before the flood gates opened.

"*Lysi, Morakkari.* I am certain," she said patiently with a small nod. "Now, drink. You must have a cup every morning and evening."

And because I didn't know what else to do, I drank the foul-tasting, bitter liquid until the cup was emptied.

I closed my eyes as tears of happiness welled up in them, not wanting her to see me cry.

"What now?" I finally asked once I opened them again, once

I was able to control the sudden, overwhelming emotion at her abrupt announcement.

What now?

Words that Kivan had just asked me and now it was *I* that felt uncertain.

"You continue to live," she said, as if it were obvious. "You wait. The baby will grow and when the baby decides to come, it will."

I blew out a breath and then asked a question that I'd been wondering. "How long do Dakkari females gestate for?"

"Five moon cycles," the healer answered. Almost half of humans. It explained why the morning sickness came early.

"All right," I whispered, looking into my empty cup before looking up at her, a small, hesitant smile appearing on my face. "Thank you."

"You come see me often, *Morakkari*," she continued. "I will have your tea delivered with your meals and once the worst of the nausea comes, I have something to settle your belly too."

"Thank you, healer," I said again, rising from the low table. "I would like that."

I left shortly after, exiting from the tent in a state of happy disbelief.

I'd been so certain that I wasn't pregnant that the news had come as a shock. But the only thing I wanted right then was to find Arokan and tell him the news.

I nodded at the guards and then turned towards the base of the hill, where our tent was, hoping that he'd returned from his duties already. Hell, I practically ran there.

I only stopped short, the smile dying from my face, when I saw Hukan. She was emerging from the black vine forest, carrying a basket of something in her arm. She was alone and she peered around before she saw me.

I watched her straighten and frown, but then, much to my surprise, her expression lightened, as if she made the effort to soften her features. She even began to approach me and I stopped in my tracks, wondering why she would do such a thing.

"*Morakkari*," she greeted.

"Hukan," I said, my tone hesitant at first, using her given name since the guards were far enough away. "Is there something you need?"

Something flashed in her gaze but she shook her head, eyeing me. She gestured to the basket she was carrying and I peered inside and saw small berries, large and green in color, so dark they looked black at first. "*Kuveri* fruit. You can only find them in the southlands. We make sweet bread with them. I will bring you some, *lysi?*"

Taken aback, I didn't know what else to do but nod. "I'd like that," I said, studying her.

Had Arokan spoken with her? Was that why she was making an effort to speak with me?

"Thank you," I added, giving her a small smile. It was for Arokan's sake. She was his aunt, a blood relation to his mother. For him, I could make peace with her.

She inclined her head in a nod and passed me, on the way back to her tent, I presumed. I stared at the spot where she'd stood before I looked into the black vine forest.

Surprisingly, I felt like a weight had been lifted. Or had, at the very least, *started* to lift. Hukan's disapproval of me, her insistence that I was not strong enough for Arokan, that it would only be a matter of time before he realized that, had always been an insecurity in the back of my mind. But, perhaps Hukan saw that I was trying to be the queen he deserved.

And despite the encounters we'd had, I still wanted her approval, her blessing. She was the last female of Rath Kitala, of Arokan's line, at least until I bore a daughter. I didn't want there to be a divide between them because of me.

"*Kalles*," I heard.

My breath hitched and I turned, Arokan's voice cutting through my thoughts like a blade.

"Hi," I said, my belly warming. My two guards, a respectful distance away, departed at my husband's nod and he wrapped his arm around my waist, guiding me the rest of the way to the tent. "Wait."

I couldn't stand another moment of not telling him. Even the walk back to our tent was too long. Night was descending and we were alone at the back of the camp. It was peaceful and quiet and I *needed* to tell him.

When he frowned, turning to me, I reached my hands up to wind around his neck and said, "I just came from the healer."

His expression tightened and pulled, worried. It always amazed me how well I could read him. Most of the time, he was in *Vorakkar* mode. He kept his emotions tightly concealed, to be strong for his horde.

But around me, he didn't. He let me see what he was feeling. He was Arokan with me, not the *Vorakkar*.

"What is wrong?" he rasped, gripping the back of my neck, peering down into my eyes as if just doing that, he could discern an illness.

"Nothing is wrong," I whispered before I couldn't contain my smile anymore. "In fact, everything is wonderful. She told me I'm pregnant."

Arokan froze, his muscles tightening around me. "*Neffar?*" he rasped, stunned.

"We're going to have a baby, Arokan," I whispered, reaching out to touch his cheek. "I'm pregnant."

His breath hitched and then he was kissing me, devouring my lips, my words, as if he needed to consume them to believe them. I knew the feeling.

I grinned into him, knowing that he felt what I felt. From the beginning, I knew he wanted children. He'd told me many times. He'd told me that I would give him many. He'd always believed I would, while I'd been the one with the doubts.

But not now. I was pregnant. I was *happy*. I was in love with a horde king of Dakkar who had taken me from one life, only to give me a new one. A better one. A life where I felt free. Loved.

Tears pricked my eyes and ran down my cheek as Arokan kissed me. Then I gasped when he hitched me up into his arms and strode the rest of the way to our *voliki*, intent on celebrating the news in a much different, much more private way.

In my ear, he rasped, "You honor me, my Luna. I am proud to be your male."

AFTERWARDS, I lay against the cushions in our bed, flushed from pleasure from head to toe. My horde king had been thorough and insatiable and I'd loved every moment of it.

I stroked his hair, threading my fingers through it, as he rested his head on my belly. Though the baby was only beginning to grow, while it would still be a while before I began to show, Arokan pressed words into my flesh.

Dakkari words. Soft and low. Some words I understood, but most I did not. Regardless, his voice brought tears to my eyes because I knew they were words of hope, of love, of promise.

Arokan would make a wonderful father. That I knew with certainty.

Our *voliki* was quiet and warm. My husband was pressed against me and ever so slowly, his words lulled me into sleep.

Everything was falling into place. We'd arrived at our new camp safely, my brother and I had reunited, the distance between Hukan and I was lessening, and now I was pregnant with Arokan's child.

But that night, though I lay in the safety and warmth of my horde king's arms, my dreams were dark.

As dark as the black vine forest.

As if Kakkari herself was warning me what would come next.

32

"Water?" Jriva asked, the young boy sounding out the word slowly. Working with me at the *pyroki* pen, he'd picked up a few universal tongue words, *water* being one of them.

"*Nik*," I said, smiling, reaching out to ruffle his hair, just like I did with my brother. The boy grinned. "*Tei runi.*"

You go.

Jriva was due for a break. The *mrikro* still had a cough from the journey—due to the dry weather in the southlands and the dirt he'd inhaled along the way—and the elderly Dakkari decided to rest that day in his tent, at the instructions of the healer. So it was just Jriva and I working in the enclosure.

I watched the young boy nod and then exit out the gate, running towards the front of the camp where the water barrels were kept. Knowing Jriva, he would probably try his chance at charming some *bveri* meat or some of the *kuveri* sweet bread from the cooks while he was there.

Alone with the *pyrokis*, I blew out a long breath and wiped at some of the sweat on my forehead. That morning, I'd gotten a late start due to morning sickness. It had reared its head the past couple mornings, leaving me tired and pale. Arokan had stayed with me longer than he should've that morning, worried, hovering over me as I emptied my stomach into the chamber pot.

He did not like seeing me sick. He'd sent for the healer and she'd mixed together a tea, which had helped settle my stomach. After an hour resting in bed, I couldn't stand another moment in the tent, so I'd gone to the *pyroki* pen, though Arokan had protested.

I wouldn't be cooped up in the tent for the duration of my pregnancy, so I would simply push past any discomfort. Morning sickness was temporary, but the satisfaction I felt working was lasting.

A short distance away, I saw Kivan hard at work too. Since Arokan said he had a proclivity for crops—considering he'd burned the earth in order to enrich it—Kivan was planting purple Dakkari grain, which would be harvestable in just a few months, even with the cold season coming. I didn't know how long we would remain in the southlands, but Arokan seemed to think long enough to grow a small field of crops.

Kivan caught my eye and I gave him a little wave. He nodded, giving me a small grin I hadn't seen in a long time, and went back to digging out a watering trench for the field.

The sun was low in the sky, casting deep golden rays. In the distance, I heard the laughter of a Dakkari child. Even from the *pyroki* enclosure, I smelled the delicious aroma of warm, spiced meat and simmering broth wafting from the front of the camp. There would be a communal meal that night to celebrate our new home and it was the perfect, peaceful evening for one. I was looking forward to it.

Hukan emerged from between two tents, coming into sight, two baskets looped around her arms. Her eyes sought me out in the pen and then she turned to my two guards.

In Dakkari, she addressed them and I watched them exchange looks before gazing over at me.

"Is something wrong?" I asked, approaching the fence of the enclosure, brow furrowed.

"*Nik, Morakkari*," Hukan said, inclining her head, when my eyes met hers. "I was wondering if you would help me."

"With what?" I asked.

"The females need fresh *kuveri* for the grand meal tonight. Many of them and quickly. I fear I cannot gather enough on my own, so I would like to request your help."

My eyes turned to the black vine forest before returning to her, biting my lip. I was reminded that our relationship was still precarious. Her coming to me for help was surely another step in the right direction, wasn't it?

I nodded, exiting the enclosure. "Of course," I said, taking one of the baskets from her when she offered it to me. "I'd be happy to."

"Thank you, *Morakkari*," she said. "I am grateful."

As we turned into the forest, my guards followed, though, like always, they stayed a respectful distance away. It was my first time setting foot inside and I found that when my eyes adjusted to the darkness, it wasn't as frightening as I thought it would be. Curious, as we walked further and further into the darkness, I passed my hand over the black vines and they felt smooth and soft beneath my palm.

"They make a good broth base," Hukan told me when she noticed me eyeing them. "Very rich. Very nutritious. And inside, they have edible seeds, though you must boil them first."

"It seems everything can be used for something," I commented, looking around as Hukan led us deeper inside.

"It is the way of the Dakkari," she told me, walking next to me. "To be wasteful is an insult to Kakkari. And if we take something, we must replenish it."

"Is that what those golden seeds were for before we left the old camp?" I questioned. "To replenish?"

"*Lysi*," she said. "Seeds that will produce food for the next horde or the next herd of animals that passes through. You get and then you give. Even during your *tassimara*, there were seeds planted in every lantern, so wherever they landed, wherever Kakkari's wind took them, they would flourish and provide."

My lips parted. "Really?"

I'd never known. I remembered the glowing lanterns lifting into the sky that night, twinkling like stars. I thought that...wonderful.

"*Lysi*, it is tradition. It is the Dakkari way."

I'd heard that more times than I could count. *The Dakkari way.*

"Even the southlands," Hukan continued, stepping over a fallen vine, "are evidence of this."

I saw her look over her shoulder, at my guards, as I asked, "How so?"

She didn't answer. At least not right away. We walked deeper and deeper so that even when I turned, I could no longer see the warm glow of the camp.

"The *kuveri* grow this far inside?" I asked, getting a little nervous with the darkness, though I hid it as best as I could. "There's hardly any light. It's a wonder that they grow at all."

"They thrive best in darkness," she replied and after a few more minutes of walking, she said, "Here we are."

There was a small grove of *kuveri* berries growing on grey, bushy, wild plants at the base of the stones the black vines grew on.

"Let us hurry, *Morakkari*," Hukan said, already plucking some of the berries off and dropping them into her basket. "The grand meal grows near."

I nodded and helped her pick the little fruits off the nearest bush.

"Thank you for bringing the sweet bread yesterday," I commented after a little time had passed, once a quarter of my basket was filled. "It was delicious."

Hukan inclined her head. After another moment, she said, "I always enjoy when the horde comes through the southlands. It is bountiful here, is it not?"

"It certainly seems so," I said.

"Perhaps because there are no outsider settlements anywhere near here," she commented. "They are the opposite of Dakkari. Wasteful, all-consuming. They do not care of the destruction they leave behind. They only take."

My hand paused in plucking a berry off the bush. My eyes flashed up to her but her expression seemed innocent enough. "Human settlements, you mean?" I questioned slowly.

"*Lysi*," she said immediately. She looked up at me, her green-rimmed eyes contracting on me. "Oh, but you are not human anymore, are you, *Morakkari*? I meant no offense."

Yes, she did, my gut told me. She'd meant to say that, had said it purposefully to hurt me, to draw a clear line between us. Dakkari and human. In her eyes, I would *never* be Dakkari, despite her words.

Inhaling a long breath through my nostrils, I didn't want to give up. I didn't want to go back to ignoring each other's existence because it made things awkward around camp, around Arokan.

Brow furrowing, I said carefully, "Hukan...I want there to be peace between us. For Arokan's sake. He cares for you deeply. I know you have never liked me. I know you think Arokan can do better than me."

She paused in plucking as well, turning to look at me with an unreadable expression. There was a familiar flickering in her gaze, which made dread pool in my belly, which made me think that once again, we were back to where we'd been before. I wondered why it had reversed so quickly.

"But he chose me," I said, steeling my voice, needing her to understand. Softly, I confessed to her words I had not even told Arokan yet. "I love him. And I believe he loves me too. I am his queen and I am not going anywhere, no matter what you—"

I heard rustling and quick footsteps behind me. I heard the hiss of a blade and I spun around, my heart pounding in my chest, *knowing* that something was wrong.

In disbelief, I saw two Ghertun hovering over the still bodies of my guards. They were on the ground, blood pooling beneath daggers sticking from their sides. The Ghertun had snuck up from behind. They'd never even had time to draw their swords.

My basket of *kuveri* dropped to the forest floor and I gasped, backing away, their slitted eyes directly on me.

"Hukan," I said softly, swallowing past the lump in my throat, my eyes going to the daggers imbedded in my guards' sides. If only I could get to one. "We must—"

I turned around, only to find three more Ghertun standing behind Hukan. My eyes widened in alarm.

"Watch out!"

She didn't move and avoided me when I reached for her.

The Ghertun didn't make a move towards her.

"This is her?" one of them asked, that raspy, slithering voice making bumps break out over my flesh.

"*Lysi,*" Hukan replied, her eyes cold, her jaw set. She turned from me, looking at the Ghertun over her shoulder. She wore an expression of disgust as she regarded him, her lips pressing together. "You said you would not kill the warriors."

"H-Hukan," I whispered in shock. Then anger enveloped me, rage that made my hands shake. She'd betrayed Arokan, betrayed me, betrayed the horde. And now two innocent Dakkari were dead because of it.

"Hurry and take her away," Hukan snapped at them. "Before he realizes she is missing."

Realization flooded me and without another moment of hesitation, I turned on my heel and tried to run.

Only to be caught by the two Ghertun that had killed my guards. I struggled in their arms, jabbing my elbows anywhere I could, trying to turn my head to bite them. All they did was let out a disgusting sound resembling a laugh.

"Remember our agreement," Hukan said, her tone cold. "You never harm another member of the horde, never come close to our camp or the *Vorakkar* again. Do you understand?"

"Yes, female," one of them, the leader, hissed. He approached me, brushing past Hukan. I smelled his rancid breath, felt the heat of it brush my cheek, as he said, "Our king will find her quite...amusing. An enemy horde king's bride. We will be rewarded greatly."

Hukan's jaw clenched and she looked away from me.

And I realized there was only one thing left to do. I just prayed someone would hear me.

I dragged in a deep breath, about to scream as loud as I could.

"*Arok*—!"

The Ghertun's fist struck out. I felt pain explode at my temple.

Then the world went dark.

268

33

When I woke next, I smelled smoke.

My head was throbbing but I tried to keep still, to assess the situation first.

I was lying on my side in a clearing. Still in the black vine forest, I realized when I saw the jutting rocks, but I knew the forest was large. We could be anywhere inside.

My hands were tied in front of me with a rope, so tight that I couldn't move my wrists. My feet were bound in the same way, but I noticed that the rope was thin. It wouldn't take too much effort to cut, if only I could get a blade.

Behind me, I heard them. The Ghertun. I'd counted five before they'd knocked me out. Were there more now?

I heard one speak in their own tongue and I suppressed the shiver of revolt that went through me.

Suddenly, I was flipped over to my other side so that I was facing the small fire pit they'd constructed.

They must've guessed I'd woken, I thought, eyeing them with a glare, my jaw set, my head pounding.

There were still five Ghertun. Five Ghertun that had plotted with Hukan to take me away.

I was a fool.

I remembered how Hukan's attitude towards me seemed to flip so suddenly, how she'd greeted me and offered to make me sweet bread after coming out of the black vine forest. Had she met with the leader then? Had she begun to think of a way to lead me into the forest without rousing my suspicion?

She made me think that there was hope for us. She asked for my help—how that must have *grated* on her, I realized—in order to lead me into a trap. Now, my guards were dead, only because they were doing their duty. They'd never seen their deaths coming.

The leader of the group—a Ghertun with a deep, ugly scar across his jaw—crouched in front of me. His legs were like a *pyroki's*, bent heavily at the knee joint, and his feet were clawed, the bones raised. I heard those claws digging into the earth next to me as he balanced himself.

"You wake," he noted, cocking his head to the side. I smelled fermented brew on his breath and I saw metal jugs being passed between the other Ghertun. "How fortunate."

They had traveling sacks and rations, which told me they'd prepared for this journey From the Dead Lands? I remembered the leader had mentioned a *king*. A Ghertun *king*.

"You will all die for this," I told him, my voice surprisingly calm. "The *Vorakkar* will—"

His hand flashed out again and light burst in my eye. He'd slapped me this time. Hard enough for my flesh to throb, but not a punch that would have rendered me unconscious.

"Your horde king will never find us, human," the leader rasped. Then he let out that awful laughing sound as he said, "Besides, you were betrayed. It seems someone wanted to be rid of you. Why would you want to go back?"

The thought of Hukan's betrayal enraged me. "Why did you take me then, if someone wanted to be rid of me? Maybe there was good reason for that."

His expression sobered. "Because that Dakkari filth killed the king's son. One of them, at least. As penance, our king wants *you*."

My brow furrowed.

The scout. The Ghertun scout that Arokan had executed had been the king's *son*? Why had the king's son been a lowly scout?

"Oh yes," the leader said. "We have been watching you for a long time. Waiting. First, the king will take you. Then, he will take the horde king's head."

"You can't fight the horde," I scowled. "You would never make a dent. They are skilled fighters and the *Vorakkar* is the best of them all."

The leader laughed again. "We have great numbers now. An army. We have waited to strike and soon, we will not only destroy your horde. We will be able to take all of Dakkar for our own."

"You lie," I rasped.

"Never," the leader purred. His expression quieted and he cocked his head to the side, studying me. "We were very surprised to learn a horde king had taken a human as his queen."

I glared up at him, my jaw clenching.

"Then again, human cunt is...*divine*," the leader said softly, leaning towards me, his breath and words making my stomach turn. "Soft and warm and so *tight*. No wonder the Dakkari wanted you warming his furs."

I spit in his face, rage and disgust making my body tremble. Arokan had told me that he'd witnessed Ghertun attacking settlements, both human and nonhuman settlements alike. He'd told me that the Ghertun killed and pillaged and raped.

"If you touch me, your death will be slow," I promised.

The Ghertun wiped his face with his hand and then, to my disgust, licked his palm. He grinned, his slitted, dark eyes shining from the fire burning the earth, where a skewer of roasting meat turned.

"Delicious," he purred, making my belly drop in dread. Then his shoulders dropped and he leaned back. "Unfortunately, human, you are meant for our king. He would know if we had…sampled."

The other Ghertun grumbled and laughed a bit, telling me they all spoke the universal tongue. That surprised me. I thought Ghertun nothing more than barbaric, savage beasts. How was it that so many knew a second language?

I swallowed. There was no way in hell I'd let them take me to their king.

Arokan will come before that ever happens, I thought, that knowledge sinking in. He would come for me. He wouldn't rest until he found me.

I almost felt sorry for these Ghertun. Almost.

"However," the leader continued, "it seems you need to be taught a lesson, human."

He said something in the Ghertun tongue over his shoulder and my eyes flickered to one of them rummaging through his travel sack, only to pull out a short metal poker.

My breathing went shallow when he placed the end into the fire, letting it sit, turning it until the end was red-hot.

"You will be marked anyway," the Ghertun leader said, seeing where my eyes turned. "We will save our king the hassle."

Eyes widening, I squirmed in my bonds as the leader retrieved the poker and approached me. My heartbeat revved in my chest, adrenaline rushing through my system.

"*Don't touch me*," I yelled, trying to wiggle away. But the bonds were too tight. I struggled harder when two Ghertun approached and held me down, pushing me flat onto my back, tearing my tunic until my shoulder was exposed.

Panic lit my veins as I eyed the hot poker. There was a symbol at the end. Three horizontal stacked lines.

The leader got closer and I kicked out my feet, connecting solidly with his groin.

The leader cursed, hissing, and rage flashed in his gaze when he dropped to the ground, the poker falling from his hand. In the Ghertun tongue, he yelled at the two holding me down and one grabbed my legs roughly, though I thrashed.

Then the leader picked up the poker. "Human bitch," he hissed. "I'm going to enjoy this."

I screamed as the searing pain registered. He pushed the symbol deep into my flesh and nausea churned in my belly when I smelled my own skin burning.

It only lasted a handful of seconds, but the moment the poker left my skin, I struggled again, despite the chilling pain that numbed me, desperate to break out of their grasp. Inhuman sounds rose from my throat as I thrashed.

Satisfaction went through me when I once again managed to kick the leader, this time right in the jaw.

His face snapped to the side but when he turned it to look at me, I saw his nostrils flare. My breath hitched when I saw his own leg rear back.

I only had a moment to shield myself, to shield my exposed belly, before he launched a powerful kick into my side, shaking my body, my breath whooshing out of my lungs until I gasped and choked for air.

He crouched low over me again as I lay there, struggling to breathe.

I looked up at him, eyes wide, frightened for the first time because I wondered if I'd been able to protect the baby enough.

"Test me again," the leader growled, "and I'll do a lot more than mark you, human."

That was the last thing I heard before his fist flashed out again, knocking me unconscious once more.

THE NEXT TIME I WOKE, the pain registered almost immediately. My side ached, my face throbbed, and my shoulder radiated icy heat from my burn.

Overhead, I saw the sliver of the moon. From its position, I knew it was the dead of night and time was slowly creeping into the early hours of morning.

Realization hit me. I'd been gone for hours.

Arokan would know by then I was gone. In my gut, I knew he was already searching for me, but if he hadn't found me by now, if he hadn't been able to track the Ghertun that had taken me, would he find me?

They must've covered their tracks well. They must've taken me deep into the black vine forest and I wondered if Arokan would find me in time. They must have felt secure in the knowledge that the horde *wouldn't* find me, especially if they were eating and drinking and laughing at their leisure.

My eyes sought out the group of Ghertun. The fire had died to embers, but I could still see the glow of their eyes in the darkness.

They were still drinking. I watched them, trying to lie as still as possible, knowing that the darkness would shield me at least a little.

They were growing sloppy as the hours drew on. They were laughing, speaking in the Ghertun tongue, lounging about. Every now and again, one's eyes would flicker to me, but I closed mine quickly, feigning sleep.

I watched them for a long time, however. With every sip of brew they drank, a plan formed in my mind. I realized I didn't need to wait for Arokan. I could handle this myself. My husband had given me the *knowledge* to handle this myself. We'd trained for hours and hours together, for *weeks*. I just needed to time everything right.

I was a *queen* of a Dakkari horde. Arokan saw a strength in me and over the weeks and weeks that I'd been with him, I'd begun to see that strength too.

While I was no horde warrior, I could escape a handful of drunk, stumbling Ghertun, couldn't I?

I had to believe I could. There was no other option. I was running out of time before they would take me farther from the horde, into the Dead Lands.

Studying them, I saw three out of the five had a dagger on them. Good odds. I remembered the night Arokan had taken me into the forest, back at the old camp. I remembered what he'd said. That I had used his weakness to draw him close and that was when I'd struck.

I could do the same thing, I realized.

If I could taunt over a Ghertun with a dagger, I could grab it. They might be too drunk to realize otherwise. I had to hope they were.

So, I opened my eyes and didn't close them whenever one happened to look my way. I stared at them and one nodded over to me, informing the leader that I was awake.

The leader glanced over at me and I held my breath, holding his glare. He ignored me, taking another swig out of the metal jug before passing it, saying something in Ghertun that made them all laugh.

I saw one get up from the fire and go off into the dark forest. It gave me an idea.

"I need to empty my bladder," I called out.

"No," the leader replied.

"It's urgent," I said, steeling my voice.

He ignored me.

I tried again. "You really want me smelling like piss for the entire journey? Because I will go in my pants if I have to. You'll be the ones who'll have to smell me."

Even in the darkness, I saw his nostrils flare. He was quiet for a moment, making me think my idea had failed, but then he nodded at the nearest Ghertun—one with a dagger—and jerked his head towards me.

The Ghertun huffed, but got to his feet, swaying over to me. Drunker than I thought, I realized.

Good.

Roughly, he pulled me to my feet and I stumbled from how tight the bonds were.

"Loosen them," I said, "so I can walk."

"You think me dumb, human?" the Ghertun slurred.

Yes.

I didn't press my luck. I felt the leader's eyes on me so I awkwardly shuffled, though I purposefully made it seem more difficult than it was. I stumbled more than I needed to. I didn't want him to think I had *any* chance to escape and out of the corner of my eye, I saw the leader accept the jug when it was passed back around, his attention already diverted towards the brew.

The Ghertun didn't lead me far. Only far enough away where if I pissed, they probably wouldn't be able to smell it at the camp. Still, it allowed me more privacy than I would've had.

The Ghertun pushed me against a rock and grunted, "Hurry."

Heart racing, I debated what to do next. I didn't think I would get another chance to be alone with one and I needed to draw him close enough to grab his dagger.

There was only one way I could think of and I pressed my lips together before saying, "I need help with my pants."

His head jerked towards me. His drunken grin appeared, displaying sharpened, yellow teeth, and it revolted me.

Immediately, he came forward. I told myself to be still as his hands roamed down my body, as I felt his disgustingly cold flesh through my tunic. His clawed fingers came to the laces of my pants and he sliced through them with one flick. The waist loosened.

My breathing went shallow. Alarmed, I wondered if this had been a good idea, especially when he pressed his lower body into mine. My belly churned when he tilted his head and licked a line up my throat, over my cheek, with his slimy tongue.

"I do not care about the king," the Ghertun slurred. "I haven't had a human cunt in a long—"

With a sudden jerk, I gripped the hilt of his dagger and pulled it free. Before the Ghertun even realized what was happening, I sank the blade deep into his belly—right where Arokan told me to during our training sessions—feeling the hard scales give surprisingly easily.

His eyes flashed to me in shock and he stumbled back, but not before I twisted and pulled the dagger free.

For one stunned, silent moment, he looked down at his wound, one leg giving out underneath him.

My hands shook and I stared at him, feeling the heavy weight of the dagger in my palm.

He was the first being I'd ever wanted to kill. I didn't know how I felt about that, not yet, but I would do whatever it took to survive, to get back to Arokan, the horde, and Kivan. I would do whatever it took to keep my growing baby safe.

The Ghertun fell with a loud thud, blood spilling from his wound. I saw his eyes roll back, but not before he let out an anguished, angry cry, alerting the leader and the other Ghertun at the clearing.

Then he was dead.

I heard the leader shout. Through the black vines, I saw him racing towards me...the other three Ghertun not far behind.

34

I was running out of time.

Immediately, I bent down and sawed the dagger back and forth over the bindings at my feet as hard and as fast as I could. If I wasn't able to run soon, they'd catch me. And who knew what they would do if they did.

Thankfully, the rope was as thin as I originally thought and it didn't take long for the sharpened, bloodied dagger to snap through the bonds. Without another moment of hesitation, with my feet freed, I turned and sprinted away as fast as I could, pumping my arms at my sides, just as the leader and the three Ghertun reached the body of the fifth.

I heard the leader curse, heard one Ghertun stumble over the body, but I continued to run. I might not have been strong, but I *was* fast and I used that to my advantage.

What I didn't count on, however, was how dark the forest would be. Hardly any moonlight—what light there was from the crescent moon—penetrated through the canopy of the thick vines. Only shafts of it, here and there, helped illuminate a clear path for me, but I feared that the Ghertun would have better vision in the dark. I knew the Dakkari did. Darkness was a weakness of humans and I had no room for weakness. Not right then.

My breath came out in panicked, loud pants and I made an effort to quiet it when I heard rustling behind me, when I heard the leader give orders to his Ghertun, not too far away. They'd lost sight of me in the thick darkness, but they were experienced trackers as scouts. I wouldn't underestimate their ability, considering they knew this forest better than I did.

Though I continued to run, I tried to be as quiet as possible. But my footsteps were loud and I feared that running was drawing their attention even more.

As I ran, I cut the bonds tying my hands, though I was clumsy and managed to nick my wrist. It didn't matter. At least I wasn't tied, at least I would stand a fighting chance if one of them found me.

Pain exploded in my shoulder, right over my burn, when I ran straight into a vine-covered boulder I hadn't seen and my body spun, landing heavily on the earth.

Panting, I pushed up and heard the leader's voice. They were close.

Not too far in front of me, I saw a shaft of moonlight illuminate a large, jutting rock, with a fissured crack right down the middle. It would be big enough for me to squeeze into.

Slowing my breathing, I went for it. Holding the dagger close, I squeezed myself into the small space, the rock pressing tight around me. At the last moment, I saw a broken fragment at my feet and I paused before picking it up. I stepped out from my hiding place, cocked my arm back and threw the rock as far as I possibly could, in the opposite direction.

The forest was silent as I heard it clatter off another rock and then I squeezed myself back inside the crack when I heard the leader's voice sound again. They'd heard it. Good.

A few moments later, I heard quick footsteps approach. I dragged in a silent, deep breath, holding it. A few yards away, I saw two Ghertun pass, though I couldn't tell if the leader was one of them. They ran in the direction of where I'd thrown the rock and when they passed, I let out my breath slowly, relieved.

I felt blood drip down my hand from the dagger. Ghertun blood. It was still warm but I refused to think about it. Still, I wiped my hand and the dagger on my pants until they were clean.

I don't know how long I waited, but I kept quiet. I *listened*. In the distance, far enough away, I heard loud Ghertun voices carry, bouncing off the boulders, echoing back to me. I listened until I didn't hear them anymore and I prayed that they'd continue on in the direction of where I'd thrown the rock, far, far away.

When I felt it was safe, I slowly wiggled out from the crack, still clutching the dagger tight, and turned in the opposite direction. I didn't run. I kept my steps light and quiet, using the boulders to shield me from sight just in case.

My heart froze in my chest when I heard anguished screams in the distance. Breath hitching, I realized it was from the direction the two Ghertun had gone.

Their yells filled the forest and I stilled, placing my back against a boulder as I listened, heart pounding.

Then, bright relief filled me when I heard *Dakkari* orders echo from that direction.

Arokan.

They must have found the two Ghertun. Hope filled me and I spun back around, quickly striding in that direction.

Arokan, Arokan.

I could see him soon. I could feel his arms wrapped around me. I could feel safe.

Those thoughts spurred me into a jog, wanting to see him, *needing* to see him.

The closer I got, I heard more Dakkari words filter through the forest. I was gaining on—

My breath left me when I was suddenly tackled from the side, the cool bulk of a Ghertun pinning me down.

I hit the ground *hard* and my burned, already injured shoulder knocked against a nearby boulder. I felt a *pop* at the joint.

My scream echoed through the forest.

"*Human bitch*," the Ghertun leader hissed in my face, making to reach for the dagger in my hand, though I struggled underneath him. "You will pay for their lives."

In the distance, I heard a roar shake the forest.

Relief. *Arokan*. I knew it was him.

That knowledge filled me with determination and I swiped out the dagger quickly, managing to cut down the leader's arm. He hissed in surprise but when I made to stab his belly, he rolled off me to avoid it and I used that opportunity to jump to my feet.

I began to run—

Only to land facedown when he grabbed my ankle, my teeth chattering together, my lip splitting. My shoulder twinged and I cried out, feeling him grab higher on my leg.

I rolled and saw that the leader was trying to pull himself up. I kicked, thrashing. I connected with his face. His grip loosened on my legs. I kicked him again with my other leg, finally managing to break free.

I felt the ground begin to vibrate. I recognized it. I knew that the *pyrokis* were approaching fast, a lot of them by the sound of it. I heard the echo of it grow louder and louder.

I jumped to my feet and looked at the Ghertun leader lying on the earth. He seemed to recognize that his time was limited. He heard the Dakkari coming, same as I.

"Surrender," I gasped, trying to catch my breath, holding out the dagger, keeping my eyes on him, "and your life might be spared."

He let out that awful laugh. "Even you know that's not true, human." I tensed when his arms flexed, when he prepared to push off the ground. "I will take my chances with *you*."

He lunged. Though I saw it coming, though I was *ready*, I was unprepared for his speed and he knocked the dagger out of my hand before I even blinked.

Behind me, I heard a *pyroki* burst into the clearing. The Ghertun's eyes widened and he stumbled back, prepared to flee. I turned and saw Arokan swinging off Kailon, his blade already unsheathed.

The Ghertun didn't make it far.

With a furious roar, my horde king swung his sword, plunging it into the leader's belly, right where his heart was. He was dead the moment it penetrated.

The leader immediately fell facedown, but Arokan was already turning to me, the dead Ghertun forgotten.

His expression was thunderous. His eyes were wild, his chest heaving with roughened breaths, Ghertun blood splattered across his chest and face.

My lips parted. I'd never seen my horde king so...undone.

Relief made tears prick my eyes as his arms came around me, swinging me up against his chest. I bit my lip when my shoulder pulled and he gentled his strength when he noticed me holding it peculiarly.

"Luna," he rasped in my ear. He was shaking, the muscles in his arms and shoulders and chest vibrating with the adrenaline coursing through him. "Luna."

Just then, the rest of the horde warriors broke through the clearing, surrounding us.

"There were f-five," I told him. "I killed one earlier."

Arokan's expression pulled and he turned to his *pujerak*, whose eyes I caught. Arokan's arms tightened around me as he said, "There is one more. Do not return until he is dead."

The *pujerak* inclined his head. He called out to the horde warriors and they rode out. They would comb through the forest, I knew. They wouldn't stop until Arokan's orders were carried out.

Arokan swung us both up on Kailon. Exhaustion was starting to weigh on me. Now that I was safe, all I wanted to do was sleep. I was still cradled in his arms and I rested my head on his chest, listening to his heart race.

My horde king looked down at my face, his expression tightening at whatever he saw. Rage entered his gaze, hot and furious. I realized he was doing everything he could not to explode.

I reached out to touch his cheek and he closed his eyes, his nostrils flaring, cupping my hand with his. He brought his forehead down to mine, gently.

Rasping, he said, "I feared...*vok!*"

He stopped with a curse and I could still feel him tremble against me at whatever he thought.

"Take me home, Arokan," I whispered.

Beyond words, my horde king nodded and he spurred Kailon into a sprint back towards camp.

35

"You're sure I can't do anything, Luna?" Kivan asked quietly, squeezing my hand.

"No," I said, giving him a small smile that I hoped reassured him. I was lying in bed, propped up by a plethora of cushions. It was early morning, not even a few hours after Arokan had found me. Dawn was just beginning to break over the sky and already, I'd been patched up by the healer, my arm popped back into place, and I'd had some tea for the pain. "I just need rest."

Kivan nodded. He looked tired. He'd been up all night too. I'd learned that it had been *Kivan* who'd alerted Arokan that something was wrong. He'd seen me go into the black vine forest with Hukan, though he hadn't thought anything of it at the time. However, once he saw Hukan exit alone, without me or my guards, he went to find Arokan immediately.

"I'm glad you're safe, Luna," Kivan whispered down to me. He squeezed my hand and then rose from the bed. "I'll see you later."

I nodded and watched him go. My *piki*, Mirari and Lavi, had already come by and I knew they were outside waiting for my brother, to ask him about me. Both, apparently, were overcome with guilt, though I couldn't understand why. I'd dismissed them yesterday evening, to go let them prepare for the grand meal.

The moment my brother exited the tent, Arokan stepped inside, as if my husband knew I'd needed that time with my brother.

Arokan was still quiet. Even though the last of the Ghertun had been hunted down, he was still furious. I could tell. I'd never seen him this way before and it worried me.

"Come here," I ordered. Silently, Arokan walked to his side of the bed and slid in beside me. He drew close, careful of my injured shoulder, of the burn, and positioned me so I lay my head in the crook of his elbow.

We hadn't had time to talk. I almost feared what to say, considering how the circumstance had come about.

"Arokan," I whispered, turning my head to look at him. "Did you...did you find the guards? Their bodies?"

I couldn't stop thinking about them. If I'd never gone into the forest with Hukan...they would still be alive.

"*Lysi*," he said. "They will be given a proper burial. A warrior's burial."

I nodded, trying to meet his gaze, but he was looking down at my burn. At the Ghertun marking. His eyes were frozen on it, though I knew he'd seen it when the healer put healing salve on it.

Suddenly, he said, "Hukan did not try to flee when I put her under guard watch."

My breath hitched. I hadn't told him it was Hukan, not directly. But judging from what my brother had said, my husband had put together the fragmented pieces. He knew that his only blood relation, his mother's sister, the female that had once saved his life, had betrayed him.

My fingers sought his hand. His palm was warm and he gripped my hand tightly, as if afraid I would let go.

"I'm sorry, Arokan," I said.

"She will face her punishment," Arokan said, his voice strange. "She will face Kakkari."

I didn't know what that meant, but I wasn't certain I wanted to know right then.

"I know you love her," I said, looking down at our entwined hands. "I know this is hard for you."

"For me," he repeated slowly, turning my face to look at me, his brow furrowed in an expression that looked anguished. "*Kalles, you* were betrayed, taken, beaten, *burned*…your—your pant lacings were…were ripped—"

I sucked in a harsh breath, realizing what he was saying, and I turned in his arms, ignoring the twinge in my shoulder. Taking his face in my hands, I whispered, "They didn't touch me, Arokan. Not that way."

He closed his eyes and tears pricked my vision. The things he must've thought…

"Arokan," I whispered, stroking his cheek. "My body will heal. The healer said the baby is safe. *I'm here with you.* That's all that matters."

"The burn will remain," he said, his voice hardening. "The memory will."

I went silent. I knew it would. I would forever remember the feel of a dagger sinking into Ghertun flesh, of a shocked expression, of the realization that I'd killed him.

But I would do it all over again if I had to.

"I failed you," he said.

I gasped. "What?"

"I did not protect you," he said, looking at me, that emotion that I'd seen when he'd entered the clearing in the forest right at the surface. "The dark things I thought when I realized you had been taken, when we could not find you as the hours went by…*vok*, Luna, it was the worst moment of my life and I have experienced many of those. I failed you. When I swore to protect you, when I swore you would be safe. I am sorry, *kassikari*. Please forgive me."

Hearing him apologize was almost as wrong as his words.

"Arokan," I said, taking his face again. "Listen to me. You did *not* fail me. Don't *ever* think that again."

He shook his head.

"Stop it," I whispered, my throat clogging. This was why he'd been quiet, I realized. Because he believed he'd been responsible for what I suffered. "Arokan, you did save me."

He closed his eyes. "I found you because I heard you scream."

"No, that's not what I meant," I said. When he looked at me, I said, "I meant that you gave me the strength and the knowledge and the training in order for me to survive. Without that, I don't think I would've."

He dropped his head to my shoulder, letting out a rough breath.

"I tried to stay calm," I told him softly. "I watched them. I came up with a plan. You remember that night in the forest? When I drew the blade on you?"

He nodded.

"I remembered that night too. I did the same thing. I got one alone and close. I managed to get his dagger and I did what I had to do. I cut him where you taught me to," I said, "to protect myself and our baby. Then I ran. I hid and then I heard the horde coming. The leader...he must've seen me. He was desperate by then, but you came before he could act on it."

Arokan looked at me and I watched him process my words.

"I know that you think you failed me, but you didn't," I whispered, leaning forward to give him a small kiss. He breathed me in, his fingers delving into my hair. "You didn't. It breaks my heart knowing you think that."

"I want...I *need* to kill them again, *kalles*," he rasped. "For hurting you."

I stroked his hair, felt his tail wrap around my thigh. I knew that feeling wouldn't go away for a long time.

However, his words made me remember something.

"Arokan, there's something else," I whispered.

"*Neffar?*"

"The leader," I started, looking at him. "He said the Ghertun have a king. Did you know that?"

Arokan's lips pressed together. "We heard reports, *lysi.*"

"They were going to take me to him," I told him, eliciting a growl from my husband. "Apparently the scout that we found at the old camp...that was one of his sons. He wanted revenge. That's why he took me, because he knew it would hurt *you*. The leader said...he said that the king is planning to take all of Dakkar, that he has an *army* big enough to succeed."

"It is a concern, *lysi,*" Arokan rasped, "but the Ghertun do not know how many Dakkari warriors we have. I can assure you, *kalles*, that any army he has is no match for us."

I relaxed, nodding. After a moment, I whispered, "I *was* frightened, Arokan. I won't deny that." He tensed beside me. "But only because I feared for the baby. I feared that they would take me away before I ever saw you again."

He blew out a long breath that ruffled my hair, his arm tightening around me.

"I was frightened too, Luna," he confessed softly, his voice guttural and raw. "I have never been so frightened in my entire life."

My chest squeezed because I heard the truth in his voice.

"Promise me you'll stop thinking you failed me, Arokan," I said, seeing his irises contract at my words. "Promise me."

His jaw clenched as he said, "I will do my best, *kalles*. That I can promise you."

It would have to be good enough. It would take time to move past this, to move on. It had shaken us both, I knew, but I knew that it would make us stronger. I didn't doubt that.

I took his hand again. I leaned forward and pressed a gentle kiss to his lips and then I pulled back and said, "I love you, Arokan. No matter what, I love you. I regret not telling you sooner."

He leaned his forehead against mine. His voice deepened as he said, "I love you too, my Luna, *rei kassikari, rei Morakkari*. I think I have from the very first moment."

36

Two days later, when the sun sank just below the horizon, Hukan was standing before the raised dais, before Arokan and me.

Night was falling. Her judgment was coming. The horde was assembled, the mood somber, the air so thick with tension, with anger, with disbelief, that I felt it as tangible as a touch against my skin. It weighed heavy in my lungs as I sat beside Arokan.

I was dressed in gold, my shoulders and thighs bare. On my skin, for all the hordes' eyes to see, was the Ghertun marking that had been burned into me. The healer had offered to cut it from my skin, so as not to be reminded.

However, I wore my burn like a badge now. I didn't want to erase what had happened simply because it hurt me to think of it. It had happened. I accepted it. I moved on.

Just like Arokan's scars, it had become a part of me the moment they'd burned it into my skin. I wore the marking of an enemy and it would forever be a reminder. I accepted that too.

But it also reminded me that I survived. I came out the other side, not the five Ghertun who had taken me.

And now, Hukan would answer for her betrayal. She was standing there, unchained, dressed in nothing but a white shift dress, her feet bare, her hair undone.

Arokan had just finished recounting her crimes for all the horde to hear. He had finished revealing her conspiracy with the Ghertun to take me to their king when he said to her, "You have betrayed us all, Hukan of Rath Kitala."

I couldn't help but flinch when he used her given name, a public disgrace. It pained Arokan, I knew it did. I wanted nothing more than to reach over and take his hand, but I was his queen and I had to be strong. I would sit beside him as he did his duties as *Vorakkar*.

"She is not Dakkari," Hukan hissed. "I did this for *you*. It was always for you."

Arokan's hands clenched into his throne, but otherwise, he held his emotions in check.

"She is Dakkari," he argued, his voice deep and hard. "As is the child she carries in her womb at this very moment."

A murmuring went through the horde and Hukan's face paled. I jerked my head over at Arokan before I looked at my brother across the way. I hadn't told him just yet, but he inclined his head when he saw me watching, as if to say it was all right. He was watching Hukan's trial with Mirari standing right next to him.

"A child," Hukan said softly. Her eyes flashed to me. To Arokan. "I—I did not know there was a child."

"*My* child," Arokan growled. "A child of Rath Kitala, your *own* line. You betrayed my queen and you betrayed your own *blood*."

Hukan was shaken by the news. For all her hatred of me, it seemed she held no hatred for my child. Because my child would share her blood, the blood of my husband, of his mother.

Before Arokan delivered his judgment, I knew what it would be. He'd told me before the trial had begun. Dakkari were never executed for their crimes. Instead, they were to face the judgment of Kakkari. They were exiled into the wild lands, never again to have the comforts and security of a horde. They were given a single dagger with which to live or to die. If Hukan somehow reached an outpost, it was up to their leader to allow her admittance or not.

A lonely, uncertain, and harsh existence awaited her.

Tears pricked my eyes thinking about it. Not for Hukan's sake, but for Arokan's. This was a female he'd grown up loving and respecting. A female that had looked after him after his own parents had been murdered by the Ghertun. Yet, she'd conspired with them to betray me, to betray him.

I didn't feel sorry for her. She'd made her choice. She hadn't denied it when she'd been confronted and two Dakkari had been murdered because of her.

My heart ached only for Arokan, for the difficult decision that he'd had to make and the grief that would always haunt him because of it. He would always live with this decision.

Arokan jerked his head at two Dakkari warrior escorts that would lead Hukan out into the wild lands, far away from the horde. Arokan stood from his throne. He descended the steps of the dais and stopped in front of his aunt. From his belt, he drew a dagger, which he gave to one of the escorts.

"This was my mother's dagger," he said. "May it serve you well."

And then he bent his head low and spoke in Hukan's ear. A goodbye, I knew. Perhaps even a thank you, for all that she had done for him up until that point. Because for all of her faults, she had protected Arokan when he'd been a child. She had given him council whenever he sought it. She had been his only remaining family.

I didn't know what was said. It was a moment only for them

and my heart twisted in my chest when Hukan reached up to touch Arokan's cheek.

Then she looked at me. Our eyes held for a brief moment. I saw hers flicker over my healing split lip, the bruises on the side of my face from the Ghertun leader, the burn that took up half my shoulder.

Her eyes dropped to my belly, where my child grew.

"You are at the mercy of Kakkari now," Arokan said, breaking her gaze. "Pray that she is merciful. Pray that she is more merciful than I."

Hukan's head dipped.

Then she turned away slowly, towards the warrior escorts.

Wanting to give Arokan comfort, I descended the dais to stand beside him. Discreetly, I slipped my hand into his as we watched the two escorts, on their *pyrokis*, lead Hukan away. I squeezed his hand as we watched them grow smaller and smaller in the distance. The entire horde remained silent, watching until darkness fell over Dakkar. Watching until Hukan could be seen no more.

She was lost in the wild lands now, never to return.

Arokan kept a tight grip on my hand and I stood there with him, long after the horde members left, until it was just the two of us, staring into the dark night.

AROKAN'S EYES were closed as I smoothed the washing cloth over his shoulders, over his chest. The day had been hard on him, the grief still raw.

The water was warm around us, in our bathing tub, our skin pressed together. I spread my fingers wide over his chest, felt his strong heartbeat underneath my palm. Steady and slow.

I didn't ask him if he was all right. Of course he wasn't. I couldn't make the pain go away. Time would help heal it, but it would always be there, like a scar. A reminder.

And I was doing my best to comfort him, but I worried that it wasn't enough.

His eyes opened and he looked at me. He caught my hands and brought them up to his lips before he slid his own hands down my body to rest against my belly.

"I don't even know what to say this night," I confessed, licking my bottom lip, the cut stinging.

His eyes met mine. "Tell me that you love me," he said, his voice guttural, deep.

"I love you, Arokan," I whispered into his ear. Words just for him. Though my shoulder was still healing, I brought my arms up to rest on his shoulders, wrapping my hands around the nape of his neck, holding him close.

"Tell me that you will be with me always," he murmured.

"I will be with you always," I said softly, "until my last breath."

"Tell me that…" he trailed off, meeting my gaze. "Tell me that you forgive me, for taking you from your village the way I did."

My brow furrowed. I'd never known that he'd had doubts about that, about how we'd been brought together.

"There's nothing to forgive," I told him truthfully, the water trickling as I shifted over his lap. "I didn't understand it at the time, Arokan, but I realize now that it was a blessing. *You* were a blessing. You gave me a more complete life. You help me enrich it every single day."

His shoulders loosened. His gaze softened. It was a look just for me.

My heart fluttered in my chest. Leaning forward, I kissed him, slow and soft, memorizing him though I knew I had no need.

And I knew, right then, that our future would be bright.

That day, the past couple days, had been bittersweet. They had been difficult, emotionally, physically, for both of us, for all of us. I knew that there would be more difficult days ahead. With the uncertainty of the Ghertun threat, with the challenges of horde life, with the cold season approaching, the days ahead would be unpredictable.

But I knew, without a doubt, that as long as Arokan was at my side, as long as I was at his, we could face anything. Together.

When the baby came, when I brought our son or daughter into this world, we would be even stronger.

"Although," I said, pulling back slightly from his lips to tease him, wanting to make him smile, "I'm *not* sure I forgive you for that time you tried to force-feed me *bveri* meat."

He made a surprised sound in the back of his throat and I was satisfied when I got a hint of a grin from him. "Stubborn *kalles*," he murmured. "You fought me at every turn."

"You liked it," I whispered.

He gazed at me, brushing his fingers over my lips. His expression was serious when he said, "I would not have had you any other way, *rei Morakkari*."

EPILOGUE

Two moon cycles later...

MY HANDS FISTED into the furs, crying out when Arokan slammed deep into me, shaking my whole body, chattering my teeth together.

I moaned, *"More!"*

His fingers flexed at my hips, pleased.

I was on my hands and knees before my horde king. I'd woken him that morning by slipping between his thighs and gently sucking on the head of his cock. Not a moment later, he'd flipped me over, ready to give me what I'd so nicely asked for.

Beneath me, my growing breasts bobbed with every thrust and I felt one of Arokan's hands cup them, felt him tweak my nipples in a way that made me groan.

So good.

My horde king knew every place to touch me, knew how much pressure to use, how to angle his hips just right to hit that perfect, sublime spot inside me. He knew when I was ready to come, he knew when to hold me on the edge or just let me fall. He read me as easily as I read him. He knew when I needed soft and slow and he knew when I just needed to be fucked and he happily gave me whatever I wanted.

"*I love you I love you I love you,*" I breathed, gasping, beyond thoughts and almost beyond words. I was right on the edge. "*Arokan!*"

Arokan groaned behind me. He loved when I said that and I told him I loved him multiple times a day.

Then I was orgasming around him, my breath catching in my throat. I couldn't even scream. My mouth was wide in a silent cry as pulses of intense pleasure shot through my body.

My arms shook and Arokan caught me before I fell face-down into the furs. He brought me up to my knees, my back pressed against his front, and he continued to piston his hips into my sex.

In my ear, he rasped, "*Rinavi leika, rei Morakkari. Lo kassiri tei. Lo kassiri tei.*"

You're beautiful, my Queen. I love you. I love you.

One of his arms banded just beneath my breasts. One came to rest over my large belly, where our baby grew.

Then Arokan was bellowing out his release into me, as jets of his seed filled me, his hips rocking faster and harder.

He sucked on the sensitive spot just below my ear, nibbling it with his sharp teeth, as he rode out his own orgasm, and then we both collapsed into our furs.

Chest heaving, I cuddled into my husband's arms, our naked bodies intertwined. After I caught my breath, I laughed, the sound husky and happy. I turned into him, peppering kisses over his jawline, his cheekbones, the bridge of his flat nose, running my hand over his hard, muscled, tattooed chest.

"Insatiable," he rasped, his eyes closing. "You will drain me of life before the child comes."

"You love it," I whispered.

But he was right. Pregnancy made me insatiable. *Almost* as insatiable as Arokan, and he was a hot-blooded Dakkari horde king in his prime.

The past couple days, however, I'd been particularly ravenous. Arokan had gone out on patrol for close to a *week,* tracking a pack of Ghertun—almost to the Dead Lands—that had proven themselves more cunning than the rest. He'd just returned and I was making up for lost time.

"I do," he agreed, though he groaned as he said it.

"I'll let you sleep tonight," I promised.

He opened one eye to peer at me, as if to say, 'oh really?'

I grinned. The worst of my need had passed and I was content to lie in my husband's arms. I'd missed him terribly while he was gone. I'd worried about him every moment, lying awake at night praying to all the deities in the universe, to Kakkari and Drukkar, to keep him safe, to bring him back to me. Every patrol he went out on was like that. It never got any easier.

But he was the *Vorakkar.* He had a duty to his horde to keep them safe, to keep *me* safe. So he went. He went out on long patrols and didn't return until whatever threat they'd happened upon was eliminated.

Arokan looked at me, his eyes warming as they drifted over my features. I felt his love for me in that gaze. It was like sinking into a hot bath after a long day, warm, relaxing, satisfying.

His hands reached down to cup the baby. We were lucky enough not to experience any complications, considering that he was Dakkari and I was human. But already I could tell that the child would be big. Rightly so, considering the size of the father.

"Still two months to go," I commented. The healer believed that I would carry for the full five months. Already, my back, my ankles were killing me. I was ready for the baby to come *now*. Soon, I wouldn't be able to continue working with the *pyrokis*. I would have to sit outside the enclosure with the *mrikro* and shout orders to Jriva.

I smiled. That wouldn't be so terrible. I could munch on *hji* fruit, just like the *mrikro*, as I did it.

"They will pass slowly," Arokan murmured, "because we anticipate her arrival every moment."

Her.

Arokan believed it was a girl. A horde princess. I didn't know why. He just told me Kakkari had shown him in a dream. He told me I would bear him a girl first, then three boys before another girl.

Five children. I'd told him that we should get through the first pregnancy before we thought about more, but somehow I knew that Arokan was telling the truth. We would have many, many more children together and the line of Rath Kitala would be strong again.

Considering that Arokan had lost Hukan to the wild lands—no one had seen or heard reports of her—I was glad to give him many children.

Outside, we heard a warrior call out to Arokan and my husband's arms tensed. Immediately, we shared a look and then slid from our furs, our time together cut short. There was always something, some matter to deal with in the horde. It came with the territory. More often than not, our mornings were interrupted.

I dressed with my husband, wanting to check on the *pyrokis*. We were on the cusp of the cold season and we'd begun to build nesting enclosures for the pregnant females, so they could give birth. I wanted to make sure the construction was continuing at a swift pace, since we were running out of time.

We exited the tent together and I blinked, my breath

hitching in surprise. From our tent, we could see the vast wild lands of Dakkar, though were situated at the back of the camp.

And right then, I saw over fifty *pyrokis* with their warrior riders, idling just outside the camp border. Before us, flanked by two warriors, was a tall, broad, bare-chested Dakkari male, with shoulder-length, dark *blond* hair—a color variation I'd never seen on a Dakkari. His eyes were light too, the circle of his irises gray.

He was *handsome*, I couldn't help but notice, with strong, proud features, though his mouth was pressed in a serious, almost grim line.

Another *Vorakkar*, I realized, my lips parting.

I'd never seen another horde king, but there was no doubt in my mind, judging by the way this male carried himself, from his commanding presence to the scars that I saw drifting over his shoulder, that he too was a leader, just like my husband.

My suspicions were confirmed when Arokan stepped forward, a small grin playing on his lips. The two males clasped arms and greeted one another in Dakkari. When the blond's eyes came to me, Arokan stepped back and draped his hand over my hip and said, "*Rei Morakkari.*"

The blond *Vorakkar* inclined his head to me, his eyes dropping to my growing belly before going to the Ghertun burn at my shoulder. He looked at me, something going through his gaze, but said in the universal tongue, though it was more accented than my husband's, "It is an honor, *Morakkari*. I have heard tales of you throughout the hordes."

His eyes returned to my husband.

"We were passing by on patrol. I wanted to pay my respects and offer my congratulations on your *tassimara*, though it was long ago."

"Thank you," Arokan said. "Stay for a meal. Your warriors and *pyrokis* can rest. There are matters we should discuss."

About the Ghertun, I knew.

The blond shook his head. "There will be time for that, but not now. I have also come to inform you that the *Dothikkar* requests his *Vorakkars* in *Dothik.*"

Arokan absorbed the news. "About the Ghertun?"

"*Lysi,*" the blond said. "We do not come together often, but this is a matter of importance."

Arokan inclined his head in confirmation. He looked at me and then asked, "When?"

"When the moon is full," the *Vorakkar* replied.

In three weeks, I knew. I sighed silently. Arokan would be gone again, but I knew that it was inevitable. If the Dakkari king wished to gather his *Vorakkars* to discuss the Ghertun threat, then Arokan had to go. It was important.

I nodded at Arokan when he looked at me and he squeezed my hip. "I will be there," my husband replied. His eyes tracked over the fifty *pyrokis* just outside the camp and he asked, "Where are you heading?"

"A human settlement to the east," the blond replied and my head jerked to him. His gaze flashed to me. Carefully, he said, "The numbers of a *kinnu* herd grow dangerously low. We suspect hunting."

Dread pooled in my stomach and I couldn't help but say, "They only try to feed themselves. Before the cold season comes."

"Even still, *Morakkari,*" the blond *Vorakkar* said, "these are the laws of the *Dothikkar*. We must investigate."

From the corner of my eye, I saw my brother appear, Mirari next to him. Lately, they had been inseparable, despite the rocky beginning of their friendship. And I was glad for them.

My brother held out his hands at his sides, as if to ask what was going on. I nodded at him, reassuring him, and the *Vorakkar* turned and saw him.

When the blond turned back to regard me, I told him, "My brother and I came from a village, probably much like the one you will find on your journey. We only tried to survive and it was a hard life. We were desperate and hungry and foolish." I felt Arokan's gaze and it gave me strength to say, "Now, we *live*. We live a free life, a happy life, because of my husband's mercy."

The blond *Vorakkar* absorbed my words. I didn't know if they would have any effect, but I would try. I would always try.

"We only ever needed mercy," I finished, hoping he understood what I was trying to tell him.

The blond *Vorakkar* regarded me closely. His gaze was intense, as if he could see to my very bones. Arokan was the same way, quietly intelligent and observant. In the back of my mind, I wondered if all *Vorakkars* were like this.

Yes, I decided. They had to be.

The *Vorakkar* said, "I will think on your words, *Morakkari*. But I make no promises."

"That's all I ask."

The *Vorakkar* inclined his head again, his gaze returning to Arokan. "We will take our leave."

"*Lik Kakkari srimea tei kirtja*," Arokan said.

I'd never heard the combination of those words before, but I thought they meant something like: *may Kakkari watch over you.*

"You as well, brother," the blond *Vorakkar* replied. His eyes met mine. "May Kakkari protect you all."

Then he left, his two warriors flanking him. My breath hitched when I saw his back. Just like my husband's, it had been stripped by the whip. I would never get used to the sight.

Then, we watched from outside our tent as the *Vorakkar* led his warriors away on their *pyrokis*, kicking up dust as they went.

Heading east.

"He is merciful, Luna," Arokan murmured in my ear. "He is a good male. But just like all *Vorakkars*, he must be strong too."

"You can be all three," I told him, turning in his arms, looking into my husband's eyes. "*You* are."

Then he said something I didn't expect. "Only because you

have made me so. Only because you have made me a better male, a better *Vorakkar.*"

I smiled. "Then I have hope. Maybe he will go to that village and find his *kassikari.* Maybe he will have no choice but to be merciful and she will make him better for it."

Arokan grinned, leaning his forehead down to touch mine.

"There is always hope, *rei Morakkari.* You have taught me that too."

Claimed by the Horde King
Horde Kings of Dakkar Book #2

She broke their laws. Now, he has come to punish her...

In my human settlement on the hostile plains of Dakkar, I am an outcast, a strange girl orphaned since birth, alone, and dreaming of a life I don't have. I hunt to survive, though it is forbidden, though it breaks the strict Dakkari laws that we all must follow.

When my desperate actions catch the attention of a Dakkari horde king—a cold, powerful, and merciless warrior leader, with eyes like flint and a body like steel—he seeks to punish me...and he succeeds.

But then he does the unexpected.

Instead of taking my life, he claims me as his own.

Available now!
Visit www.ZoeyDraven.com for more information.

ABOUT THE AUTHOR

Zoey Draven has been writing stories for as long as she can remember. Her love affair with the romance genre started with her grandmother's old Harlequin paperbacks and has continued ever since. As a Top 100 Amazon bestselling author, now she gets to write the happily-ever-afters—with a cosmic, other-worldly twist, of course! She is the author of steamy Science Fiction Romance books, such as the *Warriors of Luxiria* and the *Horde Kings of Dakkar* series.

When she's not writing about alpha alien warriors and the strong human women that bring them to their knees, she's probably drinking one too many cups of coffee, hiking in the redwoods, or spending time with her family.

Visit her at www.ZoeyDraven.com.

Printed in Great Britain
by Amazon